THE THRALLS OF FATE

IN THE SHADOW OF SIN:
BOOK ONE

BY
ALAN HARRISON

Cover design by MiblArt
Map by Cornelia Yoder

ISBN 9781838132811 (paperback)
ISBN 9781838132804 (ebook)

II

For those who believe they are free

The Lands Of
ALABACH

High Sea

Elis Point

THE NORTHERN REACH

Col

Mhórtos Isle

The Sonnet

The Tragedy

Steel Mountains

Tán

Penance

Rustlake

The Glenn

Roseán

Point Grep

See inset

Eternal Sea

Tornadh

THE CLIFFLANDS

Móráin Sea

Ongar

Ardh Sídhe

THE WOODLANDS

Lough Aislinn

Móna Bog

THE WETLANDS

Hunter's
Den

Boughal

The Hazelwood

The Academy

Rosca Umhir

The Godsring

Dromán

Caillin Wood

THE MIDLANDS

Omen

Mount
Selyth

THE GODLANDS

Tine

Dainge

Terrian

Gulf of Bhreacain

THE FLOODLANDS

THE KINGLANDS

Bhuaim

Mule Mountains

Tulcha

Scrimán

Scearri

Dungaló

Cruachán

Ronnagh

Legend

★ Capital

● City or Town

■ Point of Interest

〜 Lake or River

∴ Wetland

🌲 Forest

Gorán

Isle of Lorcan

Sea of Storms

Miles

0 10 20 30 40 50

(Inset map)

Rustlake

The Glenn

The Scalp

Roseán

Point Grep

CONTENTS

PROLOGUE

Padraig Tuathil, Captain of the City Guard, stood before the door to the royal quarters. Iron-bound oak towered twelve feet overhead, flanked by torches with flames struggling in their sconces.

The Pyromancers never stood a chance. He wiped sweat from his brow as the image of the dying men burned through his mind. *What hope is there now?*

He sighed deeply. Usually, the thought of having to confront King Diarmuid terrified Padraig, but tonight he reckoned he'd rather take his chances with the king than face the undead horde scaling the castle walls.

Móráin Hall lay behind him, leading up to the royal quarters via stairs carpeted red. Once the central social hub of the inner keep, now it sheltered hundreds of frightened women and children from the violence outside. Mothers tried to hush their crying babies, while others prayed for the Gods to save them. The sounds of weeping and frail lament filled the air, but it did nothing to drown out the cries of battle from across the moat. Amongst the crowd, two young boys played dice beneath a portrait of St. Lorcan.

They're faring far better than those in the Cathedral. The thought struck his heart and weakened his knees. *Aideen...I should have stayed with you.*

Padraig looked up at the two Simian sentinels who stood on either side of the studded oak door. They had not moved, not when he arrived, not as he stood before them in indecision.

"I...I need to see the king," Padraig said.

One of the Simian guards looked down. He was a full head and shoulders taller than Padraig. Plated mail made up most of the guard's mass: slab upon slab of blue-tinted steel. Beneath a spherical half helm, a stern face of black fur glared down. The guard's heavy lower lip was quivering.

Gods above and below. Even the Simians are frightened.

"There's nothing wrong with being afraid," said Padraig, trying to sound braver than he was.

"We are not here tonight to be afraid," replied the Simian, his voice booming, yet clear and articulated. "We will guard the people of Cruachan with our lives, and we will fight back this enemy to our last breath. All this, we will do without fear."

Padraig swallowed a smile. *This one isn't half as good a liar as Farris was. The damn turncloak had that much to be proud of.*

The cries of battle outside amplified as the door swung open. The king had every window of his chambers spread wide. Amidst the odour of smoke and burning bodies from the city, the stench of alcohol hit Padraig like a wine-soaked blanket.

Thainol. Another gift from Farris?

Across the room, King Diarmuid Móráin, Third of His Name, Nineteenth Incarnate, lay slouched and drunk against a windowsill.

"The North Wall is on fire," he whispered, as if to himself.

"Yes, sire," said Padraig, not sure what else to say. The North Wall wasn't the only thing on fire; the city's entire commercial district was ablaze. "I had my Pyromancers stationed upon the wall when the horde first approached but...."

He struggled to find the words. Witnessing it firsthand had been bad enough, but recounting the atrocity made it seem even more real.

"Their own flames were turned against them," Padraig continued. "And after they died, a foul power raised their charred bodies to turn on their own brothers-in-arms."

Diarmuid shook his head. "Truly a power greater than the Gods. And why did you leave the battle?"

Padraig fell to one knee. "The city is almost lost, Your Grace. I have come to escort you from the castle as we make our final stand. We raised the drawbridge, but the undead are crossing the moat. Arrows do not slow them. Spears and swords do not slay them. I fear it is only a matter of time before they are inside the keep."

King Diarmuid's eyes remained closed. "Do not fear, Padraig. I have already accepted my own fate. You must do so too."

Padraig was well used to slurred insults and verbal attacks from the drunkard that ruled the kingdom, but this was far more unsettling. He slowly stood.

"The women and children have gathered in Móráin Hall, Your Grace. They pray and sing for our victory. I don't plan on dying tonight, but if I must, I will be on my feet. None of my men fled when the horde approached, and none begged for mercy when we were overwhelmed. They died bravely because they fought for your honour—for the honour of the kingdom."

The king remained silent.

"They came in riding on horses and bears," Padraig continued, gesturing to the window. "On mountain lions and beadhbhs from the Glenn: wild animals, untameable in life. Their army grows larger as our men die. They marched on the Academy of Dromán and took a thousand battlemages into their ranks. If they take this city, they will truly be unstoppable. Although we don't know where this enemy came from, all we can do now is *fight*."

Deep in concentration, the king still did not respond. Padraig studied his face, looking for any hint that the king had not yet given up, but only frightened eyes stared back. The king's golden locks hung loosely on either side of his face; beads of sweat ran down his brow.

"Power," he said. "Power forged by mortals, buried deep in knowledge they are forbidden to understand."

He took a seat by the table and poured himself a drink.

"Your Grace?" said Padraig, moving towards the king. Such a strange thing to say... Was that some sort of poem? A lyric from a song? Most of what the king had said tonight didn't sound like his own words. Padraig sat down beside him.

"Do...do you know who brought this upon us?"

"I once believed I did." The king drank deeply, staring blankly out to the west through another window by the mantel. "I cannot see the cathedral from here, Padraig. What of the smallfolk?"

"They were gathered there once the horns sounded," said Padraig, trying his best to cast away the mental image that descended upon him. "But we were not able to protect them from the horde. I put my best men there, but..."

I should have protected her myself.

"...but they have joined those storming the moat."

The king bowed his head. "You were not the only one with family there, Padraig. Many more will be forced to fight their loved ones tonight." He poured himself a glass of thainol. "Here, drink with me."

The clear liquid acquired a fiery glow as it filled the glass, reflecting the inferno outside. Diarmuid handed the drink to Padraig, holding it between two extravagantly ringed fingers and a chubby thumb. The captain knew better than to refuse anything offered by the king, especially alcohol.

One drink for courage, and I'll join my brothers at the gate.

"Long live the Triad," said Diarmuid, raising a glass.

"And blessed be the Trinity," whispered Padraig.

King Diarmuid didn't flinch as the alcohol trickled down his freshly shaved chin. He lowered the glass and looked expectantly at Padraig with those brilliant blue eyes said to have been inherited from Lord Seletoth Himself.

Padraig forgot his manners, and promptly drained his own glass. The inside of his throat shrieked as the thainol passed, bringing water to his eyes and searing his chest. Once the burning subsided, his body fitfully exhaled the pungent fumes, forcing a second taste upon him.

And to think the Simians prefer this over our fine wines. He immediately felt quite drunk. *At least it works.*

"Ha!" laughed the king, leaving Padraig unsettled by the sudden change in mood. "Farris swears it's distilled from potatoes and grains, but all this time I'm sure he's been bottling his own piss!"

Diarmuid picked up the bottle. "He gave me this one a year ago, right before he left. He said it's from one of Penance's finest reserves, worth a small fortune, apparently. I was going to keep it for a special occasion, but it seems the fall of my realm will occur long before any royal wedding."

The king chuckled softly as he took another drink.

He's back to his old self, at least. Padraig dried his mouth with the back of his hand.

"Has there been any word of Farris since he left?"

It seemed like the right question to ask, although the city would likely fall within the hour.

Diarmuid stood and made his way back to the window. "I swear I saw the speck of an airship sailing through the northern sky earlier, but it couldn't—"

Padraig started, knocking his chair over.

"An airship?" he echoed. "Has Penance sent its fleet to save us?"

He saw nothing but smoke in the sky, though. The king sank to his knees and buried his face in his hands, weeping.

"Farris is dead. She showed me the signs. She gave me a chance to prevent this, and I tried. Oh, how I tried! But no matter what I did, like water running through my fingers, everything just slipped away. Fate is a cruel mistress, for only now I understand."

He looked at the ceiling, tears running down his cheeks.

"It was me! My actions caused this! I thought the Silverback was the one she spoke of. I thought I could change the tides of fate, and I have paid dearly for it."

King Diarmuid stared up at Padraig, his voice growing hoarse.

"But was I supposed to ignore her? Should I have sat by and waited for everything to crumble?"

Padraig squatted beside his king, resting on raised ankles.

Gods help him, he's lost his mind.

"Nobody could have predicted this, Your Grace. There was nothing we could have done."

Diarmuid grabbed Padraig by the scruff of his neck and pulled his face close. Every ounce of thainol was thick in his breath.

"I *saw* it," he wheezed. "I had a chance but—"

Screaming women and children interrupted the king. Padraig's heart plummeted.

They've breached the keep!

King and captain both turned towards the oaken door, now the only thing separating them from the massacre. Children cried for their mothers, mothers cried for their Gods, but the Trinity remained silent. The few guards stationed in the hall cursed and yelled as they fought, though it was difficult to distinguish the sounds of the living from the dead.

Without hesitation, Padraig grabbed his sword and bounded for the door.

I cannot die hiding with a drunken sot.

"Don't leave!" King Diarmuid, still on hands and knees, crawled towards the captain. "Don't leave me here alone!"

Padraig stopped. "I made a vow that I would protect the weak and innocent, even if it costs me my life."

"No, please!" said the king, grovelling at the captain's feet. "I don't want to die alone; I don't want to die alone!"

His voice dropped to a whimper, and tears filled his eyes.

"She told me that I'd die alone."

CHAPTER 1: MOURNING

Morrígan rose as they carried her mother's coffin into the chapel. She did not look as it passed.

She turned her attention to the stained-glass window behind the altar: a depiction of the birth of King Móráin to the Lady Meadhbh and Lord Seletoth. The figures wore cloaks of bright green and red, now shining emerald and ruby as the sunset spilled light into the hall. The new-born baby was gleaming and golden, holding an axe in one hand and a shield in the other.

If our ancestors claimed this land from the Simians using magic, then what use were an axe and a shield?

The mourners returned to their seats, and Morrígan followed suit, shivering as a frigid sea breeze rolled through the chapel. She wore a loose-fitting tunic with large sleeves, fastened by a grey belt woven with intricate, interlocking patterns. Two wooden pins held her jet-black hair in a braid, though not nearly as neat as usual.

She always did a better job at keeping it tidy than I could.

Sorrow crept forwards from the back of her mind, but Morrígan fought it with clenched fists and gritted teeth.

From the altar, Daithí the Blessed cleared his throat. The old druid served as a stark reminder that this was indeed a funeral, and Morrígan's mother was, in fact, dead.

Dead.

Looking for another distraction, she turned her attention away from the stained-glass window, now focusing on the facial features of the druid. Thick grey curls framed a blemished red face, bloated from decades of indulging on wine and ale.

He often drank at The Bear *with father. . .*

Morrígan shook her head as the image of the killing field flashed before her; the troll, the corpses, her father galloping away on horseback, and her mother lying dead in the morning mist.

As the old druid spoke, he caught Morrígan's gaze and smiled. His blue eyes sparkled in the dusk's golden light, peering out behind his nose, round and bulbous . . .

Just like a troll's.

There was no avoiding it. Her mother was dead, her father was gone, and she was alone.

"We thank the King, the Lady, and the Lord for giving us life so we can live to love one another." Daithí spoke with a hollow monotone, rolling through each syllable as if he didn't care for the words themselves. "This gift is ephemeral, so we must fill our days with as much love as we can. That's how Aoife Ní Branna lived. She filled her life with the love she shared with her family, her friends, and her neighbours.

Today we pray that she'll continue to do so, in the Plains of Tierna Meall for eternity."

Nothing was said about the others who had died that day, but Morrígan counted them off in her head.

The mountain troll had killed two of the five strange travellers before it reached the farm, but Morrígan couldn't remember what they looked like. The other three had attempted to fight it right before her eyes. The first was crushed inside his own armour, dying as valiantly as he had fought. Another, a woman dressed in white, was bludgeoned to a pulp by the beast's bare fist. Only the third, a Pyromancer, had survived, but he lost his arm in the struggle. The sound of tearing flesh and bone was still fresh in Morrígan's ears.

And then, Mother. . .

She pulled her mind away from that memory, trying to recall the faces of the strangers as the druid droned on.

Where did they come from? Why did they bring a troll here to Roseán?

Morrígan pictured the trio travelling together across the Glenn and found herself almost smiling at the thought.

A warrior, a mage, and a healer: just like in the stories.

Closing her eyes, Morrígan imagined what it would be like to leave Roseán with formidable allies, searching for fame and fortune. She pictured herself returning someday to a hero's welcome, with all the same faces and places unchanged since she left. The bards would sing of her adventures, and she'd be remembered for generations.

But who will sing about those who died today?

A hand touched her gently on the shoulder. "Morry, it's time to leave now; the service is over."

Morrígan reluctantly returned to reality. Daithí the Blessed had finished his sermon, and the other mourners slowly filed out of the chapel. Only her uncle, Yarlaith the White, remained.

A lump formed in Morrígan's throat as she caught sight of her mother's coffin, left alone on the altar. She wanted to ask about what would happen next—whether there'd be a wake or a burial ceremony—but those questions brought grief, and Morrígan was desperate to talk about something else. Anything else.

"How's the Pyromancer holding up?"

"Ah," said Yarlaith, his brow furrowed as if caught off-guard. He fidgeted with the collar of his healer's robes; its white cloth was grey, like the few wisps of hair left on his head. "The mage is doing...well. It's a miracle he survived, but there's nothing divine about the pain he's in right now. He's lost a lot of blood, and I doubt I'll be able to save his arm . . . but he'll live. More importantly, Morry, how are you doing?"

"Fine," she mumbled, hoping Yarlaith wouldn't pry any further. They made their way out into the chapel gardens in silence.

The flowers were slowly dying with winter on the way, but their colour still shone along the path. The road from the chapel twisted and turned downhill towards Roseán's town centre, lined by tall trees with leaves of autumn gold and brown. The Harvest Moon would be in just a few more weeks, but the thought was bittersweet.

Mother always loved the festivities more than anyone . . .

No, she would not dwell on it. She needed to be brave. She needed to be strong. At fourteen years she was almost a woman grown, and only widows and children cried. Not mages, or knights, or adventurers.

"I must return to my patient," said Yarlaith as they turned towards the High Road. "You should go to *The Bear*, Morry. You aren't the only one in grief today. Put on your brave face and inspire the others to be strong."

Morrígan forced a smile and looked up at Yarlaith. She didn't think it was very convincing, but the old healer nodded in response.

"That's it," he said, clasping his hands together. "In the meantime, I'll prepare the spare room for you." For half a second, the smile that perpetually shone from his face faded. "Just, don't enter the clinic while the door is closed. Some of these medical procedures are incredibly delicate, and Fionn is in a lot of pain."

He smiled again. "That's the Pyromancer's name, by the way. Fionn."

***

The sun threw scarlet rays over the sea as Morrígan made her way to *The Bear and the Beadhbh*: a crooked, two-story building at the centre of Roseán's town square, and the only business that remained open after dark. The two Reardon brothers from the forge sang out of key at the entrance of the tavern, flagons of cider in hand.

Morrígan scowled as the memory of her father resurfaced. He was one to start drinking as soon as the sun set, regardless of the season. She pushed past the two drunkards, their song finishing with a tuneless crescendo.

Morrígan was immediately met with the thick aroma of bacum smoke as she stepped into *The Bear*. Roars of laughter and slurred toasts clashed with the sound of a bard strumming a lute. Passing him, Morrígan caught a quick glance of Taigdh, the innkeeper's son, shuffling through the crowd to deliver drinks to their patrons.

Peadair has him working too hard. Taigdh should have been at the chapel with the rest of them.

Spirits were high, despite the funeral service less than an hour before. That was the way it always was in Roseán. Funeral festivities were something that Morrígan had grown used to long ago. If an elderly villager died of natural causes, it was typical for the men to get together, raise their glasses, and make a toast to the inevitable cycle of life. "That's just the way things are!" they'd say.

But there was nothing natural about Mother's death.

A man dressed in black mumbled as Morrígan took a seat at the bar. She didn't bother with a response.

Probably more empty condolences anyway.

All morning, the villagers of Roseán had been saying the same thing: "She's with the Lord now." "Everything happens for a reason." "It's all part of the Lady's plan." Sometimes it seemed as if everyone just repeated what they heard from other funerals.

Morrigan fought against the tears that filled her eyes. Mr. Cathain, the undertaker, sat across the bar. The old man nodded solemnly towards her; he seemed to be the only one who realised there had been a funeral today.

The bard laughed and plucked a light, uplifting chord that caused Morrigan's fingers to curl into fists. He broke into an energetic, jolly reel, and villagers clapped along to its bouncing rhythm.

Sir Warts, Sir Warts, a hero of sorts,
And so, our story began,
When a hog of the North, donned a shield and a sword,
And ev'ryone thought him a man.

Sir Warts, of course, was called to the courts,
Where the noblemen made him a knight,
But a jesterin' fool, stood high on a stool,
And sought to make ev'rything right.

"Sir Warts! Sir Warts! I fear I must thwart,
Your plan to live amongst men,
But my eyes they are wise, and see through your disguise,
Vile mountainous hog of the Glenn!"

Sir Warts, of course, thought none of the sort,
And sat there in silence instead,

But hearing the slander, the Earl stood in anger,
And lobbed off the jester's head!

The crowd cheered, but Morrigan saw a hint of remorse in the bard's eye.

He's only playing what they want him to play, she realised, her anger fading. She scanned the room, taking note of those who were singing, and those who remained silent. *They sing and dance to celebrate Mother's memory, but they drink to forget their own grief.*

Peadair appeared from behind the bar and placed a glass in front of Morrigan.

"Apple and pear cider for the lady! No, no, don't worry about paying, not at all. Consider it a token of our commiserations. I'm deeply sorry for your loss, Morrigan, we all are. Taigdh will be glad to see that you're doing well."

"Thank you, Peadair." Morrigan forced herself to smile, remembering Yarlaith's words.

Before she could elaborate further, Peadair vanished to serve another customer.

Across the inn, Taigdh tended to a rather large table of revellers. He seemed suited to the role of assistant innkeeper, but quite different to the little boy Morrigan used to pass notes to at the back of Yarlaith's reading lessons. It was a sad thought, that Taigdh would probably be working and living in the inn for the rest of his life. He was only a year older than Morrigan, but he was certainly wiser than most of the drunkards he served.

She drank her cider alone as she studied the huge mural behind the bar that gave the inn its name. A large black bear stood on hind legs, locked in combat with a beadhbh. The flightless bird of prey clawed at the bear, its black beak like an arrowhead, its long, feathered neck the shaft. Bears and beadhbhs were said to be often found fighting over prey in the Glenn, but Morrígan didn't know of any who had explored the poisonous valley.

"Um, Morrígan?"

Darragh, the butcher's boy, stood by her side, his gaze averted from hers. He was a short, chubby lad, with a huge mess of red hair. He rubbed his hands together, as if unsure what else to do with them.

"I...I just wanted to say that, um, I'm sorry for your loss."

Morrígan tapped her foot against the barstool. "What exactly do you have to be sorry about, Darragh?"

His eyes widened, and he began shaking his head. "No, I didn't mean it like that, I...I just—"

Morrígan suppressed a grin. Taigdh had always been much better at making Darragh nervous than she was. But those days were long gone.

"Relax, Darragh," Morrígan said. "I meant that in jest. I really do appreciate your kind words. Please, send your father my regards."

Red faced, Darragh nodded, his eyes focused on the floor. He excused himself with a mumble.

Morrígan spent most of the night alone after that, watching as the bard continued to sing loud and boisterous songs at his audience's request. A group of young girls sat up with the bard and sang along, escalating the small performance into a full festival of music. The bard brought music from the Seachtú of the south, while the girls taught him the local songs of the Clifflands.

As the night went on, more and more people danced and sang. A wide circle in the centre of the inn was cleared, making more room, but it didn't stop some people from climbing on the furniture.

Despite the atmosphere, Morrígan couldn't help but wonder about the adventurers, and why they had come through her little village by the cliffs, on that morning of all mornings.

It was only because of the king's new taxes that her family had been working so early in the first place. After the troll killed her mother and the travellers who tried to fight it, the beast turned towards Morrígan. Only then did the sun rise, its light turning the troll to stone before her eyes.

Morrígan shivered. *It's probably still there, petrified, looking over the farm...*

After a particularly long and exhausting number, the bard cleared his throat and thanked everyone for their participation. When he said that this was the liveliest inn he had ever visited, the crowd cheered, though Morrígan reckoned he said that everywhere he played.

"Now, for one last song..."

He picked up the lute and strummed a single chord. Already anticipating what was to come, Morrígan jumped to her feet and stood up proud and straight. When the bard sang, everyone went quiet and did the same, but Morrigan always liked being the first one to rise for the Ballad of the Trinity. It was a sign of disrespect to the Gods if you didn't stop what you were doing and pay attention, so being the first to do so made Morrigan feel like she was more devout than anyone else. The bard sang the song sweetly, but he was drowned out by a chorus of drunken patrons, each trying to out-pride the other.

A thousand ships sailed across,
Long leagues of intrepid waters,
Our homes were lost, our lands destroyed,
But paradise still called to us.

Most of the villagers sang along dutifully, but one person did not stand with the others. The large man sitting in the stool beside Morrigan faced away from the bard, drinking to himself. She tried to ignore the blatant display of disrespect and continued singing with the others.

Armed with faith, and led by the Lord,
We found this sacred country,
With hills of green, and rich of soil,
Móráin declared it heavenly.

At this point, several others had stopped singing, their attention focused on the patron in black. Still, he remained silent, hunched over his frothing pint of ale. Morrígan leaned over to get a closer look at the man's face. To her horror, she saw that he was not Human.

With the watchful eye of the Lord,
And the guiding hand of the Lady,
King Móráin, will forever reign,
Through the Penetrance of Divinity

The bard played on regardless, as people around him whispered to each other and pointed at the stranger. Morrígan, however, was still shocked at the sight of his face.

A Simian!

She had never seen one before. He wasn't fully dressed in black; thick brown fur covered his arms, his head, and his face. He continued to drink deeply through dark, protruding lips.

So Seletoth will watch our land,
And Meadhbh will weave our fate,
But tonight, we raise a single glass,
To Old King Móráin the Great.

During the final drawn-out note, no one paid any mind to the bard. He feebly presented an upturned hat to the crowd, but everybody slowly edged towards the Simian. The stranger kept drinking, and this seemed to worry the villagers even more. Eventually, Ciarán from the mill spoke up.

"Excuse me, sir, you should show more respect!"

The Simian slammed his drink on the table, startling those nearby. He turned in his chair, facing the mob for the first time.

"And what have I done to offend you, little man?"

Ciarán cleared his throat and raised his chest, perhaps to not look so little.

"You've disrespected your hosts. The least you could do is stand for our Ballad, but all you lot are alike: ignorant of everything the Trinity has done for you."

Some nodded in agreement, but others looked away in shame, as if they knew it was a poor choice of words.

The Simian stood. He loomed two feet over the speaker; three, perhaps, considering how Ciarán shrank in fear.

"You should read a book, Human," the Simian barked, "instead of listening to jesters for your history lessons. This one seems to have left out the verse where your people slaughtered mine...how they used their magic to enslave us."

He motioned towards the bard, but the singer had disappeared. It looked like Ciarán wanted to do the same.

"It was not our choice!" Another voice came from the crowd. "We gave your kind a chance to live alongside us!"

The Simian snorted. "You gave us a choice between giving our lives to your Gods or to your swords."

"And you chose neither!" called a third voice. "You've done nothing but spit in the face of the Trinity ever since we let you rats live!"

Rats? Morrigan stole another glance at the Simian. *But he looks nothing like one...*

The hairs on the Simian's arms stood on end, and his hulking body quivered slightly. He seemed as if he could snap at any minute, but his face remained calm and emotionless.

Morrigan leaned away from the Simian as much as she could. *Gods, he could probably kill us all if he wished.*

Ciarán suddenly grew brave again. He pointed at Morrigan.

"This girl lost her mother today!" he shouted. "You deny our Gods, so tell her what you believe! Tell her the fate of her mother was nothing but bad luck!"

Leave me out of this! Morrigan wanted to say.

But the Simian gave no response. Instead, he looked straight into Morrigan's eyes. His were dark and unblinking, lined with emotions Morrigan couldn't quite grasp. In silence he stared for some time, before clearing his throat.

"I have nothing to tell you, little one," he said. "My words are as empty as the prayers of these fools. Listen to them, and they'll blind you to the truth: your mother will not live forever in Paradise. Instead, she will live on in your memories."

The Simian finished his drink and slammed the empty cup on the bar. The crowd started to part as he took a step the door, but the Simian stopped. He glanced back at Morrigan.

"Cherish the moments you had together, instead of praying for those that will never come."

With that he strode through the tavern door, slamming it as he left.

After a moment, the little man spoke up. "Don't listen to what that heathen said, Morrigan; your mother is waiting for all of us in Tierna Meall right now, and we know it."

Others chimed in with similar sentiments, and Morrigan thanked them. Still, the more she thought about what the Simian said, his words seemed to make a strange kind of sense.

The Simians or the druids may be wrong, but in another way, Mother can still live on through me...

Despite how brave and strong she had pretended to be, it all disappeared in a flood of tears.

She's dead. She really is dead.

"Ah, he had no business coming in here, making her cry like this!" said one of the villagers. "Those rats, I tell you, they don't care about anyone's feelin's but their own!"

"That's 'cause they were born without souls, they can't feel nothing!"

"Aye, rats will never understand what they don't have. That's why they fought against us, 'cause we've got mages and healers when all they've got are their smoke and their steam."

Morrigan tried to hide her tears, but there were too many people around her.

"I...I want to go home!" she cried, jumping from her chair, and hurrying towards the front door of the inn.

As she left, Peadair rang his bell, signalling closing time.

"Have you no homes to go to?" he bellowed, over and over, half in jest as he always did. "Have you no homes to go to?"

Outside, Morrígan started into a run.

Mother. Gone. Really gone.

She reached the northern side of the town square, taking the High Road towards her uncle's house.

Without Mother, without Father, what's left for me?

As tears streamed down her cheeks, Morrígan's feet carried her to the front door of her uncle's house. She pressed a hand against it.

How could this happen to me? Rage boiled in her stomach as she pushed the door open.

Morrígan barely took two steps into the house when a sudden scream split the silence, a howling from the clinic further down the hall.

Yarlaith's patient!

The image of the young Pyromancer flashed through her mind; his arm being twisted and pulled from its socket with a sickening crunch.

Part of Morrígan wanted to peek through the clinic's door and see what was happening...but she recalled her uncle's words. A delicate procedure. A young man in great pain. A warning that neither should be disturbed.

Morrígan slowly turned away from the cries of pain.

She made her way upstairs towards her uncle's spare room in the landing. Upon her freshly made bed sat a strange, folded fabric. As she approached, Morrígan saw that this was some sort of cloak made of out black feathers. Next to it lay a letter, which she promptly read:

To my dear Morry,

I know this is a day you will be happy to forget in years to come, but I did not forget that this was supposed to be a special day. This is a cloak made from the feathers of a beadhbh from the Glenn, and quite popular amongst travellers and adventurers these days. Wear it at night, and I promise you will be safe.

With love, Yarlaith

Her uncle's unique signature adorned the bottom of the note, each letter looping extravagantly into the next.

Morrigan picked up the cloak and threw it over her head. It fit well around her shoulders and draped low without touching the ground. She crept into bed and cried herself to sleep, wrapped safely in her birthday present.

Chapter 2:
The Double Agent

Farris woke up drunk, not quite sure where he was. With a stretch, he dragged himself from bed, his head throbbing, his mouth as dry as the Dustworks of Penance.

He stumbled across creaking floorboards towards a nearby window, hoping the view outside would provide a clue to where he was. With delayed, deliberate movements, he pulled open the shutters and grimaced as sunlight stabbed his eyes.

Once his vision cleared, the morning commotion of Cruachan's markets greeted him, with people buzzing around clusters of squalid stalls dotted along Barrow's Way. It was a familiar sight. Farris figured he was probably in one of the inns that lined the North Wall of the capital.

He glanced across the room and cringed at the sight of the half-clothed female Simian sprawled across the featherbed.

I must have gotten stupid-drunk again.

Suddenly aware that his naked body was on display to all outside, Farris slunk away from the window and crouched down to put on his trousers. He spotted his leather tunic thrown over a chair in the corner of the room, then tiptoed across the floor.

The tunic was heavy; its concealed weapons and brass buckles rattled as he pulled it on. He tried to quell the clamour, but concern for his sleeping hostess vanished once he spotted a sink against the far wall.

He went over and twisted the tap, putting his parched lips to the running water. Although he didn't believe in heaven, for that moment alone, Farris experienced paradise.

A jaded voice interrupted his bliss.

"You must be pretty thirsty, considering the state you were in last night."

Ah, a perceptive one! Farris turned to face her, suppressing a grin. *The Crown would do well to hire you as an agent in their ranks.*

She was pretty enough, though her body wasn't quite as supple as Farris's typical bed-mates. Still, a captivating smile revealed teeth that would have been beautiful if they hadn't been stained sallow from years of thainol and bacum abuse.

The details from the previous night slowly came together in Farris's mind, but none brought him much relief. Her name was Jane, a barmaid working in *The Stained Glass*, and it wasn't the first time Farris had found himself in her bed. Still, he couldn't remember why he had been drinking so much the previous night.

"Marc, are you going to stay for breakfast this time?" Jane sat up and reached for a grey blouse on the floor.

Farris scanned the room, hoping to find some clues. "How late was it when I arrived at *The Glass*?"

Jane giggled. "We were about to close when you came barging in, stinking of thainol and shouting my name. You seemed happy to see me...happier than now."

Farris turned and splashed more water onto his face, rubbing his damp, bloodshot eyes. He picked his head up to see a drained, weary face staring back at him from the grimy mirror above the sink.

This is not a good day for work.

He paused for a moment, listening intently; the faint hum of a resonance-crystal swung gently through the silence.

"No!" Farris frantically patted the dozens of pockets hidden throughout his tunic. "Jane, do you hear that?"

She didn't answer, but instead stared back with beautiful, confused eyes.

Farris swore as he spotted a tiny crystal lying by his feet, glowing white and resonating softly.

The king wants to see me again. He was probably summoning me all morning. He picked it up.

A forgotten fear twisted his stomach. There could only be one reason why he'd be called again like this, on such short notice.

He knows. The bastard knows we tried to poison him.

He bolted towards the bed and snatched a leather boot, squeezing it on his foot. Dropping to his knees, he searched for the other.

"What's wrong?" asked Jane, rising to her feet.

The boot lay at the other end of the bed. Farris grabbed it and pulled it on, then made his way towards the door.

"Marc, where are you going? Aren't you even going to say goodbye?"

"Something came up...I need to go." Farris Silvertongue had earned his reputation amongst the Simian rebels by being an excellent liar, but this certainly wasn't his morning. "I'm sorry."

"No," she said firmly, bounding forwards and grabbing his hand. "That's not good enough. Am I just supposed to wait until you get drunk again? Marc, I want to be with you..."

Farris sighed, fingering the crystal in his other hand. *She has no idea who I am. If she knew I worked with the Silverback...*

But what was he supposed to tell her? Where could he start?

She doesn't even know my name.

"It's best that I go. You...you deserve better than me."

"Sin's stones," she cursed, rolling her eyes. She let go of his hand. "Can't I decide myself what I deserve? Am I supposed to believe you running off again is somehow doing me a fucking favour?"

"No, you don't understand."

"Oh, I think you'll find I understand perfectly well. You want me to think that you're some sort of cold, emotionless person who I'm better off without, but I know you, Marc. You're *scared*. Scared of what we might become if you dared show me any level of honesty!"

Farris paused. How could she know so little and so much at the same time?

"Fine," he said, turning to leave. "Maybe you're right. Maybe I am just afraid."

"Well, you're welcome back whenever you grow a damn spine." Jane followed him to the door. "But as sure as the Tower still stands, I'm not expecting that to be very soon."

Farris nodded and left, descending the stairs two at a time. Perhaps there was some truth to her words, but he didn't think on it for long. By the time he reached the bottom of the steps, his thoughts returned to the king.

We should have waited...

The air outside was colder than usual; it brushed through the hair on Farris's face and brought gooseflesh to his skin. Beneath the silver sky, stalls and stands stretched down Barrow's Way right over to the Grey Keep: the seat of King Diarmuid, Third of His Name, Nineteenth Incarnate. Its presence roared with power; its mass dwarfed the rest of the city. Farris felt himself sober up immediately.

I could run. I could make my way back to Penance and...

But he knew it wouldn't be that easy. He had spent three years infiltrating the Crown, and he knew how powerful its reach was. Even now, spies could be lining the streets, hidden, watching his every move.

Merchants and farmers tried to force their wares upon Farris as he rushed through the market. A toothless Human waved carrots above his head, shouting, "First crop of the year!" even though carrots were in season for the past two moons. Beside him, a young woman was in heated discussion with a Simian merchant over the price of a bronze candlestick. One glance told Farris she was being cheated.

Further up, a bearded preacher stood atop a wooden platform, dressed in fine clothes that Farris was sure were stolen. The Human gestured to the sky.

"Our Lord Seletoth dwells upon Mount Selyth!" he screamed to a group of young men. "The journey may be dangerous, but we must go, brothers! Give to the Lord! Your coin can bring about our salvation!"

Actors living in a city of lies.

As he reached the castle walls, double-wide wooden gates opened, and a procession of knights and soldiers marched out to a loud fanfare of noise and colour.

"Bandits to the north," muttered a young Simian. A crowd had gathered to see the brave men off. "They're ambushing caravans on the roads that bypass the Glenn. The sooner Santos's tunnel is finished, the better."

"Aye," agreed Farris, spotting a group of Geomancers in their ranks. "I dream of the day our two great races are brought together through Simian technology."

It was mostly true. It was only a matter of time before the Silverback declared war on the Crown.

Brought together by Simian technology indeed.

Farris broke away from the crowd and made his way to the open gates when an old Simian beggar grabbed at his ankle.

"Please, sir, Humans broke my legs when I didn't pause for their prayers. Now I cannot work to feed my family. Have mercy..."

The beggar half crawled across the ground, propped up with a wooden walking stick under his elbow. Torn rags covered his legs, bent and useless.

"I have no coin now, brother, but I will return later. I promise." It was the first truth he told all day.

"Have a nice day, and a bountiful harvest," replied the beggar dully, his eyes drifting back to the crowds.

As Farris crossed the courtyard, both Human and Simian servants busied themselves with work in the royal gardens, lush with flowers of every colour imaginable. A young female Simian tending to some roses waved to Farris but called out another man's name. Farris wasn't sure if she was referring to one of his own aliases or had mistaken him for another. To be safe, he smiled and waved back extravagantly before disappearing into the Grey Keep.

The crystal still hummed in Farris's pocket as he crossed Móráin Hall. Eighteen pewter busts of dead kings lined the walls, along with portraits of the twelve Holy Saints of the Trinity.

In the early days of the kingdom, the Church had a habit of raising any Human to sainthood in response to carrying out good deeds. Amongst those pictured were Lorcan the Architect, Durnadh the Blacksmith, Aisling the Healer, Moira the Hunter, and Mhórthos the Bard.

Farris couldn't help but stare at the last portrait. The bard's beady eyes leered out from under thick eyebrows, his mischievous smile half-hidden beneath a beard, pointed and black like a spearhead.

Mhórthos...what he'd give to be able to see me right now.

Farris couldn't help but see the poetic justice in his predicament. Simian separatists were a fringe political group, though Farris suspected most Simians were at least sympathetic to the cause. It was still commonplace to see loyal Simian guards and soldiers within the ranks of the Crown. However, some claimed this was concerted effort by King Diarmuid to quell Human-Simian tensions in the capital.

But Farris personified this gap, both a spy for the Simian dissidents and one of King Diarmuid's most trusted agents, like something straight out of one of Mhórthos's tragedies.

When Farris tore his gaze away from the bard, a trembling anxiety took hold of his body. His vision blurred, and his chest grew tight, his heartbeat quickening. The hall went spinning; he barely caught himself in balance. Eyes focused down on the crimson carpet beneath him, he took a deep breath.

It'll pass. It'll pass. Give it another moment and like the others, it will pass.

He exhaled slowly, focusing on every movement of air through his lips. He took another breath and tried to calm himself, but a different thought surfaced.

They know. They all know, and they're waiting for a chance to strike. This was the last straw, and now they know.

He lost control of his breathing and fell to one knee. *We should have waited. We should have fucking waited before we tried to poison the bastard.*

Then the anguish vanished, his heartbeat returning to its natural rhythm. Farris stood and regained his composure, checking to make sure nobody had seen him. He smirked.

They don't know, of course they don't! If he did, he would have sent the Wraiths for me instead of a crystal wave.

Two Simian soldiers guarded the door to the royal chambers. Their blue-tinted armour shimmered in the waning torchlight. Farris couldn't help but wonder what side they'd fight on when the time came.

He reached into his tunic for the crystal. "I have been summoned by the king," he said. "It started earlier this morning." The guards eyed the crystal carefully, then stepped aside.

Inside the royal chamber, King Diarmuid sat at the end of a long, gold-bound oak table. His face was red; from wine or anger, Farris couldn't tell.

Perhaps both.

As he entered, another man, standing, swung around to greet him. Farris knew him well: Padraig Tuathil, Captain of the City Guard.

"I hope I'm not interrupting," said Farris.

Padraig smirked as the Simian crossed the room, his footsteps muffled by the carpet.

"Ah, Farris Turncloak! Have you come to bring us the heads of more brothers-in-arms? Or have you any left, at this point?"

"Those men weren't my brothers," said Farris, resisting the urge to raise his voice. "I was acting on behalf of His Grace, and I succeeded where you and your men failed."

"My men failed because they weren't *traitors*."

"Enough!" The king waved at both Farris and Padraig with the back of his hand.

"Apologies," whispered Farris, sinking to one knee.

"As you were." King Diarmuid made a motion with a jewelled hand, one finger pointing upwards. "I need to speak with you in private. Padraig, leave us be."

"Yes, Your Grace."

As he passed, Farris spotted a thick coin-purse tied to the captain's belt.

Another bribe from the Black Sail?

He listened carefully as the door closed behind Padraig. There was a brief silence before two pairs of footsteps moved away. He closed his eyes and unravelled the rhythm of the fading strides.

He dismissed the guards so he could listen in on our meeting.

The king stood, his hands fumbling as if he didn't know what to do with them. "Have you brought me any news from the waterfront, Farris?"

"I delivered the Black Sail report yesterday," he said carefully, "but you know how slippery these smugglers can be. My informants will need more time."

The king sighed. "Of course, of course...I remember now, you brought me another bottle of thainol. How could I forget?"

Farris's heart soared as the king gestured towards the bottle, still sealed with the poison inside undisturbed. Only during the frostbitten winters in the Dustworks did the sight of a single bottle of thainol bring such happiness. This one had been shipped from Penance and placed directly into Farris's hands with instructions to give it to the king. One sip, Farris was told, would render any man infertile.

If he doesn't know about the poison, then why have me summoned on such short notice?

King Diarmuid's eyes remained fixated on the ground. His lips quivered.

"Is there something wrong, Your Grace?"

The king looked up at Farris, his radiant blue eyes laced with terror. "I...I was attacked."

It was not the response Farris expected. "Attacked? By whom?"

The king closed his eyes. "By...they were...Simians. Dissident Simians, allied with the Silverback."

"Impossible!" Farris exclaimed. It really was impossible; the Silverback would never attack the king without letting Farris know first, especially after so many years of careful planning. "When did this happen? Where was it?"

The king buried his face in his hands.

"Last night. Santos was leading me down to inspect the progress of the railway. We were halfway between here and Penance when we were ambushed. They murdered Santos and my guards, but I escaped."

"And what of the rebels? Have they been caught?"

"No," said the king hesitantly. "They were gone when I came to. Padraig has men stationed in the tunnel now."

Farris stared at him, his mind reeling. Something didn't add up.

"So, the attackers just left you there? To die?" Farris added the second question to make it seem less like he was questioning the king's account.

"Savages," growled Diarmuid, his face turning red. "We've given them too much, Farris. The bond between the Crown and the Triad is as strong as ever, but all it would take is the action of a single individual to spark a bloody civil war."

War... Farris suppressed a shudder. With generations of peace since the Fall of Sin, none had ever even attempted to take the life of a king. Even the Silverback didn't want to kill King Diarmuid outright. This much Farris knew for sure. So why an assassination attempt?

We worked so hard to make the king trust me. The Silverback would never throw all of it away like this.

"What do you propose we do?" he asked, trying to fill the silence.

King Diarmuid leaned forwards over the massive, oaken table.

"What do we do?" he asked, with the whisper of a madman. "Isn't it obvious? We *strike*. We take the City of Steam!"

Farris focused on his breathing, the anxiety creeping its way back in. "Is that what you want?" he asked. "To start a war with the Simians of Penance?"

"Not yet," said the king, mopping sweat from his forehead with a white silk handkerchief. "We need to build up our defences first. I'm garrisoning battlemages in every settlement across the Clifflands as we speak and raising taxes across the kingdom to fund them."

Farris nodded, slowly. *The smallfolk won't like that one bit.*

"But mages alone won't win the war," the king continued. "The Triad's Skyfleet is far too powerful. I need you to travel to Penance to destroy it."

Farris managed to keep a straight face. "Anything for the Crown, my liege."

The king walked to a south-facing window overlooking the waterfront. Dozens of vessels—from tiny fishing boats to giant galleys—were tied along the piers. Further out were three airships, floating above the water. Farris recognised two instantly. Both *The Horizon* and *Cumulous* were common sights in the city. The third was a newcomer. It was no more splendid or larger than the other two, but it looked *powerful*. Four large engines surrounded the gargantuan gas cell, instead of the two that commonly adorned the continental models.

"It's called *The Glory of Penance*," said King Diarmuid. "It was built last year to cross the Eternal Sea. The Triad pulled its funding just as it was complete, so the captain is taking a trade route until he gathers enough coin for a proper expedition."

"Very exciting."

"Yes," said the king, curtly. "Many have lost their lives to the Eternal Sea, for no ship could conquer it. But this..."

"It could find a new home for the Simian people," whispered Farris, his mind rushing at the possibilities.

Don't smile. You have orders to destroy the Skyfleet.

"You will travel on that ship when it leaves for Penance tomorrow at dawn." King Diarmuid pulled out a roll of parchment from inside his robes and handed it to Farris. "You will board under the identity of a Simian named Chester who will be travelling as a passenger. I am told he bears a resemblance to you. Keep your head down and nobody will question you. Chester has been told that—"

"—the ship leaves at noon," finished Farris, who had already opened the parchment and began reading.

"Four other agents will be on board," continued the king. "They'll have similar instructions, but you will never see them, and they will never see you. Once the ship docks at Sin, seek out a druid by the eastern front. Ask him about my health, and he will respond with the words, 'The Lord and Lady protect him.' After that, things will move quickly."

Farris stared at the parchment.

"You commit those words to memory, Farris, and destroy the parchment."

"Of course, Your Grace," the Simian muttered, his mind far away.

I must tell the Silverback. As soon as I arrive at Penance, I'll warn him.

But what of the other agents? What would happen if he never spoke the code to druid? Would they carry on the mission without him?

Perhaps I can silence them. Perhaps they will never make it to Penance.

"Do you understand your orders, Farris?" asked Diarmuid, his voice sterner than before.

"Yes, Your Grace," Farris said weakly. "If I may be excused, I'll make my preparations."

"Yes, agent. Godspeed."

Farris pulled out his pipe and a line of flint from his breast pocket. With a well-practised flick and a twist, he put his lips to the spout and inhaled the soothing smoke. He closed his eyes as the smoke filled his lungs, clearing out the vapours of anxiety.

The king laughed, quickly returning to his old self. "Be sure to enjoy that, Farris! You know these ships don't allow that kind of stuff on board. You'd burn it straight out of the sky!"

Farris stopped and turned, puffing smoke out from the side of his mouth. "Of course, Your Grace. You know I'm more careful than that."

With that, Farris pressed his shoulder against the door, swinging it open forcefully. Padraig Tuathil collapsed on the floor as the Simian tumbled over him.

The king roared again with laughter. "Very careful, of course!"

Farris jumped to his feet as a bewildered Padraig held a hand to his own face.

"What is *wrong* with you? You could have broken my nose!"

Farris shrugged. "And you could have been standing somewhere sensible."

He held out a hand and helped pull the captain to his feet, keeping his other hand hidden from view.

"I seem to have dropped my pipe." Farris gestured to the floor. "Could you help me look for it?"

It was the captain's turn to laugh. "Oh, I would be glad to if I didn't have this damn city to protect."

Padraig marched off towards the barracks in the western wing, wiping dust from his cloak as he went.

Farris smiled and picked his pipe up from the ground. He bowed to the king and closed the door, straightening himself before walking out through Móráin Hall.

When he reached the gates of the castle, he was greeted with the same pleas of help from the lame beggar. Farris walked over and casually dropped Padraig's coin-purse in front of the old Simian. The beggar scrambled over to it and leapt in the air with delight when he saw it was full of gold.

Farris sighed as he watched the beggar pick up the bag and run off to the market in the distance, leaving his wooden walking sticks behind.

Actors in a city of lies. From the highest noblemen to the crippled beggars, we do what we must to get by.

CHAPTER 3:
THE GARRISON

A cold morning breeze sliced salt and moisture across Morrígan's face; she tasted smoke in the air. Roseán was not far from the Simian city of Penance, and soot and steam often came carried in on northerly winds over the Glenn. Sometimes airships flew over those jagged peaks, but on the day Morrígan's mother was buried, the sky remained empty and grey.

Most of the same villagers who had attended the funeral were gathered in Roseán's cramped graveyard behind the chapel. People shuffled as they crowded around the gaping hole in the ground, careful not to step foot on any of the other surrounding graves. A coffin sat at the bottom. Morrígan committed the image to memory, knowing it was the last time she'd ever be this close to her mother.

There was some comfort in the routine; Morrígan couldn't deny that. Still, she couldn't help but feel slight disgust as Daithí the Blessed described her mother with the same vague, clichéd phrases as he did at every burial.

"She was a kind woman, a caring mother, and a loving wife."

Morrigan clenched her jaw tight. *She never loved him.*

The sound of iron scratching stone punctuated the priest's words as four men shovelled dirt on top of the coffin. Yarlaith would often use his own Geomancy for village burials, but the healer was still busy in the clinic. Morrigan could still hear the Pyromancer's screams from the previous night.

"She was well loved by the community," Daithi continued, "and she would have loved to see all of you gathered here today."

Morrigan glanced over her shoulder to gauge the size of the crowd. *Then why didn't they ever get together for her when she was alive?*

"Though short, her life was full of laughter and love. There is nothing more terribly tragic than the death of someone so young and beautiful."

She was more than her youth. She was more than her beauty.

Morrigan closed her eyes and blocked out the rest of the druid's words. She wore her new beadhbh cloak, fastened tight against the wind. One of the strange adventurers had been carrying the feather and down of a skinned beadhbh, and Yarlaith had Mrs. Mhurichú, the local dressmaker, fashion it into a cloak. It fit her well, but Morrigan was more interested in the other implications her birthday present carried.

They travelled through the Glenn. They explored the poisonous valley, and only one lived to tell the tale.

Although Roseán was situated just several miles from the Glenn, she knew very little about it. Yarlaith had once said that every plant and flower in the valley was poisonous, and every bird and beast a predator. Its mountains acted like a massive, natural shield separating Roseán and the Clifflands from the Simians of Penance to the north.

Morrígan recalled the Simian's words from the previous night. Surely, he meant well, but part of her struggled with the thought of there being nothing...*after*. No Tierna Meall. No life. Nothing. How could anyone live a happy life without knowing where they would end up? She knew little about Simian culture, but they did hold funerals of sorts. She had once read about great furnaces where the Simians would burn their deceased, releasing the remains into the air in the form of fumes.

This was a disturbing thought, as the Church claimed that only in the pure, undisturbed form of a buried corpse could one live forever. To interfere with the dead was a sin worse than murder itself.

A murmur rippled through the crowd, signalling that the ceremony was coming to an end. Morrígan, didn't stir, and instead stood staring at the grave.

"Morry, are you alright?"

Taigdh appeared by her side, but she barely turned to look at him.

"Yes," she replied. The word felt like a lie before she even said it.

"We're all heading back to *The Bear* now," he said. "Sorcha and Darragh are coming too, but if you want to stay here instead, we understand."

Morrigan nodded. As she did, a mound of dirt upon her mother's grave quivered, just slightly.

"Did you see that?" said Morrigan.

"No?" he said, taking a step closer. "What was it?"

"I saw something move. Just now, in the grave."

"What?"

"There look! It's happening again!"

Morrigan pointed a quivering hand down at the grave. There, several pebbles and stones trickled down the mound, as if the ground beneath them was shifting.

"It's just the soil settling," said Taigdh, shaking his head. "It's nothing."

"How can you be sure?" Morrigan's voice rose. Taigdh balked in response. Behind him, Darragh and Sorcha, the dressmaker's daughter, caught Morrigan's eye.

"What's the matter, Morrigan?" asked Sorcha. She approached and casually slipped her fingers inside Taigdh's. Morrigan pretended to ignore that.

"The grave, the soil, it's moving. Look!"

The three looked at the grave; none were polite enough to object. After a moment of waiting, another tiny shift in the soil caused more grains to come loose.

"There!" cried Morrigan. "Do you see?"

Sorcha sighed. "It's nothing, Morrigan. It's probably the wind, or—"

"It's not the wind. It's like something's moving down there, something—"

Morrígan gasped as the realisation came to her. "What if she's alive?"

Silence. On hearing those words, Taigdh, Darragh, and Sorcha all stood still, averting their eyes from hers.

"Morry," said Taigdh. "You know that's not possible."

"I don't know!" she snapped. "And you don't either!"

Sorcha took a slow step forwards, then raised a gentle hand,

"Morrígan," she said, lips pursed in caution. "Back when your uncle told me that my father died, I didn't believe him at first. Even when I saw Dad lying dead in the clinic, I still thought he was alive. Yarlaith explained what would happen next, the measures he would take to ensure nobody else in Roseán would contract the pox that killed him, but I didn't care. I didn't care because my father was already dead."

And I don't care about your life story.

"What I'm saying, Morrígan, is that you've been through a lot. Sometimes your mind will lie to you. Sometimes you'll start thinking thoughts that don't make sense, or thoughts that'll do nothing but bring harm to yourself and those around you. These next few days will be the hardest, but we'll be there for you."

"That's right," Darragh chimed in. "We'll be here, no matter what."

"You can talk to us about anything," said Taigdh. "Even if you don't think it's important, even if you don't think anyone else cares, you can always talk to us."

"Thank you," said Morrígan, forcing a smile. "I just want to be alone, though, for a little while longer."

They bade her farewell, and Morrígan was left staring at the grave.

But I know what I saw...

The remaining villagers each shared their condolences as they left. Morrígan thanked Mr. Cathain and his son for helping with the funeral, and Mrs. Mhurichú for the beadhbh cloak; the dressmaker seemed happy to see Morrígan enjoying her gift. Ciarán from the mill, Peadair from the inn, and Fearghal the butcher all bestowed their sympathy, and she thanked them graciously. The Reardon brothers from the forge each shook her hand, leaving her fingers with a dull ache.

Is this it? Am I supposed to go back to a normal life now?

She paced slowly after the villagers, unconcerned of where they were headed. Maybe they'd return to *The Bear* for another night of festivities. Or perhaps Fionn the Pyromancer had made a full recovery and was ready to tell her why he and his companions chose that damned morning to lead a mountain troll to Roseán.

Either way, it was difficult to care what happened next. All she wanted to do was fall into her mother's arms again and cry. To hear the sound of her voice. To feel the warmth of her embrace.

Peadair walked slightly ahead, deep in hushed conversation with Ciarán and Fearghal. Morrígan knew it was rude to eavesdrop, but she couldn't help but listen.

"—the railway. That's why they did him in. Those tracks under the ground were supposed to unite Penance and Cruachan. Man and Simian, brought together with something even tighter than the Iron Concordant."

The butcher shook his head vigorously. Fearghal was a loud man, almost incapable of whispering. His voice grabbed the attention of more than those who were listening.

"Bah, it doesn't make any sense. None of it does. Why would the Silverback assassinate one of his own?"

"Because it was *Santos*," insisted Ciarán. "His trains were getting in the way of the separatist movement."

"Separatist?" roared Fearghal, "Is that what they're calling themselves now? The only thing the Silverback wants separated is King Diarmuid's head from his shoulders!"

Peadair placed a hand on Fearghal's arm and shushed him, nodding back towards Morrígan. The butcher lowered his gaze and mumbled apologetically.

Some people broke away from the crowd as they made their way down the High Road.

Going to get drunk again. But she didn't care; she wanted to hear more about this Silverback...

"The Simians claim they've changed their ways since the Fall of Sin," said Peadair. "They say that they've learned, that they've left the days of dissent behind. But all this with the Silverback and the railroad—"

Peadair cut himself off as the town square came into view. Immediately, Morrígan saw why.

Four groups of men dressed in solid, bright colours had gathered in the centre of the village. Reds, blues, greens, and greys, they stood still as statues in a strict, military manner.

"Soldiers!" gasped Peadair. Morrígan followed as they hurried down the High Road, walking almost at the pace of a jog towards the Square. Excitement rose like a balloon in her chest.

Maybe the king found out about the troll! Maybe he sent them here so nobody else would have to die like Mother did!

As she got closer, she noticed one soldier in solid green armour adorned with bright medals, standing before the rest. He wore a cloak, fastened with a brass brooch that glimmered in the sun. His stern face surveyed the crowd.

By the time Morrígan entered the Square, a crowd of villagers had already gathered before the stranger.

"—and I assure you, the Crown has brought in these measures to ensure your safety during such dangerous times."

Peadair and Fearghal stood at the edge of the crowd, where Morrígan joined them.

"They've announced the king's new taxes," whispered Peadair. "The Crown now claims an eighth of our profits, in place of a tithe."

"Curse their eyes!" swore Fearghal. "What right do they have to march in here and take our earnings like this?"

"The king's divine right," muttered Peadair, throwing a smile towards Morrígan. She smiled too, then noticed her uncle weaving through the crowd just over the innkeeper's shoulder. Yarlaith the White seemed far more exhausted than usual.

"What's going on?" Yarlaith asked in a breathless rasp.

"Taxes," said Peadair with a knowing nod. He had been the one who warned Morrigan's parents about the impending increase the day before the troll attacked.

A strange thought occurred to her. *We never would have been working that early, alone on the farm, if it wasn't for these new taxes. If it wasn't for them, would Mother still be alive?*

"That one has the look of a Geomancer," noted Yarlaith. Behind the speaker, a crowd of hooded soldiers stood grouped together by their colour. Morrigan counted twelve of each. Yarlaith leaned closer to Peadair, keeping his voice low.

"And they're not carrying any weapons..."

Peadair raised his eyebrows. "Battlemages! But why bring half an army to spread the Crown's news?"

"It may not be as simple as that," said Yarlaith, nodding towards the speaker. "From that one's insignias, I'd guess that he's a colonel, and the number of mages behind him equal that of a full battalion: forty-eight."

"I don't like where you're going with this, Yarlaith."

The colonel pulled out a roll of parchment from under his cloak. "There is another measure that His Grace has taken to guarantee your safety in these tremulous times. Point Grey is not far from here, and the Crown has seen that it has been fortified with his royal forces. His Grace recognises that there are many who are not protected by stone walls. For your safety, he has garrisoned battalions in every major and minor settlement along the Clifflands."

He gestured to the men behind him, each standing tall and proud in attention. "These are men I have trained for the field myself. They are honourable and brave warriors, and they will put the safety of this village first. You have my word." He paused and searched through the parchment in his hand. "Now, could the landlord of *The Bear and the Beadhbh* please make himself known?"

All eyes turned to Peadair.

"Aye, that'd be me. What do you need?"

"A word, please."

The crowd parted once the colonel stopped speaking, but Morrigan and Yarlaith made no move to leave.

The colonel approached Peadair and held out a hand, but the innkeeper didn't shake it.

"If it's a round you want, you'll be paying like all the other folk."

"Ah," said the colonel. "That won't be necessary." He handed Peadair the parchment he had been reading from. "This is a writ of accession, signed by the king himself. It demands you to hand over your property to the Crown. Until His Grace says otherwise, my battalion will be stationed in your inn."

Dumbfounded, Peadair took the document from the colonel and stared at it, though Morrigan knew that he couldn't read.

"*The Bear*," he said eventually. "No, this is preposterous!"

"This is the law, and His Grace has declared a state of emergency given the growing threat of the Simian dissidents."

"You can't have it!" he said, pointing a finger at the colonel. "This inn is my life; it's been in my family for generations."

"I'm afraid you have no choice in the matter. His Grace has signed the writ in sacred blood. I am obliged to execute its orders, and you are obliged to follow them. This will only be temporary, and there will be compensation."

With that, the colonel untied a large coin-purse from his belt and threw it to Peadair.

Peadair caught the purse in both hands. "There must be some kind of—"

His words were silenced as the bag fell open in his hands. Morrigan stood on the tips of her toes to steal a peek and saw the unfamiliar shimmer of gold inside. Judging by the size of the bag, she reckoned there must be more than a hundred coins in there.

The colonel smiled. "And there will be another one of those for every moon we are here. Now, my men need to rest. Can you give me the—"

"Keys!" shouted Peadair, scrambling for his pockets. "Yes! Here you go! Let me know if you need anything else. Anything else at all!"

The colonel held out his hand again, and Peadair shook this time.

"Colonel Eodadh, at your service."

"Ah, Eodadh, great name. Strong, of the Old Tongue. I look forwards to meeting you again."

The colonel bowed deeply and returned to his men. From the waning crowd, Taigdh emerged, a strange combination of dread and confusion upon his face.

"Da', what's going on? Who are all these people?"

"Ah, nothing to worry about, Taigdh," said Peadair softly, taking out a handful of coins and letting them fall back into the bag. "The colonel and his men will be moving into *The Bear*, just until all this Silverback business blows over. Just think of it as a paid vacation."

"What are you talking about? What about our home?"

Peadair placed a hand on his son's shoulder, lifting the bag up and down with the other. "We can live wherever we want, son. We could even build an inn over in Point Grey, so your mother can still be with your grandmother. Would you like that?"

For a second, Taigdh's eyes met Morrigan's.

"For the time being," said Yarlaith, stepping in, "you're free to stay in Morrigan's old family home, if that's okay with her, of course."

The two men turned to Morrigan. She nodded vigorously.

"That would be perfect, Yarlaith!" exclaimed Peadair. "We could move in there while we get ourselves sorted. Can I get you to send Moire a quick crystal-wave too?"

"Of course, Peadair. Feel free to drop by whenever you can."

Yarlaith sighed as Peadair and Taigdh strolled towards the inn, the former walking with a spring in his step.

"Come, Morry," Yarlaith said. "It's getting late."

Morrigan and Yarlaith made their way to the High Road, past the rows of motionless soldiers. Once the mages were out of earshot, Yarlaith spoke in a cautious tone. "The other villagers won't be happy when they learn that their watering hole has dried up, not to mention that a battalion of soldiers will be sharing our village."

Morrigan nodded slowly, not sure what to say.

First Father, then Mother, now Taigdh. It won't be long now until I'm the last one left.

They walked past the graveyard and the chapel in silence. The ground shimmered golden under a thick blanket of damp autumn leaves, squelching with every step. Upwards, the road curved gently with the shape of the hill. Yarlaith's house rose ahead of them.

I suppose this is my home now too.

"I don't like these developments, Morry." Yarlaith gave her a pensive glance. It was like one of his reading lessons all over again. "Why do you think the king would want to send his forces here?"

She knew by the tone of his voice that he already knew the answer. "Is it because of the troll? Have they come to protect us?"

Yarlaith sighed. "I wish it were that easy. They have come to protect us, yes. But not from trolls. Have you heard talk lately of one named the Silverback?"

"I heard Peadair mention it earlier. He was talking about someone named Santos too. Who are they? Simians?"

Yarlaith paused, struggling to find the right words. "I see no reason to hide anything from you, Morry; there are troubling times ahead. A small rebel movement in Penance has been growing over the past few years, and now it seems like they're ready for war."

"But what about our generations of peace?" asked Morrigan.

"It isn't enough for Silverback," said Yarlaith, his eyes somewhere far away. "He wants complete freedom from the Crown, and he and his people will do anything to achieve it."

"The separatists..." whispered Morrigan.

"Terrorists," spat Yarlaith.

"And Santos? I heard Peadair mention something about a railway."

"Santos was the Chief Engineer of Penance. He and King Diarmuid planned on building a railway underground to connect Penance to Cruachan...north to south. It was meant to be a beautiful convergence between Human and Simian cultures."

"What happened?"

"They were both attacked by the Silverback's terrorists while inspecting the railway. The king barely escaped with his life. Santos on the other hand..."

His voice trailed off; he put his trembling hands inside his cloak. Morrigan had never seen him so shaken.

"Why would Silverback kill one of his own?"

"I never said this made any sense," said Yarlaith. "The Simians are people, just like us... but there are some who are not content with simply beating their chests."

As they crossed Yarlaith's garden towards the house, Morrígan's thoughts returned to the villagers of Roseán. How long will the battlemages remain in *The Bear*? Was the Silverback really such a threat to a quiet little village?

When Yarlaith opened the door to his house, another thought struck Morrígan. "Yarlaith, what will the villagers do now with *The Bear* being closed and all?

Despite the seriousness in his tone earlier, Yarlaith laughed. "Well, Gods forbid they're forced to abstain for a little while! But with these recent developments in the capital, I suspect sobriety will be the least of their worries."

CHAPTER 4:
FARRIS SILVERTONGUE

It didn't take Farris long to track down his informant at the waterfront; Old Donal rarely strayed far from the docklands of Cruachan.

Farris found Donal picking through the contents of a discarded crate of spoiled fruit by the pier. The little hair he had left was as thin and fair as his skin, so the beggar was easily mistaken as a Human.

That's strange. It's past noon, and he's still sober.

"Is that you, Donal?" he called. "You're paid far too well to be feasting on scraps."

Old Donal snorted. "Ha! Scraps? These Humans are fools to be throwing away such ripe food." He picked up one particularly brown apple. "Some of 'em have even started fermentin'!"

Farris grinned as he scanned the docks. The scent of freshly caught fish rose up to meet his nostrils, as mongers and merchants crowded the wharfs below. A single longboat stood tall out over the quay, while dozens of thickset men busied themselves with its cargo. No airships were tied up at the dock, though, for only the southern waterfront was large enough to house the colossal Simian crafts.

"I've got another job for you," said Farris, keeping his voice low but his tone amiable. "Perhaps the most important job you'll be given this side of winter. If you succeed before nightfall, I'll pay you double."

Old Donal turned to face Farris, wet pieces of fruit dripping from his lips. "Must be special, but I'm a busy man. Can't be expected to drop everything at such short notice, y'know? How about tripling me pay, and I'll even share some of this fine produce with ye?"

He took another moist bite from the apple, chewing loudly as Farris pretended to consider his offer.

"Fine," he said. It wasn't as if Donal was being paid very much in the first place. "Three times your usual fee. The job is simple, but our time is short. I need you to find out everything you know about a Simian named Chester."

Donal paused and raised a single, sceptic eyebrow.

"That's all?"

"More or less. He'll be travelling as a passenger on *The Glory of Penance* tomorrow."

Donal's pensive eyes glanced towards the sky. "She's just arrived today. A beauty of a sight, so she is. You should be sure to catch a glimpse 'fore she sets off."

Noted. I might even make a day of it.

"There's one snag, though," said Donal, a smile curling from his lips.

Farris sighed. "And what would that be?"

"*The Glory* isn't a ferry-ship. It's got cabins and such, but no passengers. I could get a list of her cargo no bother, though."

Farris swore to himself. *Sin's stones! Chester was meant to be travelling as a passenger.* The more Farris thought on the king's words earlier that morning, the less sense they made. *Don't they even know what kind of ship I'm supposed to be on?*

"Just find out what you can about Chester." said Farris. "I'll return here at sunset."

Donal laughed. "That long? Sure, I'll be able to tell you everythin' about him by then, from the food he had for breakfast, to the name of the last woman he fucked!"

***

Although Farris lived just a hundred yards away from *Derelith's Pawn and Brokers*, he still felt a familiar surge of excitement when he pushed through those old wooden doors. Once the base of operations for the Simian dissidents of the city, today it was completely empty save for Derelith, its proprietor.

"Farris Silvertongue! How the Holy Hell are you?"

He bolted around the counter to greet Farris with an enthusiastic handshake. As they shook, Farris's eyes were drawn towards a golden chain sparkling against Derelith's white shirt. The chain held a gold pendant, triangular, with three crooked spirals in the centre.

"It's been too long Farris. Far too long!" he said, eventually releasing Farris's hand. Derelith was a clean-shaven young Human and certainly didn't seem the type to run an illegitimate business, fencing and laundering for the Thieves' Guild of Cruachan. As quickly as it had appeared, the look of pure glee and excitement vanished from Derelith's face.

"But, are you sure it's wise to return? Even after all this time? We're still on a hiatus here, you know, as far as the City Guard are concerned. What with the Guild being disbanded and—"

"I am well aware of our current situation," cut in Farris. "Only a matter of grave concern would bring me here."

The pawnbroker's expression darkened further. "And what would that be?"

"You mean you don't know?" asked Farris, irritated and surprised. "Aren't you still in contact with Penance?"

"Of course, and the Silverback himself has been keeping me filled in on your actions with the Crown. Last I heard the king trusted you enough to take that bottle of poisoned thainol Samson brewed up. They say that the Móráin line will be put to an end soon, 'cause of you. But if you ask me, I reckon it would have been easier to just kill the ol' bollocks."

"Well, it seems that's exactly what the Silverback tried to do. Last night. There was a failed assassination attempt on the king."

Derelith's brow furrowed. "No...no, that's not possible. Wasn't the whole point of this operation to keep him old and infertile? To what end, I don't know, but the Silverback insisted this was how we fight them."

"Indeed," said Farris. "And I didn't spend the past three years digging through old medical records on the royal family to have the Silverback ignore all the information we sent him."

Derelith shook his head. "I told you before, Farris. It's a tough pill to swallow. An immortal king?"

"Immortal *kings*. The Church has been teaching this for a long time, Derelith. The king's sacred bloodline is kept pure and intact by a gift of immortality, passed on from father to son since Móráin the First was born to Lord Seletoth. They call it Divine Penetrance."

Derelith wrinkled his nose. "I thought you didn't believe in any of that shit."

Farris didn't answer. Debating religion was not what he came here to do.

And I don't even know what to believe anymore.

"The Silverback saw my evidence," said Farris. "And that was enough to convince him all of this is real."

"Well, it looks like he changed his mind."

"Fool!" Farris roared, baring his fangs at Derelith. "They tried to kill the king with *hitmen!* They attacked him as he was being escorted through the tunnels. They killed Santos, too, along with his Simian guards."

Derelith shrank back in fear. "No!" he whispered. He held a pale hand to his face. "There's no way...he wouldn't harm Santos! They've had their disagreements, sure, but skies above, he's Nicole's father!"

"Well, he's dead. The king's preparing for war, and he's planning to strike Penance, directly. I'm flying out with four other agents of the Crown tomorrow morning to stage the attack. I just need to send a quick crystal-wave to the Silverback."

Whatever colour remained in Derelith's face faded. "I won't have access to another crystallographer for another three days, Farris. Two, if I threaten some of the right people."

A creeping, burning terror began in Farris's chest. He fought against it. "Fine, so what else can we do to warn them?"

Derelith didn't respond immediately. His gaze fell to the store's wooden floor. "I'm... I'm sorry. You know how cautious we need to be with this Church stuff. We can't just stroll down to our local mage and get him to send a message to Penance."

Farris closed his eyes. Bright sparks of light danced in his vision. His throat went dry, and he fought to get the words out.

"We...we could kidnap one, a crystallographer. Kill him afterwards and..."

But he knew. He knew well that no courier or carrier pigeon could make the trip in less than a day. The Church's crystals were the only means they had to warn the Silverback.

Derelith looked up at Farris. "What if we just tell everyone about the king's plans?" He spoke slowly, as if not convinced by his own words. "If everyone in Cruachan knew, surely the news would reach Penance by nightfall."

"No..." whispered Farris. The truth had manifested itself in his mind before their meeting had begun, but only now did he acknowledge it. There really was only one way of stopping the attack on Penance.

I have to go with them.

"Nobody else can know," said Farris, his voice low. "Not until we get a foothold on what's really going on. King Diarmuid has left me blind on the details of the attack, ignorant to the identity of the other agents on board the ship, but I'll find them. I'll kill them on the ship, before they reach Penance. We'll end all this *quietly.*"

Derelith closed his eyes and nodded slowly. "Sure, that'll probably put us a full head and nose ahead of the king. But is it worth endangering the population of Penance, just for the sake of keeping the upper hand?"

Farris paused, and chose his words carefully.

"Derelith, I've been working for the Crown for three years now. I know how they work. If we expose their plans now, with no proof, they'll use it against us. It's possible that they killed Santos themselves and blamed the Silverback, just to justify attacking Penance. They're ruthless, but they're *naive*. There's been no major conflict in this country for well over a hundred years, and the Crown has forgotten what it's like to fight a war. You saw how easy it was for us to manipulate them during the Thieves' Guild crisis."

"How easy it was for *you*," corrected Derelith. "Don't be passing your ingenuity there onto me. All I did was watch."

"Fair point," said Farris. "And you saw how quick they were to hire me without question afterwards. What kind of organisation does that?"

"One run by a drunkard with a golden crown."

"Precisely. Sure, the Crown has more men than we do. The Crown has more money than we do. The Crown has more reach, more infrastructure, and more power than we do, but they've so much more to lose. We've got men in all the right places, and we've learned far more about them than they have about us. The best part of it, the reason why I'm willing to risk my life, and maybe even the lives of those in Penance, just to keep this edge, is that they have no idea how far we've come. To them we're a lone fly that refuses to be swatted, but they have yet to see the swarm. Their underestimation of our strength is the only hope we have of winning this war."

Derelith stood in a thoughtful silence when Farris finished. He had embellished on some parts, of course, but the Human certainly seemed convinced.

"Alright, Farris. I'll keep this information to myself. In the meantime, I'll try my best to find out what really happened in those tunnels."

"Thank you, Derelith. I better get back to work. There's plenty to do."

"Stay strong. You've already got half the kingdom fooled, what trouble will a few of the Crown's agents cause you?"

Farris smiled. "Let's hope they cause enough trouble to give me a good excuse for killing them."

**

The sun was still shining by the time Farris returned to the docklands. Most of the daily freights were already docked, and only a few labourers and stevedores remained to tend to the last cargo.

Fortunately, Old Donal had returned to his post. His gaping, toothless smile was enough to tell Farris that he had completed his task.

"Chester the Lucky!" he announced. The old beggar was visibly drunk. "Chester the Lucky was born thirty-three years ago in the Steamworks of Penance. He drinks unflavoured thainol and smokes pre-rolled bacum cigarettes. The colour of his hair is a similar shade of brown to your own, so I'm told. I did never find the name of the last woman he fucked, but his wife is called Penny, so it could be that."

Farris sighed. "Have you got any useful information?"

"Cool your coal!" The beggar held up his hands in submission. "I haven't gotten to the best part yet! In Penance, Chester excelled at mathematics, engineering, and astronomy. He moved to Cruachan at a young age to study the art of navigation and trained with the crew of many airships known to frequent this fine city!"

"Oh no," said Farris. "Please tell me you're joking."

"Chester the Lucky earned his title from regularly winning the wages of other crewmembers of *The Glory of Penance* and..." He paused. "Bollocks! I've just gone and ruined the best part. He's one of the ship's navigators! I was all over the city, trying to find out about those who'll be travelling onboard. The Church has three special passengers, top secret stuff, but none are Simians. I was about to give up until I thought to ask about the crew."

The Crown really is a joke. How in the name of Sin am I supposed to impersonate a damn navigator?

Farris reached for a small bag of silver stags concealed in one of his inside pockets.

I'll need to find him. I'll need to meet him and impersonate him well enough to get on board.

Getting by as a passenger would have been a challenge enough, but to act as Chester the Lucky for a whole day, surrounded by his peers and crewmen...

"Where can I find him?" he demanded, thrusting the bag of coins into Donal's hands.

"He drinks at an old tavern not too far from here. *The Gutted Fish.* You can reach it by heading—"

Farris already knew the location of every public house and brothel in the city. He stormed off into the dusk and vanished before Old Donal noticed he had been paid four times as much as usual.

CHAPTER 5:
HARVEST

"I told you, I don't want to talk about it."

The Pyromancer, Fionn, crossed his arms, ignoring Morrigan's gaze. She scowled.

How could anyone be so stubborn?

"Leave him be," said Yarlaith. The old healer walked ahead of Morrigan and Fionn as they made their way through the town square. All around, the villagers made preparations for the Harvest Moon festival later that night.

"I don't have time for this," said Fionn. "I need to reach Point Grey by nightfall if I'm to catch the last ferry to Penance."

What are you hiding? Morrigan studied the Pyromancer's face. The more she did, the more she doubted he actually was an adventurer. He certainly didn't look like one, with his silky red robe and his soft, porcelain skin. His eyes looked as though they had never seen battle, and his lean body was more like a dancer's than a warrior's.

But his arm... His right arm was twice as big as his left: a hulking mass of muscle sprouting from a slender shoulder. Morrigan had first wondered if he had been a blacksmith; the Reardon brothers of the forge had once told her that this was a typical trait of a blacksmith, spending all day hammering away with one arm. They claimed that they too would be grotesquely disproportionate if it wasn't for the hours of weight-training they did every other night.

This explanation didn't suit Fionn, however. His arm looked *unnatural*, as if it didn't belong to him at all.

"Why are you going to Penance, Fionn?" asked Morrigan, despite another irate look from her uncle.

Fionn didn't answer immediately. His lips moved slightly, as if mouthing the words he wanted to say, but a sharp voice cut him off.

"That's enough, Morry!"

"But Yarlaith—"

"I said enough! Can't you see he's in shock? Leave him alone!"

Morrigan stood dumbfounded. *He never so much as raised his voice before.* She watched in silence as her uncle placed a hand on Fionn's oversized shoulder. The young mage looked up at the healer.

"Yarlaith?" he said with a quivering tone. "The voices...will they ever stop?"

"Quiet," whispered Yarlaith. "You're going to be okay."

***

That night, the Harvest Moon loomed over Roseán, full and red; it illuminated the night's sky and would have allowed the farmers to spend a little longer tending to the final crops of the season if weren't for the festival. Though the sun had set less than an hour ago, the revellers were already in a drunken stupor, dancing in circles around a bonfire in the centre of the square.

Morrígan sat alone next to a long wooden table lined with bottles of cheap ale and wine. Peadair had taken it on himself to provide alcohol for the evening, free to all who yearned to forget that their beloved *Bear* would be in hibernation for the unforeseeable future.

Many in the village had blamed Peadair for being so submissive to the king's orders but seemed happy to forget all about it with a free pint of ale in their hands. Morrígan had even overheard the Reardon brothers complain about the battlemage's presence a few nights previously.

They curse the soldiers and their magic, yet they're happy to use Yarlaith's fire-crystals to kindle their forge.

Morrígan turned her attention back towards the villagers. There was a band of musicians by the bonfire, playing merry songs of folk heroes triumphing over greedy noblemen.

I wonder if the nobility sing similar songs about the small-folk?

She watched the villagers dance and sing. Around the perimeter of the Square, a group of battlemages stood guard, with green hoods pulled low over their shadowed faces.

"Geomancers," muttered Yarlaith, approaching from behind. "Do you know much about them, Morrígan?"

Morrígan didn't answer right away. She hadn't forgotten how he had yelled at her earlier, even if he wanted to pretend he had.

"They manipulate the earth," she answered, refusing to look at her uncle. "They can move soil and sand."

"Well, that doesn't sound very useful." He chuckled softly to himself. "What use is a full battalion of soldiers playing with dirt? Is there anything else in the earth they could manipulate?"

She would have preferred to walk off, to leave him standing alone, but the answer suddenly came to her.

"Metal," she said. "Geomancers can manipulate ore, can't they?"

"The Firstborn's weapons couldn't penetrate Simian plate-mail during Móráin's Conquest," said Yarlaith, the bonfire dancing in his eyes, "but their magic was capable of bending and twisting it. I can't imagine it was a pleasant experience for the Simian soldiers inside."

He gave Morrígan an inquisitive look. "So what else do you think they could manipulate?"

She watched the Geomancers closely, imagining how they must look toiling the earth, great boulders rising beneath their feet...entire mountains at their fingertips....

"The troll," she whispered suddenly, her heart leaping from her chest. "The petrified troll!"

The stone beast was still there, just outside the village, standing over her family's farm like a statue commemorating the slaughter. None of the villagers had been able to pick it apart with their hammers and axes. It seemed as if troll-stone was quite stronger than the earthly kind.

"Yarlaith, do you think they could move it?"

The old healer smiled. "Well, there's no harm in finding out. Why don't you ask one of the Geomancers yourself?"

"Me? Why...why me?"

Yarlaith sighed and placed a hand on her shoulder.

"Morrigan, you see the way the villagers react to the military presence. We are on the brink of war, but many are reluctant to see their protectors as anything more than strangers who invade their streets and claim their taverns. The soldiers are alienated from the community they are sworn to safeguard, and that must take its toll on morale. If anything, they'd be happy to help, if it aids in having the villagers see them as sharing the same interests as their own."

Morrigan agreed. Besides, watching the horrible stone troll being disposed of would surely be a spectacle.

She left her uncle at the edge of the gathering, fixed her hair, and brushed dust from her new cloak. Yarlaith had said that the beadhbh feathers didn't match the theme of the festival, but she had ignored him: it was different, and that was festive enough for her.

As Morrigan crossed the Square, she spotted Sorcha, dancing in circles with the other villagers. She was wearing another one of her mother's dresses, designed in the style of high nobility. White and spotless, it appeared to radiate with its own light as she leapt gracefully around on the tips of her toes. Her soft, blond hair kept its perfect shimmer and shape while she whirled faster and faster, quickening to the tempo of the music. All eyes were on her, hands clapping to the beat, but Morrígan shrugged and carried on towards the battlemages.

They wouldn't think she's so pretty if it wasn't for her mother's dresses.

"Um, excuse me?" asked Morrígan as she approached the nearest Geomancer. He stood tall like a statue, moving only his eyes to look down at her. When he spoke, his voice grated with the rough accent of Cruachan.

"Yes, ma'am, is there anything I can help you with?"

"Have you heard about the troll, just outside the village?"

Morrígan surprised herself with how difficult it was to say those words. She began to rehearse the story in her head, but she couldn't bring herself to even picture the scenes from that horrible morning, let alone describe them out loud.

Fortunately, the mage nodded.

"Yes, it was a terrible tragedy, and we hope our presence here can help prevent anything of the sort from happening again."

"Would it be possible for the troll to be moved, somehow?" she asked. "With magic?"

The mage frowned pensively and called for another Geomancer stationed nearby.

"Berrían," he said as the other solider arrived. "The petrified troll out near the Teeth. Do you reckon it could be moved?"

Berrían paused. A thick beard clung to his face like mottled dirt, a stark contrast to his light, sandy hair. "Perhaps, but it'll depend on a few things..."

Morrígan was more than eager to learn. Her father used to be a jack-of-all-trades, and he had told her before that craftsmen are always pleased to talk at length about their work if you showed any interest. It was one of the few useful things he had said to her, although he'd been trying to justify the amount of time he spent drinking in *The Bear*.

"What exactly does it depend on?" she asked.

"See, our magic is capable of manipulating the earth," Berrían began, enthusiasm showing in the speed of his speech. "This lets us bend and shape the earth and Her fruits with ease.

"Now, we can manipulate natural metals, too, but if you take one metal and make an alloy out of it, like steel, then it gets a bit harder to work with. The armour of the Simians is far removed from iron and quite difficult to take control over, though still within the power of any Geomancer worth his weight in dirt."

"And stone?"

"Oh, stone is easy—far easier than the Simian stuff. But a petrified troll...that may be a matter of flesh."

"So?"

"None of the Six Schools of magic can manipulate flesh. White mages may heal wounds and cure ailments, but the flesh itself is never manipulated directly. If the troll's flesh has been petrified, then it cannot be moved. However, if the troll has turned into stone—normal stone—then it could be done."

The mage was rambling, but Morrigan was enthralled by his words. The first soldier, who had been nodding away as Berrian spoke, added his own pair of coppers.

"We certainly won't be able to carry it away," he said, "but we might be able to throw it off the cliff, if we're near enough. I wouldn't be surprised if Eodadh let us give it a shot. We've little else to be doing here anyway."

Berrian scolded the first mage, and then assured Morrigan that the entire battalion was busy protecting the village from harm.

"We'll ask Colonel Eodadh if we can spare some mages to take care of the troll for you."

"Thank you, sirs," said Morrigan. "Your kindness is beyond measure. If you'll excuse me."

She crossed the Square again, weaving between the dancing men and women, and eyeing those sitting along the cobblestone curb, drowning out the band's music with their own slurred verses.

Morrigan tried to picture her mother dancing with the others, but she was having trouble conjuring the image. Sometimes she forgot that her mother was dead and had to remind herself that she was never coming back. But on rarer days, she found it hard to imagine what her mother even *looked* like, as if she were trying to recall a vivid dream fading from memory as morning turned to noon.

Nothing had really been said about her father on the day he left them for dead, but Morrígan couldn't bring herself to care. "The king is planning on raising taxes," he had said the morning they had set out to work on the farm before dawn. "We'll need to open the stall before the greengrocers do."

That morning, Morrígan's mother had another black eye.

She would always start an argument whenever Father came home drunk, but he'd always be the one to finish it.

She turned towards the High Road, away from the festivities, and the band played on.

One month...one month and they've already forgotten.

She made her way up the dark, barren path towards the chapel.

I haven't forgotten, Mother. I'll never forget.

The rusted iron gate to Roseán's graveyard was left slightly ajar. Morrígan had been visiting her mother's grave every night, but she rarely saw anyone else pay their own respects.

They make such a big deal out of it all, the funeral, the burial, but afterwards, they leave their grief with the dead.

The path twisted through rows of weathered tombstones. One had a statue of St. Moira—the patron saint of hunting—at its head. Her features had been completely worn down to the vague shape of a Human face, and a layer of moss had wrapped itself around the inside of her longbow. The words on the stone were far from legible. The Reilighs were a family of hunters who lived just outside the village, but Morrígan doubted the grave could belong to one of them; stone statues were awfully expensive.

Some gravestones were better kept than others, but some looked as if they never had anything written on them at all. Many were overgrown with grey, twisting weeds, and Morrígan had troubling imagining that once they would have been surrounded by flowers.

Eventually, she came to her mother's resting place. Unlike the others, this one faced away from the graveyard, out over the High Road and festivities in the square. Morrígan could still hear the faint sounds of singing and laughter.

She knelt before the grave. Still relatively new, Morrígan had been making sure it wouldn't fall to neglect like the others. And she was proud of it. The flowers had been handpicked and arranged by Morrígan herself, and Mrs. Natháin the mason had advised her on the best stones and rocks to use. Tiny white pebbles were spread out along the surface, with blue and white flower petals dotted around the edges.

The tombstone itself was inscribed with words far clearer than the others:

"Aoife Ní Branna. Beloved mother, wife, and friend. She lived and died in the Light of the Lady, AC 360-403, and shall now live forever in the plains of Tierna Meal."

The Light of the Lady... If she lived and died by the fate weaved by Lady Meadhbh, that's hardly worth celebrating. Why would her path lead to death? Why would we be destined for nothing but sorrow?

She closed her eyes, fighting back tears. *What's the point? What's the point in living if the Gods can just send a troll from the Glenn to take it all away?*

The Pyromancer's face flashed before her, his eyes laced with something between fear and sorrow as it had been earlier that day. For a moment, Morrigan hated him. After leading the beast that killed her mother to the village, the least he could do was explain why he did it.

She shook the image from her head and reached out to touch the words on the stone, leaning on one hand on the surface of the grave. When she shifted her weight, however, she felt something crumble softly underneath. She shrieked and recoiled.

It's happening again.

Carefully, she crouched down to bring the stones to eye-level. Where she had placed her hand, the ground had sunk slightly, causing some of the pebbles to roll inwards towards the inundation.

A slow terror began to rise in her chest. She remembered how the soil had shifted on the day of her mother's burial, how it had led her to believe her mother was somehow still alive. Now, her mind turned towards another more realistic, sinister revelation.

Someone was here. Someone has been tampering with—

Before she could finish that thought, a cacophonic chorus of crows tore through the silence. Looking up, she saw a cloud of birds dissipating into the crimson moonlit sky. She scanned the surrounding area, searching for whatever it was that may have startled them.

She slowly walked past the grave, towards the ledge that led down into the village. Both her hands were balled into fists, ready for whomever, or *whatever*, was beyond.

Then, in the corner of Morrigan's eye, she saw something shift and vanish along the road below. She squinted through the darkness. A second dark shape darted down the road, every bit as silent as the first. Her eyes followed the winding path as more things made their way towards the square. One shape caught the light of the moon, illuminating a creature she had seen many times before, on the mural of her local tavern: a long, feathered neck, stubs of wings folded over its back, and a rounded, black beak.

Beadhbhs!

She spun on her heels and darted towards the square.

As the gravestones and statues rushed past her, Morrigan's gaze remained fixated on the thin line of smoke spiralling up into the sky. Following the High Road back to the square would take too long. She could save time by cutting through the hedgerows.

I'll warn them. The battlemages, they'll hear my voice before they see the beadhbhs.

She rushed to cross the road but froze as four more beadhbhs came stalking through the darkness, close enough to touch. Their bodies were as black as the night that engulfed them, but the harvest moon gleamed off crimson eyes. None seemed to notice Morrigan, standing in the middle of the path, even as they brushed her cloak.

Once they passed, Morrigan darted to the hedgerows and pushed her way through towards the rising smoke. Some of her footsteps found moist, muddy terrain, but she didn't slow.

When she emerged, she found herself on a lower part of the High Road, looking right down over the Square. The musicians had taken a break between songs, and most of the revellers had stopped to refill their tankards. Two Pyromancers stood with their backs to Morrigan, facing the open bonfire.

"Beadhbhs!" she screamed. "Coming down the High Road!"

The two mages reacted without turning towards her. One made a complicated gesture towards another group standing guard by the inn.

"Colonel!" called the other. "Beadhbhs!"

At the same time, a dozen black birds charged into the square. They shrieked and screamed as the villagers tried to flee, but more birds came pouring in from all directions. They moved with startling efficiency in groups of two or three. A pair of beadhbhs struck down one man, and for a full second, all Morrigan could hear was the sound of their talons slicing through his flesh. Terror tore through her body, freezing her limbs and bringing water to her eyes. No matter how hard she tried, she could not run.

But the mages made no move to flee. A proud, strong command tore through the chaos. Amongst the unfolding massacre, eight red mages formed together in a row behind the bonfire. In unison, the mages roared a single, unintelligible word, and the bonfire split into three streams of flames. Each stream found a feathered target. Even as the birds burned, the fires never crackled or swayed. Instead, they rolled smoothly around the black bodies as they fell.

Colonel Eodadh stood before a group of blue-robed mages, who shuffled into position near the well. The colonel called out another strange command in a language Morrigan didn't understand.

The silent Hydromancers gestured towards a pair of beadhbhs chasing down a young man on the other side of the square. With a flick of the mages' wrists, long shards of ice erupted from their hands and shot towards the birds like spears.

Morrigan found her courage and made a break for it. Two more beadhbhs appeared on a roof over her head, but as they jumped, a howling wind cast them off in another direction.

"Run!" yelled a mage dressed in grey. With a sweeping gesture, he sent another pair of beadhbhs flying.

Morrigan darted across the square towards the Low Road. A whirlwind of fire crossed her path, but she felt no heat as it passed. It collided with another pair of beadhbhs, wrapping around their bodies as they shrieked and burned. The smell of charring flesh flashed through Morrigan's nostrils.

Most of the villagers had fled the square, and only the mages remained to fight the beadhbhs. The Geomancers formed a line in front of the retreating villagers. They hefted their slings, armed with tiny pebbles. As Morrigan watched, the pebbles flew from the slings with vicious accuracy, splitting beadhbh skulls.

"Let none flee!" roared Colonel Eodadh. He too wielded a sling and sprayed a shower of stones over another group of beadhbhs. The beadhbhs moved to escape, but the mages had spread to route them out.

As the last bird fell to a bolt of fire, the colonel called another strange order. The mages dropped their weapons and scattered to tend to the wounded.

A dozen wounded bodies littered the square, though the charred and broken corpses of the beadhbhs vastly outnumbered them.

Not far from where she stood, a Geomancer placed his hands over the wound of a moaning villager; his stomach had been split open from corner to corner, his entrails spilled out on the stone.

"Sir! There's not much I can do for him here!"

The colonel appeared beside Morrigan as she stared at the wounded man, bile rising in her throat. His guts glistened purple and blue in the light of the bonfire, his blood thick and dark.

"Green-cloak, can your hold keep him alive for a little longer?"

"Yes, sir," said the Geomancer.

The colonel nodded. Morrígan thought he was about to tell the Geomancer to give up, but instead he turned and called out to the other Geomancers. They stopped what they were doing and darted to their commander's side. Amongst the wounded villagers, one man lay next to the centre wall, a white cloth covering his face—the man Morrígan had seen fall when the beadhbhs first attacked.

He was a labourer from the Mahon fields. Gods, would more have joined him if I hadn't warned the mages?

"Green-cloaks!" cried the colonel. "Take him up to the healer's house at the end of the High Road. Berrían, you help Niall keep him stable."

"Aye!" said Berrían. He knelt and helped the first Geomancer tend to the wounded man. They were using magic to stop the bleeding, but they could do little to close the wound. The mass of purple innards, although exposed, still seemed intact. The injured man gasped for a breath he couldn't catch, his eyes rolling to the back of his skull.

Then his body rose from the ground upon cobblestones that arranged themselves like a bed, suspending him in the air. The colonel gave another order, and the two mages sprinted out of the square with the wounded man. Morrígan followed.

She wasn't particularly fast, but she was just able to keep up with the mages. Every so often, she caught a glimpse of Berrían and the Geomancer Niall as they rubbed at the villager's wound.

Morrígan ran ahead of them when they reached the house. The door was unlocked, and she pushed her way through into the clinic at the back.

"Here," she said, pulling a bed out from the wall. It was set upon wheels, and the two Geomancers spun it under the floating bed of stone. With a sweep of a Niall's hand, the stones rolled away, and the wounded man landed softly onto the bed.

"Where's your uncle?" asked Berrian, rolling up his sleeves.

Instead of answering, Morrígan went across the room and pushed open the door to Yarlaith's study, now vacant.

"Yarlaith!" she called, but only an eerie draught replied.

"Never mind!" cried Niall. "Where does he keep the papaver oil?"

"There." Morrígan pointed. "Beside that yellow bottle."

"What's going on here?" roared Yarlaith's voice from the study, though Morrígan was sure it had been empty seconds ago.

The healer pushed his way past Berrian and Niall and waved his arms widely over the man's wound. In an instant, the dark snakes of the man's intestines slithered back into his belly.

Yarlaith produced a needle and thread from the sleeve of his cloak, and masterfully sewed the man's skin closed in seconds. Morrígan watched in awe as he went about his work, cleaning the wound with fluid strokes of alcohol and spirits.

"He will stay with me for the night," said Yarlaith, firmly, gesturing towards the open door. The battlemages took the hint and thanked him before leaving.

Only when he and Morrigan were alone did the gravity of the situation dawn across the healer's face.

"Morry, are you hurt? Are you okay?"

Morrigan nodded, but her mind was in another place.

"This wasn't normal what happened tonight," he said. "It shouldn't be taken lightly. Are you sure you're alright? Do you want to get some rest?"

"No," she said, surprising herself with a smile. "I want to learn magic."

Where were you, when the Great Tower fell,
In the Shadow of Simian Sin?
The mountains roared, the air went still,
And the Earth shook from within.

Where were you, when the Great Lord stood,
In the wreckage of its remnants?
He forbade us to leave the that terrible place,
And with that He sealed our Penance.

Excerpt from The Fall, AC 157

CHAPTER 6:
THE SEVENTH SCHOOL

Winter rolled over Alabach in the form of a snowstorm, but being so close to the Eternal Sea, the Clifflands only suffered hail and winds. Still, these carried a biting chill that came creeping across the ground, leaving ice in the cracks of the stone troll that still loomed outside Roseán.

The colonel's orders cut through the silence of the onlooking villagers. His nine Geomancers split into two groups, positioning themselves either side of the troll. The villagers whispered all around Morrígan, but her gaze remained fixed on the stone beast. It stood on two muscular legs as thick as tree trunks, twenty feet tall. Its head sat on a stump of a neck, agony etched upon its petrified face. Stone lips protruded and curled out from its mouth, exposing cracked, crooked teeth. Nostrils flaring and eyes bulging, it still seemed to be alive under the stone.

Gods. Please let them move it.

But even as the Geomancers struggled, the troll did not budge.

They changed position, now spacing themselves evenly in a circle around the troll. They cursed and yelled and grunted with determination as they tried again, but to no avail.

"What are they hoping will happen?" whispered someone behind Morrígan.

"Fools," murmured another. "All they need is a good pivot—"

Heat began to rise in Morrígan's face, but she tried to ignore them. Across the field, Colonel Eodadh threw down his cloak and joined in the effort himself.

If only I could help...

It had been two months since Morrígan had asked Yarlaith to teach her magic, but the healer had been too busy with his own private experiments and scribblings to even show her the basics. She had assumed that he'd have more free time now, considering Fionn the Red had left the clinic, but this seemed to cause Yarlaith to work even more frantic and frequently than ever. He had said that the Academy of Dromán was looking to fund his research into the alchemical methods used to re-attach Fionn's arm. Apart from that, Morrígan knew little else about his work.

One by one, the mages dropped their arms. Sweat soaked their faces and dripped onto their tunics. Still, the troll hadn't moved an inch.

"I told you! I told you they couldn't do it!" said Fearghal to nobody in particular. "What a bloody waste of an evening."

The butcher turned back towards the village; the others meekly followed, but Morrígan remained behind. With her uncle busy with his work, she didn't have much else to do for the evening.

The colonel called out to the Geomancers with some strange arcane word, and all nine immediately stopped and stood in attention; the troll leered on behind them.

"Dismissed," he said.

The soldiers broke formation and wandered back to the village, mumbling to one another. Morrígan caught Berrían's eye, and he threw his shoulders up in an apologetic shrug.

Dusk crept in overhead, but with the sky covered by a dead sheet of grey clouds, it was impossible to tell where the sun was setting.

Colonel Eodadh remained behind.

"There's nothing more we can do," he said. "I believe Berrían already explained that this may be a matter of flesh, not earth. It seems that the troll itself has been petrified, and now bears no similarities to stone."

"Yes," said Morrígan, bowing her head.

The colonel broke away and walked over to the troll, rubbing his hand across its shin. Its legs were bent in a crouching stance, arms covering its face from the direction morning had come. From here, Morrígan could see the exact spot her mother was killed.

Grief's familiar claws scratched against the inside of her throat. Her lip quivered and her mouth went dry. Tears filled her eyes.

If only we didn't have to work so damn early that morning.

"Is there nothing else that could be done?" she asked. "What if we tried with all twelve?"

"No," said the colonel. His tone was harsh and reproachful. "It is not a matter of magnitude. Not even a thousand Geomancers would be able to move the troll."

"Is there no other way?" Morrígan looked up at the troll's hideous, deformed face. At that moment, she wanted nothing more than to never have to see it again.

"Not with magic." The colonel pulled up his hood and turned to leave. "Why don't you ask the Simians to lend you an engine?"

As he left, Morrígan considered his suggestion, even though it was meant in sarcasm.

Magic has so many rules and boundaries. Simian engineers must be far freer than our mages.

There were still no developments from Penance or Cruachan. Some of the more cynical and imaginative residents of Roseán had started to dub the conflict "The Invisible War." They claimed that the king never was attacked, and the story nothing but a fabrication to give the Crown a mandate to raise taxes and declare war on Penance. It all sounded a lot like paranoia, though. Many of the villagers were uneasy since the Harvest Moon festival.

It wasn't the beadhbhs that put them on edge. It's the fact they've grown sober.

Peadair had given away the last of his alcohol that night, and there had been nowhere for the villagers to drink since.

The evening was quickly growing cold, with darkness setting in from the east. Morrígan wore only a simple gown and cardigan, for Yarlaith had forbidden her to bring out her beadhbh cloak again, considering those that attacked the village.

She stood by herself a little longer, fantasising about the day she'd learn magic and leave Roseán to study in the Academy. She had seldom left the safety of her tiny village, and it had been hundreds of years since Humans had even stepped foot outside of Alabach, in fear of the Grey Plague that drove them from their homeland.

We don't even know what the plague was. She looked to the misty peaks of the Glenn to the north. *How can everyone be so content with living out their lives in a cage?*

The view of the Glenn was serene and silent; the local wildlife retired earlier and earlier each night with winter setting in. The mountains stood before her, drained of colour in the waning light, like a dusty oil painting. The overgrown grass of the surrounding fields stood completely still, separated by thick, motionless hedgerows like stone walls.

It was the stoic tranquillity of the scene that made the movements of the dark figure all the more jarring. Morrígan squinted through the dimming light and saw something shaped like a man — a very large man—creeping towards her. It grew clearer in her vision with each step.

A Simian!

She recoiled in horror as the stranger approached, but he too paused when he saw her. For a tense moment they looked at each other, alone in the empty field, in silence.

Is he here to harm me?

Although his arms and head were exposed, the Simian wore a heavy chest-plate, tinted deep with blue. He carried a simple leather pack over one shoulder, and his fists seemed strong enough to crush stone. His dark, hairy face was stern and stolid, but there was a hint of apprehension in his eyes. After a moment's breath passed, he spun on his heels and bolted up towards the Glenn.

"Wait!"

Morrigan gave chase. The Simian must have been a spy of some sort, watching the Geomancers at work. If there were others nearby, Morrigan needed to know.

But he couldn't be a threat. He wouldn't be fleeing if he was a threat.

The Simian's long muscular legs carried him far quicker than Morrigan's, but he was still within sight as the mountains rose up overhead.

Maybe he can help. Maybe he can get his engineers to move the troll.

Still, she carried on, even as her breath ran short and the Simian disappeared into the hills ahead of her.

What if the others were right? What if there really isn't a war? What if we've been given false information about the Simians this whole time?

It was only now that she realised how close she was to the mountains. The Teeth of the Glenn stabbed the sky, rooted deep into the ground before her. Morrígan stopped to examine her surroundings, hills and winding paths extending out in every direction.

Where did he go?

She considered her options. It was getting late, and soon it'd be too dark to continue searching.

She turned back towards the village, but something caught her eye. The rocks of the mountains were uniform all around her, like a man-built wall, but several feet away, the smooth stone turned rough. She followed the shape of the stone. A dark, yawning hole stood at its base.

Morrígan went to examine the opening. It was perhaps six feet tall and widened even more as it descended into the ground.

But large enough for a Simian?

From the maps in her uncle's study, she knew that Penance was beyond the Glenn, and it was likely that this tunnel burrowed right through into the Simian City of Steam.

Morrígan left her fear at the cave entrance. Curiosity guided her into the darkness.

Carefully, she slid down over the cold, damp stone. She found herself let out in a larger chamber.

The ceiling spanned high overhead, with stalactites hanging down like sharpened teeth, each covered in a smooth layer of white mineral. The walls were uneven all around, some bearing exits and tunnels extending out in different directions. One had some light shining through. Still aware of how night was falling quickly outside, Morrigan walked towards it.

How could I have lived so near these cliffs, without ever have seen these caves?

Running water trickled all around, as if a thousand streams ran through the ceiling and the walls, but there was not a drop of water in sight. Still, she continued.

Where the Holy Hell am I?

The tunnel widened, and Morrigan noticed that there were several hollows eroded into the walls. At first, she dismissed these as natural formations, but they became more and more frequent as she walked. When she saw three together, perfectly arranged one on top of the other, she examined them more closely. Despite all her thirst for adventure, despite how she'd tried to be brave since she entered, when she looked inside the hole, Morrigan gasped.

The sound echoed and resounded around the cavern. The shrieks of bats and the beat of their wings called back to her in the distance, but the skeleton that lay within did not move.

It was aged and decayed; its bones broken here and there. An iron claymore was clutched in its hands, the handle wrapped with dead fingers and spider's webs. Morrigan reached in and picked up the weapon. It felt heavy and awkward in her hand but helped in restoring her courage.

And besides, it'll no longer help a dead man fight.

The hollows grew more numerous and ornate as she went. Some had bags of jewels and old belongings laid out next to the dead. Others had faded inscriptions in a strange language etched above their openings. The fleeing Simian was forgotten, though it was not the dim light in the distance that kept her going. Her uncle had once said that the burial place of those who died during Móráin's Conquest was lost to the scholars of Alabach, but Morrígan believed that she had found it.

Eventually her tunnel joined up with another. This one had a stream of running water, which she followed, her imagination running wild with possibilities. Had no one really been here since the days of Móráin's Conquest? Why wasn't this place teeming with scholars and archaeologists?

As she walked, she noticed an odour, like warm, decaying meat. The further she pressed through the cave, the more unbearable the stench became. Eventually, it filled the air like it had its own physical presence, thick and heavy.

The passage finally widened into a grotto, and the river ran into an underground lake. There was an opening on the far side that led downwards into another chamber, light spilling from its entrance. Morrígan shimmied around the edge of the water towards the room, careful not to breathe in through her nose.

As she got closer, the inside of the room came into view. There were torches there, dozens of them, but those weren't what caught Morrígan's eyes first.

Wooden tables lined the walls. Twisted corpses lay upon them. Some were bloodied with torn rags, others decomposing and spilling forth rank odours. Many were missing arms and legs, but limbs and heads of all shapes and sizes hung from the ceiling on iron hooks. Slabs of wood stained with dried blood covered the ground, and strange vials of liquids and powders stood high against the walls on wooden shelves.

She walked through the room, tightening her grip on the sword.

What in Seletoth's name is this place?

Some of the corpses were of bone, while others were all flesh and no skin. Many wore bright armour of gilded gold and plate-mail, with extravagant adornments and embroideries throughout. On one table was a fresh body that Morrigan recognised as the labourer who had died during the Harvest Moon festival. His ribs were torn open, exposing the remaining organs that hadn't been devoured by the beadhbhs. Both his arms were removed and hung gruesomely on the wall behind.

Another pile of bodies lay discarded on the ground nearby. One was the knight who had been killed by the troll, all that time ago. His hair still seemed alive like fire, but blood was clotted in clumps around his face and beard.

Finally, her gaze fell onto the largest table of the room. It was arranged differently to the others, not crooked and corrupted with blood. On it lay a beautiful woman, dressed in a clear, white gown that stood out stainless against the gloom. A delicate veil shrouded her face, but it was thin enough for Morrigan to make out who it was.

"Mother!"

She wanted to scream. She wanted to run. She wanted to burn the Godsforsaken place to the ground and take her mother's body to the graveyard where it was supposed to be.

She considered the others whose bodies had been defiled in death. The labourer from the festival had died slowly and painfully, but somebody had decided that he would be tortured in death too. The bodies of the warriors who had fought bravely during Móráin's Conquest had been retired here to honour their deeds for eternity, but someone had removed them from their resting places and brought them to this...*butcher's shop*.

Morrígan screamed. This time, it wasn't only the bats and the mice that answered her, but a familiar voice.

"Let it all out, Morrígan. Terror is the appropriate response to what I have committed myself to."

Morrígan turned to see Yarlaith the White standing behind her. She gasped for a breath she couldn't catch; her heart pounded against her chest like beast in a cage.

"You...?"

"Yes, Morrígan. I am the one who defiled these corpses."

"But...why?" For a maddening second, she thought of cutting her uncle down with the claymore still clutched in her hands. But her grip was looser now than it previously had been.

"It started shortly after the troll attacked," he began, his voice surprisingly calm. "Do you remember Fionn, Morrígan? The Pyromancer? You saw what happened to him out in the field. You heard his screams of agony as I tried to heal him.

Do you remember seeing him after his recovery? Do you remember his arm?"

Of course she did. Although her mind was paralyzed with fright, it conjured up a very vivid picture of Fionn the Red and his oversized right arm, like a blacksmith's.

"I told the Academy that I re-attached his arm, but it was nowhere to be found out in the field. He was alive when he came to me, but the others were dead, Morrigan. This I need you to understand. I disobeyed our religion's most sacred laws in order to save a young man's life, and that's all that should matter. That night, in my clinic under the stairs, I sawed off the knight's arm and attached it to Fionn's body."

Morrigan glanced back at the corpse of the knight. One arm was indeed severed from his shoulder.

"That should have been the end of it," said Yarlaith. "But as I sewed the arm to Fionn's bloody stump, I felt something stir. I grasped at the flesh, and instead of healing it in the manner I've perfected in all my years of training, I felt something else. Something different. Fionn's blood was already flowing into the dead man's arm, but with a *twist*, I was able to pour life into it. The lad woke screaming and found himself in possession of a new limb."

Morrigan shook her head. Even with the very small understanding of magic she possessed, she still knew that this was impossible. *To take the limb of one person...and attach it to another....*

But none of that was important right now.

"What is this place, Yarlaith?" she said, some defiance rising in her voice. "What have you done?"

The old man smiled. "It's simple really. There was an arm: a single Human arm that I managed to breathe life back into. I could have stopped there. I could have written a letter to the Academy and gotten a nice grant to continue my own research. But I did not. I found this place long ago and used it to store blood potions away from the prying eyes of the Gods. There is a tunnel nearby that leads right under my house, and I can access it from my study, in secret.

"I decided instead to use this place to test the limits of this Seventh School of Magic. For if I was able to revive a severed arm, why not something else?" He leaned in close to Morrigan and whispered, "Why not a whole person?"

Mother!

Morrigan's heart surged with everything from loathing to excitement.

"You...you think you can bring her back?"

"No, Morrigan. I *know* I can. It will take time to get the spell right, but I know it's possible. There is another tunnel from the lake that brings you under the graveyard. With a few careful calculations, I've been able to steal fresh bodies from their graves to run some tests. I haven't been successful yet but...."

He paused and walked over to Morrigan's mother, placing a hand on her forehead.

"But I know it can be done. I have faith. Even though it goes against everything the Church stands for, I still have faith. When my work is complete, the smallfolk will rejoice, for I will have conquered the unconquerable. For only if I succeed will I not be branded a heathen and killed as one."

In silence, Morrigan considered all he said. Her mother looked so peaceful and beautiful, even in death. It almost seemed as if she were sleeping, and it was easy for Morrigan to picture her smiling and waking up. Morrigan remembered having a similar thought during the funeral.

"I...I don't know," she whispered. "I'm afraid. What if we're discovered?"

Yarlaith eyed her carefully. "I knew you'd find this place someday, Morrigan, but you didn't come in from the house. How did you get here?"

"I saw a Simian near the field," she said. "I followed him up into the Glenn. There was an entrance, a tunnel...."

She expected Yarlaith to show concern at the mention of the Simian, but he gave a sigh of relief.

"These tunnels stretch out all over the Clifflands," he said, "and it is likely that the Simian scouts of the Triad have been using them to navigate through mountains undetected. There is much at stake if we're discovered, so I'll take extra measures to hide this chamber.

"What I said before still stands, Morrigan. Are you willing to throw your life away for this cause? Colonel Eodadh and his mages serve the Church first, the Crown second, and the people last. They will not hesitate to murder anyone they suspect to be involved in something as wicked as this. You must commit to this work until we succeed, and you will not be able to walk away until it is complete. Do you understand?"

It went against all the teachings of the Church, violating everything the people of Alabach held sacred about the dead. There would always be a place for her mother to live in her memory, Morrígan knew, but if they were to be caught, the other villagers of Roseán, and even the books of history, would remember them as monsters. And they would live forever in *those* memories.

But now...now there seemed to be another way to live forever, in the flesh.

"Yes," said Morrígan. She dropped the claymore and took her mother's hand in her own. "I understand."

CHAPTER 7:
THE GUTTED FISH

The docklands of Cruachan made up almost a quarter of its capacity, with the city surrounded by sea in three compass directions. *The Gutted Fish* was situated a stone's throw from Cockle's Wharf to the south, famous for the catching, selling, and gutting of fish from Móráin Sea. The sun had set by the time Farris reached the wharf, with the lively hustle and bustle of the seafood market replaced by the stolid silence of hardworking men eager to get drunk.

Chester the Lucky, mused Farris as he approached the tavern. Unlike Humans, the title of a Simian was based on either one's deeds or appearance. Farris never understood why all a Human needed do to earn his father's name was to be born of his blood. Some people called it tradition; Farris called it entitlement. He had worked hard as a young lad in the Dustworks of Penance to warrant the name Farris the Swift. Later, at the right hand of the Silverback, he had been known as Farris Silvertongue. At the king's court, he had no full name until the Guild of Thieves incident, and now most called him Farris Turncloak. Many Simians would don dozens of titles throughout their life, but few took on as many first names as Farris did.

This morning I was Marc, today, Farris, and tomorrow, Chester.

Farris stepped into the squalid old building and noticed immediately that *The Gutted Fish* smelled far worse than its namesake. Like many inns and taverns along the quays, it served hard drinks for hard men.

And women. A particularly burly female Simian was staring him down with a single eye. A thick leather eye-patch covered what might have been another, but Farris thought it would be better to avert his own gaze than try to figure out what was beneath.

Across the room was a hearth of grey granite, with a tiny flame trying to fight out from under its coals. Two Human men sat at the bar with their backs to the fire, drinking in silence as they glared at the mirrored back wall. A barman, dressed in black, absentmindedly wiped down the splintered surface of the bar with a cloth. He was a Simian, but shorter and fatter than the lone drinker by his side: Chester the Lucky.

Chester did indeed look much like Farris, with a similar build and brown hair that seemed to shimmer bronze under the candlelight. He wore a simple grey waistcoat, open, leaving his arms and torso exposed to the cool tavern air. It was typical for Simians of lower stature to dress minimally.

But Chester is an educated man. The fine clothes of a navigator would certainly stand out in a place like this. It seemed likely that Chester's appearance was a deterrent from being robbed.

Farris figured Chester must have been given the title "Lucky" by other Simians, as Humans typically didn't believe in coincidence and sheer luck. For them, everything was attributed to the plans of their Gods, from the flip of a coin to the roll of a thunderstorm. "Life in the Light of the Lady," they called it, implying that the Goddess Meadhbh was watching over their every move.

It wasn't fate that put the bottle of poisoned thainol in the king's hands. And it won't be fate that prevents the Crown's attack on Penance.

"Two glasses of thainol," he said, taking a seat beside Chester. The Simian slowly turned his head towards Farris. His eyes were dull in colour, but their gaze was sharp and sceptical.

"I appreciate the offer, friend, but I'll be paying for my own. I'm drinking the money of gamblers and fools tonight." He smiled, revealing yellowed fangs.

"Ah," said Farris. "You play cards in the city, then?"

Chester waved a dismissive hand. "A *Human's* game, that. All kings, queens, wizards, an' knaves. On the ship, we play dice." He spoke with the bastardised accent of one who travelled often between Penance and the Southern Seachtú, addled with the typical drawl of a commoner.

He has been away from home a long time.

Farris lowered his voice slightly, lining his own accent with similar inflections.

"Aye," he said. "A good game, and *fair*."

In his years in the Dustworks, Farris had learned how to cheat at dice too. With enough skill, even the keenest eyes could be fooled by a dropped die. Farris grinned, considering Chester's name.

Perhaps the Humans are right. Maybe there really is no such thing as luck.

Farris introduced himself as Jacob of the North Wall. He didn't need to divulge more information than that, as Chester mentioned he worked aboard *The Glory of Penance* straight away.

"Ah, the long-distance ship?" Farris asked. "Are you preparing to travel to the Eastern Lands? Or heading west across the Eternal Sea?"

Chester drank deeply from his own glass and sighed. "Nah, we won't be leaving Alabach for a while now."

Farris waited for a moment in silence, but when it was clear that Chester wasn't in the mood to elaborate, he continued. "Good to see her in the sky, at least. I heard she was taking a trade route. It's a bountiful time of year for commerce, and the roads are ripe with bandits these days. The skies make a great addition to the economy, and it's ships like yours that help the kingdom grow."

Chester slammed his now empty glass down on the table, beckoning the barman over to refill it.

"Aye," he said. "Our technology *aids* the kingdom, sure. But what do they give us in return? They heal an' sell us magical crystals with one hand, shovin' taxes down our throats with the other. You know how much it is for a white crystal in this city?"

"I got one for two stags today," said Farris, immediately and proudly.

"It only costs twelve shillings for a Human! Are you aware of that? We're supposed to grovel in front of them and thank them for the *privilege* of using their magics. Do you know what taxes a Human is expected to pay for Simian steel? Not a penny!"

Farris listened intently; at least, he appeared to be. Behind his nods and his smiles, he was carefully taking note of all of Chester's ticks and mannerisms. Chester spoke with the eagerness of a good storyteller, though he lacked confidence, frequently avoiding eye contact while sitting hunched over the bar. Farris subtly mimed Chester's posture while he spoke, holding his glass with four fingers instead of the three he was used to.

I just need to fool them enough to board the ship. Once we're in the air, anything goes. Farris certainly wasn't going to learn how to navigate an airship before the morning, but he could still become Chester the Lucky, at least superficially.

"*The Glory* leaves tomorrow," ventured Farris. "Are you returning to Penance?"

"Aye," grunted Chester. "Can't wait to be out of this damned city."

"It must be a long flight."

Chester shrugged. "Not as long as other ships. We'll probably reach Penance by sundown. The length of the journey doesn't bother me, though. I'll be stayin' in the good cabin for the trip."

Chester finished his drink. Noticing Farris was almost at the bottom of his glass too, he ordered a second round.

That's a start. Farris considered his next question carefully. "But didn't you say *The Glory* doesn't take passengers?"

Chester hadn't, but he answered anyway. "Other than the odd favour for the Church, we usually don't. I'm just boarding for the trip tomorrow, not for work."

"Lucky you," said Farris, unable to contain his own excitement.

So, the Crown was right. He really is just a passenger.

"Heh, I wouldn't be so quick to call it luck," said Chester. "I was on death's bed with the bloody flux half a moon ago. Was fixed by Simian chemists—not alchemists, mind you—and I missed the first trip of the last crew rotation. Now I'm out of synch with the rest, and I'll be travelling with the other crew on the way back to Penance tomorrow. All ships got two crews these days, see, and we swap 'em every fortnight."

Farris took a long, deep drink to hide his glee. *Chester's traveling as a passenger, amongst a crew not all that familiar with him. This will be easy.* He fought back a smile. Life in the Light of the Lady, indeed.

"What do you trade?" he asked. "Simian arms and armour?"

"Just armour. We'd make a lot more money if we transported crystals instead, but we don't have a single one on board. That's what I love about *The Glory*. It's the first of its kind."

Farris leaned forwards. "First, as in it doesn't carry crystals?"

"Nope, it's the first that doesn't *use* them. Anyone ever tell you how an airship works?"

From the change in his tone, it was obvious that Chester loved talking about technology. His shoulders were more relaxed, his stature more open than before.

"See, you got an engine," began Chester, making the shape of a box with both hands, "and that needs steam. Steam comes from fuel and a furnace. Now, that's no problem for locomotives an' boats. But airships, they need gas to float too: gas that's lighter than air. That's where things get a bit complicated."

"Because it's flammable?"

"Exactly. You'd be mad to have a ship that high in the sky with as much as an ember burnin' inside. I saw an airship catch fire once. All it took was a single spark, and the whole thing turned to ash before it hit the ground. Like *that*." Chester clicked his fingers.

Farris looked on, wide-eyed and eager. He didn't know all that much about airships himself and had only been on one before. It had been docked up, however, and all the crew asleep.

"That's where *magic* comes in," said Chester with scorn in his voice. "When Elis Highwind built the first airship, he lined the engine room with a huge array of blue crystals, turning the air cold despite the blazin' furnace inside. That way, the ship could use gas to float an' steam to sail. Hundreds more ships like that have been commissioned over the past seventy-odd years, but the Church always has the final say on what goes ahead. If you tell 'em your ship plans on leaving Alabach, they don't give you their magics. Simple as that. So, there's this great big Skyfleet in Penance right now, but we can't even leave this stupid little country cause of these Humans an' their Gods.

"Then, just as we finish building a ship capable of bypassing the Church's rules, the fuckin' Triad back in Penance comes in and pulls the plug on the project! It was Borris Blackhand who gave us the go-ahead in the first place, but he only makes up a third. An engineer, a nobleman, and a king. What kind of fair government is that?"

Farris didn't answer; there was still something he was missing. He raised a hand for more drinks, hoping it would loosen Chester's tongue further. As they were being poured, Farris pried deeper.

"So, what was it that made this ship so special?"

Chester waited for his glass to arrive before answering. When it did, he took deep swig of thainol and smiled.

"It's the gas. Our chemists, they aren't like alchemists with their prayers and their robes. They discover and create. We use a new gas they made. Doesn't burn as easily. Doesn't burn at all, actually. We can have a proper furnace going, without the need to go through all that shit with crystals."

Farris took a long, steady sip.

The king doesn't know this. He told me to be careful with my pipe.

Although King Diarmuid had been half-right about Chester traveling as a passenger, nothing else he had said made much sense. Assuming the Silverback did attack, why would he leave the king alive? How would they have abandoned the dying king until another patrol came to carry him back to Cruachan, a day's journey away? How could they have ambushed him in a single tunnel and fought off his royal escort of Simian bodyguards without taking any losses?

Now there's this. How did the king not know about the ship?

Farris stared into his glass. The clear liquid inside was more viscous than water, and the candlelight refracted through at queer angles, making Farris's fingers appear much larger than they were.

"Interesting," he said eventually. "Does the Church know about it?"

Chester laughed. "Aye, the Cap'n only rubs it in their faces every other day. Another sign that our technology will someday bypass their power."

"So the crew would know about it too?"

"Of course! If you've ever worked in a cold engine room, you'd be begging to be transferred to *The Glory*. It's common knowledge around Sin and the waterfront here that our ship is the way of the future."

Farris remained silent. His last question had been direct and phrased strangely enough that he feared it would stir suspicion. Fortunately, Chester called for the barman's attention again. Farris didn't interrupt him until after he had given his coins to the barman, now the only other person left in the tavern.

"So," said Farris. "You don't usually have passengers on board, but there's some coming from the Church tomorrow?"

Chester yawned. "That's it. Doesn't happen very often, but tomorrow we'll have a knight and a pair of mages coming with us."

Farris flinched. "Is that so?"

"Aye, one's a healer, the other's a Geomancer...no, fire. What're they called again?"

"Pyro. They're called Pyromancers." He took another drink. *So much for things going smoothly.* If either of those mages were one of King Diarmuid's other spies, things would be much more complicated.

"Nothing we can do about it. The Church says jump, so we fly. Could be worse though; we took on some Wraiths a few weeks back. Those things are *unnatural.*"

Chester shuddered, and Farris recalled his own experiences with Wraiths. Whereas he was an agent of the Crown, Wraiths served the Church and the Trinity alone. Although the Arch-Canon was the head of the Church, it was widely believed that Wraiths answered to the Gods themselves, communicating directly with Lord Seletoth. Farris knew this was nonsense, but he still always felt a chill whenever he thought of the hooded figures, for the truth was more unsettling than the myth.

In his research on the king's alleged divinity, Farris uncovered an old letter dated from the early days of Diarmuid's reign. When he was a young man, the king often frequented brothels, much to the dismay of the other lords and ladies of the court. More than once, it seemed, the Wraiths had been sent out to remove any woman unfortunate enough to fall pregnant to the royal seed. The king still went on his nightly crusades around Barrow's Way, unaware of the spies that followed him. If it wasn't for them, the king's Divine Penetrance would have been passed on to a bastard son, and that would have caused all sorts of problems for the realm. Farris gritted his teeth at the thought.

The Church would rather murder innocent civilians than deprive their king of his desires.

Mention of the Wraiths brought a lull to the conversation, so Farris grabbed a chance to change the topic. He asked about news from Penance, and Chester informed him of the Silverback's bid for a seat on the Triad.

"Wants to usurp Borris Blackhand, but the old bastard's not even dead yet! The healers say he'll never recover, but there's air in his lungs still!"

"And what of the Cathal Carriga? Isn't he ill?"

"Aye," said Chester. "The lad's been sick for a while now, but he still goin' too. These political types, they really take the 'till death' part seriously."

Another round of drinks was poured, and Chester began spilling his heart out to Farris, telling him all about the family he had left behind in Penance. His daughter, it seemed, would be heading off to work as a servant in a manor out by Dromán.

"It'll be hard work, but she'll live a comfortable and honest life over there." Farris felt twinge of sympathy for Chester, who was bellowing with pride for a daughter who aspired to change the chamber pots of high-born men and women. "I'll get to see her one more time before she leaves. I can't face the thought of having to say goodbye to her."

Chester paid for the next round of drinks again. He was growing visibly drunk now, slurring and ranting about the Humans on the ship.

"Rats...rats is what they call us. We let them work with our technology, in our skies, and they have the nerve to call us *vermin*." He paused and looked over at Farris.

"Do you think I look like a rat? Do you think I look like a creature of disease an' filth?"

Farris thought it best not to answer.

"When I look in the mirror, I don't see whiskers. I don't see a tail, or a muzzle, or beady black eyes. I see something that looks like a Human, but bigger, an' stronger. As a race, we're far more intelligent than they are, that's a fact! We've forged our own brand of magic through fire and steam, and now we've conquered the *skies*. In their superstitions, the Humans will never leave this land. But there is more out there, Jacob. I've *seen* it. Humans may have taken Alabach with their magic, but someday we'll conquer the *world*."

Farris couldn't help but grin. The Silverback often spoke about the lands outside the reach of the Crown.

"But hasn't the Grey Plague claimed these lands?"

Chester guffawed. "Don't believe the lies of the Church. They would have us think that the rest of the world is uninhabitable. There are some Simian scholars who believe that the first Humans were not fleeing from a mysterious plague but were the ones who *brought* it. Many accounts, from both sides, describe how more Simians died from the foreign diseases of Humans than in combat with the invaders. I have seen the hills beyond the sea to the east, and they are just as green and beautiful as these."

Farris gestured for another round but was refused— perhaps for the best. The two Simians stumbled out from the bar as if the earth itself were spinning.

The air of the waterfront was cold and damp, and a chilling breeze cut right through Farris's chest. The two made their way along the docks in drunken silence, as water trickled and slushed below their feet. The sea was dark as the sky, and the boats and ships tied to the pier appeared to sway mysteriously in mid-air.

St. Ruadh's Canal sat eerie and still at the end of the road. It rose overhead and tore through the city in a straight line, like a ship's contrails across a clear sky. Chester started hiccupping, punctuating the silence with arrhythmic outbursts.

Farris considered the work ahead of him. There were agents on board the ship, and he'd need to find them and silence them. That much was obvious. If he failed, he could still go straight to the Silverback and have the king's druid he was supposed to meet apprehended instead.

But what if the others beat me to it? What if they succeed and we're plunged into a civil war before we're even prepared?

Chester continued to hiccup as another wave of anxiety washed over Farris. It was stronger than before. Fire raged through his skull. He closed his eyes and focused on his breathing.

It'll pass, it'll pass. Like all the other times before, it'll pass.

Chester had paused, too, and let out another audible *hic*.

"Jacob, are you well?"

A thousand fears began to surface in Farris's mind, but he tried to keep them at bay.

It'll work, don't worry. It'll work. I'll tell the Silverback about the king's lies and then I'll be home.

Through a half-open eye, Farris saw the only person that could stand in his way.

No. He is not a problem. He's a drunk and doesn't even know when the ship leaves. I'll be gone before he wakes, and I'll be home before he's sober.

The ground rolled beneath his feet, and Farris fell to one knee. He held his head in his hands.

But what if he does wake? What if he gets to the ship and warns the others?

The risk was minimal, but it was *there*, eating away at Farris's peace of mind.

The future of the Simian race and the peace of the kingdom lay upon one the shoulders of the drunkard who bent down to help Farris to his feet. The fear began to subside as he stood, but Farris realised that he no longer had a choice.

"Are you alright, J-Jacob? Do you want me to walk—"

With a flick of his wrist, a tiny blade concealed in Farris's sleeve slid into the palm of his hand. He had plenty of practice with this manoeuvre, but half a dozen glasses of thainol had taken their toll on his agility. He leapt up and sliced the blade across Chester's throat, but his aim was off, and the blade only grazed the skin of Chester's neck.

The drunken Simian spluttered with fright, raising both hands up to cover the wound. Farris plunged forwards again, this time shoving the dagger into the Simian's chest. For a moment, Chester attempted to push Farris away, but a twist of the dagger rendered the navigator's body limp.

Farris caught Chester's weight with bent knees, then slowly dragged it towards the canal's bank. With a gentle splash, the body went floating down along the dark stream of water.

Feeling a little more relaxed, Farris stumbled on home. *He won't be missed. Even if he's found, nobody will care. He's a lowly Simian, a second-class citizen.* He took a turn and made his way uphill to a row of hovels looking out over the sea. *Another dead rat in the gutter.*

CHAPTER 8:
POPPY FOR THE PAIN

Water trickled and dripped overhead as Morrígan skulked deeper into the catacombs. Even after weeks of exploration, feelings of overwhelming pride and excitement still struck her every time she discovered a new chamber. Yarlaith had said that scholars have been searching for the Lost Catacombs of Móráin's Conquest for many years, but it seemed that none had thought to check under the tiny village of Roseán.

Morrígan glazed her torch over the tunnel walls, looking for any irregularities in the stone. The rocks jutted out at awkward, chaotic angles, but every so often they formed a neat and ordered cleft, and Morrígan paused to record what was inside. This one held a skeleton shrouded by a thin, grey veil— a sign that it was once a battlemage. She noted the pair of rings on its fingers and began scribbling away in one of Yarlaith's old notebooks.

One Pyromancer: bones without flesh, no ornaments other than flint-rings.

There was word that winter was slowly melting into spring outside, for daffodil shoots had been spotted along the Sandy Road. All Morrígan cared about, however, were the caps and stalks of fungi that grew along the underground rivers, vital for her salves and potions. Between her work in the clinic and the caves, she rarely saw the sky, even if the other villagers visiting the clinic told her that the clouds had finally cleared.

Delving deeper into the caverns, Morrígan reached another fork in the path and paused to record its location, scribbling on a separate roll of parchment with a Simian inkpen. As the mole burrows, she wasn't far from the workshop, but the path back to it was erratic and winding. She took a new route that she figured would bring her back in that direction and pressed onwards, keeping a careful eye out for more burial cairns along the walls.

She came upon another chamber. This one contained a row of stone sarcophagi with the likeness of brave warriors etched upon their surfaces. She pulled out her parchment and began mapping the area. The tops of the sarcophagi were too heavy to lift on her own, but she knew that inside they contained high ranking officers and generals from Móráin's conquest, perfectly preserved by archaic alchemical oils and ointments.

Morrígan checked her updated map and saw that there was possibly a shortcut from this chamber that looped back around towards the workshop. There was a thin path across the way that looked like it led back into the eastern portion of the lake. Satisfied with her work, she pocketed her parchment, amplified her torch, and returned to her uncle's base of operations.

***

When Morrígan found him, Yarlaith was hard at work, cursing and muttering before a wooden table covered in severed limbs. In his bloody hands he held an arm, cut at the elbow.

"Morrígan! Make up another measure of balanth serum."

Without hesitation, Morrígan set to work, picking out the bottles of solutions and setting the ingredients down on a separate table kept clear for alchemy. Any contamination from a flake of skin or a drop of blood could render a potion useless, so she carried out each step with extreme caution.

She slowly heated a pot of water over an array of red focus-crystals, crushing a handful of balanth stalks in a mortar and pestle until they became a fine powder. She used a brass scales and tiny iron weights to measure out exactly six ounces of balanth, all while keeping an eye on the water, careful not to let it boil. When the powder was prepared, she added the balanth to the water and immediately transferred the solution to a second array of red crystals, enchanted to produce twice as much heat as the first. The water turned cloudy and grey as it began to boil, and the powder disappeared into the liquid. This was a sign that it was time to add the blood, which she did, dropwise, using a long glass pipe filled with gauze.

Ten per ounce, she reminded herself, counting each drop as it fell into the potion. She let the solution cool for exactly three minutes, counting on her uncle's Simian-made pocket watch, and then it was time to add the remaining ingredients. They were already prepared with the exact amounts needed so they could be added quickly. The bottles were labelled with numbers, but Morrigan didn't bother to learn their real names. She hated alchemy.

When the serum was ready, she brought it to Yarlaith, who was still fixated on the severed arm.

"Grab the swab and apply it to the elbow, right where it has been cut."

The first time he asked her to do this, Morrigan was terrified of getting too close. Now, even as the blood had grown foul and crusty around the exposed bone, she barely hesitated.

She worked in silence, blotting the liquid around the flesh of the torn arm. Nothing happened. She watched for a moment, then blotted at the flesh again.

"Stop, Morrigan," said Yarlaith, putting the arm back onto the table, defeated. "The reaction should be immediate. Are you sure you added the blood at the right—?"

"Yes! I did exactly as you asked," she snapped. "How can you expect to repeat the experiment exactly as it happened to Fionn, without another armless mage to work on?"

Yarlaith shook his head. "That shouldn't *matter*. Once the solutions and poultices are exactly as they were that night, I should be able to make the flesh my mark again. I achieved that much before I even began sewing the arm onto Fionn's body."

"What if the corpses were fresher? I found some sarcophagi today, out in the eastern tunnels."

"No, Morrigan. We've been through this. It won't make a difference. Besides, I need to focus on these limbs for now."

"But even if you take control of the arm, how will that bring back Mother?"

"This is how research works. We often must stray far from our goal to learn how we can achieve it. Necromancy has never been studied properly, and before we can even consider bringing your mother back, we need to learn how it works. Now, I must go and record these findings while they are still fresh. Can you prepare more medicine for Mrs. Mhurichú's next few rounds? We're running low."

Yarlaith sat down at his desk near where Mother lay and set to work with his writing.

"Yarlaith," asked Morrígan, all too aware of how he hated to be disturbed from his work. "I know how important all this is, I really do. I just think that I'm not all that equipped to help you, to really help you, unless I know how to perform magic of my own."

"I already told you, it wouldn't make a difference," he said, not looking up.

"You did," said Morrígan. "But you promised, Yarlaith. Back after the beadhbhs attacked. You promised you'd help me learn."

"But now you're helping *me*. As this is far more important than learning the basics of the Six Schools. I've taught you alchemy, haven't I?" He glanced up at her as he turned a page of his notebook.

"Yes," said Morrígan, with a sigh. Of course, alchemy was one of the Six Schools, but it was hardly *magic*. More like cooking. "But surely I need to know the basics too."

"And what difference would that make?"

"Well, if something were to go wrong with the fire crystals, or the balanth serum, how could I even begin fixing them without knowing how they work? And if something did go wrong, I probably wouldn't even be aware of it."

Yarlaith paused. "You've been making blood potions for almost a month now. Are you telling me you don't know how focus-crystals work?"

"I know that they produce magic, like Pyromancy, and—"

"Focus-crystals do not produce magic." Yarlaith shut his notebook with a slam. He stood and walked past Morrigan, then picked a crystal from the alchemy workstation. It shimmered with a faint crimson glow between his fingers. "They are nothing but empty vessels. Repeated instances of tiny structures that a mage can alter based on his or her own needs."

The crystal slowly turned from red to blue in Yarlaith's hands. He tossed it to Morrigan; as she caught it, she realised that its heat had vanished and was replaced with a numb, freezing aura.

"You changed it," she said. "It's giving off Hydromancy now...."

"All I did was alter the structures that make up this crystal, and now the instructions for performing red magic have been replaced with those for blue magic."

"Instructions? What instructions?"

The question escaped her lips before Morrigan had a chance to prevent herself from appearing ignorant. She expected Yarlaith to grow irritated with her questioning, but instead he smiled.

"Consider that you and I were separated by darkness over a large distance, and the only means we had of communicating was with a single torch. I would easily be able to communicate two messages with the torch. Lit and unlit. On and off. One torch can provide two discreet signals. Do you follow?"

Morrigan nodded, realising that some warmth had returned to Yarlaith's voice. From the reading and writing lessons he had given to Morrigan and her friends when they were children, it was clear that Yarlaith took great joy in teaching, especially through meandering metaphors.

"Now, if I was in possession of two torches, and we had agreed on a code beforehand, how many messages could I relay?"

Morrigan thought about it for a second.

On-off, off-on. Both on...both off.

"Four?" she said, not entirely confident in her answer.

"Yes!" exclaimed Yarlaith. "So, you can see that more torches would allow me to portray a more complex message. With three torches, this number increases to eight. With four, we get sixteen!"

He picked another red crystal off the table. The fiery glow vanished, and the crystal began pulsing with white light, some flashes long, some short.

"With five torches, we'd have enough combinations to communicate a message based on letters of the alphabet, with several more to spare for punctuation. This is the basis of crystallography. If we take one crystal, divide it carefully in half, then one side will mirror the actions of the other. I can alter the structures inside one crystal to resonate with a certain pattern, and the other will mimic the actions. Crystallographers can use this principle to relay messages across very long distances, instantaneously, in what we call *waves*."

Morrigan looked at the pulsating crystal, her mind reeling with the revelation that she now understood the basis of something as mundane as crystal-waves, something she had taken for granted all her life.

"Here is where things get interesting," said Yarlaith. "Returning to our analogy, five torches would let us relay thirty-two different signals. However, if we were to have ten torches, we could communicate a thousand different signals. If we had a thousand different torches...."

He paused, as if he knew Morrigan's mind would itself strain with the implications.

"This is how crystals store information. By switching on and off the repeated structures inside, complex instructions can be written. Crystals hold far more 'torches' than a thousand, however. The number of switches alone inside a single crystal vastly outnumbers what a Human mind is capable of comprehending. Thus, the complexity of the instructions they can carry are enough to store and perform specific spells. I generate blue crystals for Fearghal's stores, freezing the air to prevent his meat from spoiling. The

Reardon brothers use red crystals for their forge, and most of the villagers in Roseán own some white crystals to heal themselves of minor injuries if I am not around."

All of this fascinated Morrígan, of course, but Yarlaith still hadn't addressed her original request.

"And magic," she asked. "Can anyone perform it?"

"Well, the first mages were created when Lord Seletoth first set His sights on Alabach so they could fight alongside King Móráin against the Simians. Only people directly descended from those brave men and women can still use magic today. My father, your grandfather, was an accomplished healer, and I'm sure your father could have been too, if he put his mind to it. So, with the right training, you, too, could become a mage."

Morrígan's eyes widened. "So, you *will* teach me?"

Her uncle paused and glanced around the workshop with its bloody bodies strewn across the floor. He picked up a beaker full of water from the alchemy station and placed it on a table before Morrígan.

"Nothing can truly be created or destroyed," he said, "for Creation is an artform reserved for the Gods. This is the First Law of Magic, and it dictates that we can only manipulate Nature and her fruits, nothing more. If I was to take a tree and burn it, it is not destroyed; its state has simply changed from wood and leaves to ash and smoke. Geomancers can bend and shape iron and stone, but they cannot create what does not already exist. And as a Hydromancer can appear to make water vanish, all they really do is change its state to steam. Go ahead. Try it for yourself."

Morrígan paused, startled. "What? Just like that? But I don't know—"

Yarlaith cut her off. "Lord Seletoth relied on us to use magic to fight against the Simian natives. Our escape from the Grey Plague relied on it, as did the founding of this great kingdom. If He had made it so difficult to learn, we never would have come this far."

He placed a hand on Morrígan's shoulder. "You were blessed with a soul. It allows you to experience love and happiness in ways Simians can only imagine. It is this same power that allows some of us to use magic. Focus on the water, Morrígan, and harness your emotions to take control of its Nature."

Morrígan narrowed her eyes and focused on the glass. She pictured it boiling and bubbling, but it remained still. She gritted her teeth and looked inside herself, focusing now on the fear she felt when the beadhbhs attacked, her longing to leave Roseán and seek fame and fortune elsewhere. Somewhere within, it felt as if these thoughts had some sort of manifestation in her being, like tiny weights tied to her heart. As she pulled on those, she suddenly felt a peculiar dampness between her fingers.

Is this it? It certainly didn't feel very powerful, but something was there, at her fingertips, as if her entire hand was submerged in water.

She balled her hand into a fist, and a tiny ripple formed on the surface of the liquid inside the beaker. Morrígan focused hard on her feelings, on her power, but the sensation of control left her as quickly as it appeared.

"Ah! You've got it!" exclaimed Yarlaith. "Try it again, same as before, but this time, *concentrate*."

She searched inside once more, to try and recapture whatever power she found, but something else took its place. The troll, the field, her father galloping off into the distance, her mother, beaten to death against the ground...all of these images ignited pain, sorrow, anger and fear within her soul, far stronger than the other weights tied to her heart. The memory of the death of her mother suddenly seemed to materialise as a huge pendulum inside her chest.

Focusing on the pendulum, again, she felt the water particles between her fingers.

Boil it. She conjured up more memories of the day her mother died: the knight, the woman in white, Fionn's arm being torn from his body. She pushed on the pendulum, and for an instant, she acquired full command over the liquid.

The pendulum lurched violently as it swung back, and Morrígan lost control. Power surged through her body, and with a crack of broken glass, the water exploded into a burst of steam.

"Ah," said Yarlaith, tentatively, eyes closed, his mouth curling to a smile. "You harnessed power from parts of yourself you have yet to master. Those who have experienced great happiness or sorrow have the potential to become great mages, but only those who learn to control their emotions can truly master the craft."

Morrigan looked down at the broken glass in a haze. *I did it. I used magic. Real magic.*

"I can't say I'm surprised you picked it up so quickly," Yarlaith continued. "You always were an excellent student. We'll work on fine tuning your power later. Now, I need you to go prepare Mrs. Mhurichú's next round of medicine."

Yarlaith bent down and began picking pieces of glass from the floor; the pressure of the steam had spread them right across the width of the workshop.

"Can't we start on Pyromancy soon?" asked Morrigan. "I'd help with exploring the catacombs if I could kindle my own—"

"Not now, Morrigan!" snapped Yarlaith, his foul mood returning. "We have a lot of work to do, and a very sick patient who requires our undivided attention."

Morrigan turned to leave. Scowling, she walked through the cavern, past disembodied limbs and torn-up corpses, severed with surgical precision. Several alchemy stations were set up along the length of the cavern, as not to have ingredients from different blood potions contaminating each other.

Of all the bloodied and broken cadavers, only her mother's body remained intact inside her coffin, still fresh and beautiful from the funeral ceremony.

This is what it's all for. Morrigan approached the coffin. *This is why we're defying the Church and defiling these bodies. Grave-*

robbing, illegal blood potions. When we wake you, it'll all be worth it.

From behind the coffin, a large black rat emerged, trotting along the ground with its nose held up in the air.

"Stupid rodent," she muttered as she reached for a glass bottle from a wooden shelf overhead. She had seen that same rat many times before; once it had even climbed into her mother's coffin before she chased it away. Morrígan slowly raised her hand, readying the bottle, when it stopped and looked up at her. Morrígan hurled the glass bottle across the room, but the rat darted out of the way into the safety of the darkness. With a crash, the glass smashed against the foot of the coffin.

"Gods, Morrígan!" said Yarlaith, scowling. "At this rate, I'll barely have a lab left by the time we're done. Go, do as I asked. Now!"

Morrígan cursed the rat as she left the workshop. She took a short tunnel down to a trap door with a ladder dangling from the ceiling. She emerged headfirst into her uncle's study, but it had been a long time since he had studied in it. Most of the books had been removed from their shelves for ease of access in the workshop, and even his favourite chair had been brought down into the caves.

The clinic itself was dark, and Mrs. Mhurichú was asleep across the way. A special leather mask covered her face, as to prevent the spread of infection. She looked like a great bird, lying there in the darkness, the respirator hooked like a beak. Yarlaith had stored all sorts of herbs and spices in there to keep the consumption in, but they did nothing to keep Mrs. Mhurichú's snores out.

Morrígan crossed the clinic towards a small alchemy lab built into the wall and went to work in silence.

Alchemy wasn't necessarily magic, but it was often referred to as an "augment" to healing. Potions and solutions did little to heal a wound or cure an ailment on their own, but there were some forms of sicknesses that even the most skilled healer couldn't cure with their hands. As a result, most white mages were well versed in both.

If blood potions were legal, then most healers would be out of their job, Morrígan realised, carefully weighing out six ounces of willow bark. She added these to a solution, along with a measure of spores from a strange fungus, and the solution simmered softly as she added heat. She sang under her breath as she added seeds to the scales.

Willow for the fever,
Poppy for the pain,
The healers keep on healin',
But we still all die the same.

She preferred making blood potions to proper ones. There was a certain magic in Human blood that came alive when mixed with the right ingredients: magic that would always be stronger than normal alchemy. She often wondered if there was a simple blood potion that could cure the consumption that even Yarlaith didn't know about. Recipes for illegal potions were hard to come by, and it was likely that there was more out there than those listed in his notes.

Morrígan double-checked all the ingredients. The fungi spores were the only components of the potion that were supposed to cure Mrs. Mhurichú, while the others eased her suffering. The woman was still sick, though, and sometimes it seemed as if all their hard work was just keeping her barely alive.

It would be a kindness to let her die. Morrígan stole a glance at her patient, who coughed and groaned under the mask. Like Morrígan, Mrs. Mhurichú hadn't seen daylight for weeks. *What kind of life have we left to give her?*

Morrígan reached for a pen and inkwell and labelled the bottles in big, clear letters.

And besides, we'd put her body to good use.

I was away, at Mount Selyth's peak
When the Tower pierced the sky.
From there we watched, but none dared speak,
'Til the Lord Himself did cry:

"The hubris of man does not compare,
To the scale of Simian pride.
But dare they add to this Sin's height,
And see their Lord defied?"

So Seletoth went to the City of Steam
And beheld the Simians in sight.
But in silence we stayed at Mount Selyth's peak,
Dwarfed by the Tower's height.

Yes, the Tower stood taller than Mount Selyth's peak,
Before it was felled from within.
And for one short breath, Lord Seletoth's might
Was eclipsed by the Shadow of Sin.
Excerpt from The Fall, AC 157

CHAPTER 9:
THE CHIMERA

'*Accounts of Necromantic practises date back as far as one-hundred years after Móráin's Conquest of Alabach.*'

Morrígan read by the light of a sinking candle, while shadows of twisted limbs danced across the cavern walls.

'*The earliest known Necromancers were healers of the Mage's Academy of Dromán, although they were ignorant of their heresy at the time. Cadavers were used for white magic, in training and in practise, up until AC 145. Under today's legislation, all healers and alchemists from those days were as guilty of Necromancy as Earl Roth himself.*'

Morrígan circled the name "Earl Roth" with her Simian inkpen and jotted down the verse and page number in her own notebook. She had started recording *everything* she did regarding her research, from the times, dates, methods, and results of her experiments, to the conclusions and postulations that arose from them, even when reading dusty old tomes written by druids long dead.

'*In Terrían, the first Necromancer was tried and executed for his crimes. In the year AC 178, Earl Roth of House Conchobhair built a crematorium in the same style of the Simians of Penance, declaring* the crypts full and the graveyards overflowing. Some of his subjects protested, but Roth was an educated man, cunning with words and wise in the ways of magic. He convinced them to bring their dead to be burned to ashes and sent into the air. The crematorium was built and serviced Terrian for five years until a fire tore the building down to its foundations. Some records tell of how the building was struck and torn by lightning, as if a sign from Lord Seletoth himself that it was a place of sin. True enough, the floors were found to be false, and the wreckage revealed dozens of corpses, disembowelled and violated. An off-duty guard was the first to arrive at the scene, and he described how the bodies were sewn together and impaled upon bloody skewers of silver and gold. Limbs had been removed from some and attached to others, forming grotesque monstrosities bred from a twisted imagination.

'On trial, Earl Roth admitted that he had been attempting to create life from death and pleaded that he be allowed carry on with his research. He was sentenced to death by burning, and he was the last person to ever be cremated in Terrian.'

Morrigan underlined the words "silver and gold" on the page. She had read about other mages like Roth, and each had pursued the same goals through different means. Putting the leather-bound edition of *On Heresy* aside, she opened her own handbook and flicked back through the pages.

'Earl Roth used silver and gold to bind corpses together, but Callaghan the Black used a simple needle and thread.'

Both men were also healers. Based on her uncle's work, it seemed apparent they had all stumbled upon Necromancy in the same way.

She turned further back through the pages, reading her notes on the Druids of Rosca Umhir, holy men who turned to Necromancy after years of work as undertakers. There were no accounts of them binding flesh together, but they were the only ones who seemed to succeed in reviving the dead. A simple farmhand in AC 244 had claimed he saw one of the druids, manipulating a set of bones "like master would a puppet." The Church intervened, and the seven druids were hanged together, on the banks of the River Trinity.

What would the Church say about this? Morrigan turned to the table behind her, piled with assorted body parts sprawled on top of one another. She was happy that she was no longer brewing alchemical potions, for her uncle had succeeded in manipulating the limbs without them.

It was the corpses of the four sarcophagi Morrigan found that lead to their success. After they had severed the old limbs, Morrigan insisted that Yarlaith take control of them without trying to recreate the events with Fionn the Red. It took some time, but eventually he grasped one of the legs. "Necromancy is a magic of the flesh!" he had cried, as the severed leg bent at the knee.

He was thankful for Morrigan's help and set her reading history instead of slaving over hot-plates and glassware.

She scribbled into the margin of her notebook. *'The Druids of Rosca Umhir succeeded without the use of alchemy or binding, for Necromancy is to flesh as Hydromancy is to water: elemental manipulation.'*

She turned and reached out to grasp a severed arm for herself, focusing on the black markings etched into its skin. In her research, Morrígan learned that many of the corpses uncovered by the Church had strange scribblings upon them. It was widely believed that these were ritualistic symbols used for dark magic, and *On Heresy* even dedicated an entire chapter to deciphering their meaning. She knew now that those markings held no magical powers, though, and simply served as anatomical markings for where bone met flesh and blood flowed under skin. Their only purpose was to make it easier for a Necromancer to grasp at them, as Morrígan did with ease.

Regular practise with candle flames and loose rocks had honed Morrígan's fledgling power to that of a novice mage. The control over the four 'mancies came easy to her now, provided she avoided harnessing the strongest part of her soul: her pendulum. That part of her power was still hung outside her control; a dozen broken glasses and a half-charred workstation lay testament to that.

She narrowed her eyes and forced her power into the markings on the limb. The sensation of Necromancy was unlike that of other magic. Instead of feeling heat or moisture between her fingers, like Pyromancy and Hydromancy, Morrígan heard *screaming*, raging through her skull. This time, the bloodcurdling roar of a man gave Morrígan confirmation that the arm was under her control. The voice formed barely audible words in the back of her mind as she let her power flow through the veins of the arm, up into its hand, and closed its fingers into a fist.

Ground-breaking, sure, but there is much left to do.

She turned to face her mother, who still lay in her coffin, veiled and beautiful. *We are close, Mother. Closer than ever.* The season above ground was spring, turning slowly to summer. Soon, it would be a full year since her mother died, but Morrígan was far from "conquering her grief," as others from the village had said she would. Sure, she no longer cried herself to sleep anymore, nor did she flare up in anger for no reason, but she was far from moving on. She wondered what kind of person she'd be if it wasn't for her uncle's experiments. She thought about how things might have turned out if she hadn't spent every waking hour with those potions and corpses.

Would I have really gotten over Mother? Would I have fallen in love, like a normal person, and went on living a happy life?

Lost in thought, Morrígan gazed over at the coffin. From the first rumour that the king was planning on raising taxes to the day the battalion of mages came to Roseán, she thought about how much her tiny hometown had changed. The inn was gone, and Peadair had left to start a new business out in Point Grey. Taigdh, Sorcha, and even Darragh were growing up, gradually taking on the responsibilities of adults.

But where does that leave me?

It took her a moment to notice that the same fat, black rat from before stood just below the coffin, raised on its hind legs. It looked up at Morrígan, as if tilting its head in awe at the girl in black.

"Go away," she muttered, but the rat didn't move. It was unlike others in the cave, all of which fled at the sound of a Human voice. This one stood as brave as Old King Móráin Himself. Edging closer to Morrígan, it opened its mouth slightly as it raised its head, as though it were smiling.

"Scram!" she said, raising her voice, but the rat just looked on with beady black eyes.

Rage boiled in Morrígan's chest, and she picked up the seventh edition of On Heresy and threw it down at the rodent. With a sickening *crack*, the book landed on top of it.

Then there was silence.

After a moment, Morrígan got up on her feet and reached out for the tome.

The rat's neck was twisted grotesquely under ruffled fur, with all four of its tiny paws curled back in agony. Its eyes met Morrígan's, and it whimpered meekly.

Broken neck, or spine, perhaps. Serves you right.

Suddenly, the most peculiar thought crossed Morrígan's mind. With a smile, she scooped up the rat up and brought it to her uncle's workspace.

***

Morrígan walked across the beach later that day, embracing the ocean air she had been deprived of for so long. The tide washed back and forth, leaving jagged rows of seaweed and debris spaced out along the sand. Clouds of sand flies swarmed and buzzed around her as she passed, knocking into her exposed ankles; she had taken her shoes off to feel the sand between her toes.

Strange objects often washed up on the beach. The tides usually crashed in from around Gallow's Head to the north, carrying strange rusted assortments from Penance. Once, after a particularly rough storm, Morrígan and Taigdh found part of an old Simian engine amongst the seaweed. She had wanted to bring it back and show her parents, but it was too heavy to move.

I bet I could use magic now, though.

In her practises with Geomancy, Morrígan saw how it was much harder to grasp steel compared to iron. It was difficult, but just within her ability.

Yarlaith had recently brought news that her parent's estate had finally been sold. After many weeks of paperwork and correspondences, the family plot and home were handed over to a wealthy merchant from Point Grey. Taigdh and his father would still continue to rent the property for the time being, but once the summer came to an end, Morrígan would be off to the Academy of Dromán to continue her studies of magic, with enough gold left after tuition to live a comfortable life as a student.

On the beach, this time instead of rusted machinery, the sea had washed up the carcass of a baby seal. A group of crows picked at the exposed ribs, squawking and fighting over its flesh. Morrígan crouched, approaching the birds in silence. She balanced herself up onto the balls of her feet and craned her neck forwards to get a better look. There were four birds in total: three on top of the seal, and another hopping around it.

Morrígan spotted a small rock, buried in the sand. She raised a hand and pushed at her power, pulling the rock up into her fist. Using magic was so much easier now that she wasn't using her "pendulum" as she had before. She felt far more in control of her emotions, too, and by extension her soul's power.

Oh, what will the other students say when they see me arrive at the Academy, already a skilled mage?

With another subtle push, the rock flew from her hand and shot towards the birds. After a screech and a flutter of feathers, three of the crows were gone, with one left dead on the sand. Morrígan rushed over to admire her handiwork; the rock had embedded itself in the bird's chest, leaving trickles of blood mottled through black feathers. She watched as the other crows landed on another row of seaweed further down the beach.

Why don't they leave? Don't they know how free they are?

In a way, Morrígan felt trapped in Roseán. Sure, she had a means now to leave and study in Dromán...but that would mean leaving her research, her mother, behind. As much as she dreamed of some day doing both, now she was starting to realise that she may have to choose one over the other.

What would it be? Go to Dromán and leave her uncle behind, or stay in Roseán and possibly change the course of history? Perhaps by the time she graduated, her mother would be alive again. If not, she could provide even more help as a fully trained mage.

That'll take years though.

There was the possibility that they'd revive her mother before then too.

Then I'd have to leave her again, just as Father did.

The thought of her father, galloping away through the mists, still managed to boil the blood in Morrígan's heart. Even after all the time that had passed, nobody else in Roseán seemed to know what happened to him.

Maybe he's drunk himself to death and rotting in a gutter somewhere.

She gazed down at the two dead animals; a swarm of sand-flies had gathered around the seal now, replacing the crows that had torn its chest open.

The Church praises Nature as if she were a mid-summer's maiden, but in truth she's a vicious bitch.

Morrígan stooped down and picked up the crow, rubbing a finger across its feathers. A voice called from behind.

"Morrígan? Is that you?"

She turned to see Darragh standing alone on the sand. He wore a greasy, blood-stained apron that hung down over his knees.

Gods, would it hurt for him to change out of those filthy clothes for once?

"Hello, Darragh," she answered, stuffing the dead bird into a pocket on the inside of her beadhbh cloak. Her mind rushed through hundreds of excuses that would allow her to leave, but she couldn't decide on one.

"How have you been, Morrígan? I haven't seen you around town for weeks."

Morrígan shrugged. "I've been busy. I'm learning how to do magic now, and I'm helping my uncle out in the clinic."

"Oh yeah!" His eyes widened. "How's Sorcha's ma' holding up?"

"Sorcha's *mother* is doing fine. She's still bedridden and can barely move, but Yarlaith keeps telling people's she's *fine*, so go figure."

"Oh, okay. Sorry if I disturbed you, Morrígan." Darragh stood in silence, staring out over the ocean as Morrígan searched for a reason to excuse herself.

"I miss the old days," he said, eventually. "I miss the days Yarlaith used to teach us all about history and things. Before the garrison arrived, and when everyone used to drink down in *The Bear and the...the Be-a-da-b—*"

"It's pronounced 'beadhbh'!" snapped Morrígan. "It rhymes with 'cave' and 'Meadhbh.' Gods, don't you even know your local inn's name?"

Darragh's cheeks turned bright red. "Sure, just everyone used called it *The Bear,* and I've only seen it written down in words."

Morrígan rolled her eyes. "Well, what are you doing down here anyway?"

"I dunno." he began. "I often come down here whenever me da' gets angry at me. It's always nice and quiet here compared to the shop. You have no idea what it's like, to be surrounded by death all day long. Even after all this time, it still turns my stomach to see a pig get gutted."

Oh, you poor thing! She wondered what kind of knots his stomach would form if he saw even a fraction of what she had.

"It's stupid, I know," he continued, oblivious to the seal's corpse by his feet. "I just come here to get away from it all, y'know? Especially with me da' and all...."

Morrígan had had enough. "Well at least you *have* a father!" She turned and marched back towards the village, her fingers wrapped tightly around the dead crow.

***

Morrígan walked down the Sandy Road in haste, passing her old house without giving it half a notice. The cobblestones were dry, for once, and the sun overhead brushed heat over the nape of her neck. A sea breeze added salted, cold air to her unkempt hair, which hung in thick black tangles over her shoulders. She hadn't bothered fixing it up properly since she started working in the caves.

Besides, I could never do it as well as Mother did. She pushed open the door to Mrs. Mhurichú's dressmakers.

"Hello, Morry! How have you been?" Sorcha was standing behind the counter, cutting through a swathe of cloth with large dress scissors. She smiled, perky and bubbly as ever, despite the fact her mother was on her deathbed.

She's doing a much better job at pretending to be brave than I did.

Morrígan smiled, too, realising that Sorcha certainly wouldn't be wearing her brave face if she knew what they had been doing down in the caves.

The shop's lobby was quite small in comparison to the rest of the building. Mrs. Mhurichú herself specialised more in augmenting and repairing clothes than making or selling them, with most of the building reserved as workspace. Sorcha had taken over the business since her mother fell ill, and Morrígan couldn't help but admire how quickly she fell into the role.

"How much for a needle and some thread?" asked Morrígan.

"Oh, three shillings," said Sorcha, looking up from her work, "but you can just take whatever you need. I couldn't possibly charge you after all your uncle has done. How's Mother doing today?"

Morrígan sighed. "Fortunately, her condition is still stable, but she's still not very lucid. Yarlaith's doing all he can right now."

"Well that's still good to hear," said Sorcha. "I'll be over to visit again this evening if that's okay. Will your uncle be free?"

"I don't think so, but I suppose you can just come in whenever you want." Yarlaith's door was always open to those in the village, of course. Morrígan wouldn't be surprised if he came home one day to find the clinic cleared of its contents.

He trusts these people far too much.

"Thank you, Morrigan. He's done so much for us: Mother, Father, and everyone else in the village. He's a great man."

She didn't know what to say, so she just nodded while Sorcha pulled open a drawer and shuffled through an assortment of tiny swatches and threads.

"You want it in black? For your cloak?"

"Oh...yeah, sure." Morrigan was suddenly aware of how dishevelled her beadhbh cloak looked. Most of the feathers were bent and crooked, the rest of her plumage in disarray. It looked as if she had just rolled down a mountain and waded through the Glenn. Around her shoulders, some tufts had been completely torn free from weeks of wear-and-tear. The garment no longer fitted her figure and hung shapelessly over her hips.

Sorcha handed her a black roll of thread, with a slender needle struck through it. The two girls' hands touched for a moment. Morrigan never knew somebody's hands could be so *soft*. Her own were dirty and calloused from working all day and night in the caverns.

Despite Sorcha's pleasantries and fronts, a hint of disgust crossed her face. She eyed Morrigan up and down, and then stared back up at her mess of hair.

"Morrigan...where have you been?" She paused and shook her head. "I haven't seen you since...since the Harvest Moon festival and...."

"And it's none of your *business!*" Morrígan grabbed the needle and thread and stormed out of the shop, leaving three bronze shillings discarded on the counter.

***

A crowd was gathering in the Square as Morrígan walked through. Her first reaction was to ignore it, but after a second thought, she decided to join them. Indeed, the last time she had seen such a crowd gather, a battalion of mages had usurped the inn.

Maybe there's another visitor to the town....

Morrígan spotted Taigdh, standing by himself at the edge.

"What's going on?" she said, desperately trying to tidy her hair as she approached.

Taigdh turned, and his eyes widened.

"Morrígan! By the Trinity! How have you been? I thought you were already gone off to the Academy!"

He threw his arms around her, and despite herself, Morrígan hugged him back.

"Oh, I've just been busy working and studying. You know...."

Taigdh pulled back and nodded solemnly. "Mrs. Mhurichú, how is she doing?"

"Much better than before! She'll be back to her old self in no time."

Taigdh smiled, sending a shiver down her spine and quickening her heart's beat. She missed that smile, and her lie was worth seeing it again.

"We really appreciate all the help you and Yarlaith have been giving her," he said. "We can't thank you enough."

We. She was unable to keep a scowl from crossing her lips.

She turned and gestured dismissively towards the crowd. "What's going on here?"

"It's just the colonel's assembly," said Taigdh. "He gives one every week." He paused and studied her carefully. "Are you sure you haven't *really* been away? He's been doing this for the past six moons!"

For a moment, Morrigan just wanted to tell him the truth: that she had really been working to change the world, to conquer death. When she looked into his eyes, she didn't want to lie anymore. None of what she did was really *wrong*, and if anyone was going to understand, it would be Taigdh.

He'd see the bigger picture. He'd see what we want to achieve before considering what the Church would think.

She held her tongue, however, as Colonel Eodadh and a squad of Geomancers marched out in front of the crowd.

"Citizens of the Kingdom of Alabach. Under the reign of King Diarmuid, under the rule of the Trinity, and under the government of the Triad, I stand before you as a light in the dark of these troubling times."

His formalities continued as Morrigan asked Taigdh what was going on.

"Without *The Bear* to get our news," he whispered, "the only way we can learn about the Simians and the war is through these speeches."

From the corner of her eye, Morrigan saw Fearghal and another few villagers standing apart from the crowd. The butcher had his arms folded, his brow furrowed as he listened.

The colonel cleared his throat. "Today I bring grave news from Penance in the north. Borris Blackhand of the Triad has died. The Simians have elected known terrorist Argyll the Silverback as their new representative. The people of Penance are making it clear that they all stand behind the dissidents and condone their actions. Today, they've handed a third of the kingdom to a murderer."

A wave of whispers washed over the crowd when the colonel paused for effect. Morrigan studied the Geomancer's features as he watched them.

He's trying to scare us.

The Triad seated in Penance was a governing body made up of three individuals: a Human, a Simian, and a king. Although they all "governed" Alabach together, King Diarmuid was still above them, for he happened to be one of the Trinity too.

With a glance, Morrigan saw that Fearghal wasn't impressed, and she considered his "invisible war" theories.

Maybe he does have a point after all.

The colonel spoke again. "The Silverback is a criminal mastermind who has manipulated the nobility of Alabach with one hand, and now holds the kingdom by the throat with the other. His spies and scouts have infested the Clifflands, but they have seen how strong we are. They know that a mage battalion is stationed in every settlement from

Point Grey to the Glenn, and that is why they do not dare risk an open war against us. They have witnessed our strength, and they have learned their place."

Morrígan remembered the Simian she saw the day the Geomancers had tried to move the troll. It was an unsettling thought, to think that he was fleeing back to Penance to make a report.

They must know about the catacombs too, thought Morrígan, considering how he had just disappeared back into the caves without a trace. Fortunately, once the caves surrounding the workshop had been mapped, Yarlaith was able to use his own Geomancy to block off the tunnels leading inside.

"But this does not mean we have nothing to fear," the colonel continued. He pulled a parchment out from his cloak and rolled it open, presenting the words to the crowd, though most of those before him were illiterate.

"This is a report made by the Crown upon intercepting a Simian weapons cache that arrived into Cruachan recently. Captain Padraig Tuathil here describes, in his own words, that he had expected to find armour, or crystals enchanted with magic, in the smuggler's ship. However, they found weapons. Not axes and swords, or knives and daggers, but unnatural, Simian contraptions. There were three in total, made from wood and brass, fashioned to be carried over the shoulder. Using a mechanism similar to the flit-rings of a Pyromancer combined with Simian firepowder, these devices are capable of launching lead projectiles in the same manner as a crossbow but can tear through armour like *parchment*."

More worried murmurs rippled through the crowd as Morrígan tried to imagine what those weapons could look like.

The Simians were not blessed with magic, so they've begun forging their own. In their work, Yarlaith was constantly telling her about the limits of magic and the laws of Nature. *What if the Simians aren't bound by those rules? What if their power could exceed ours?*

The crowd began to disperse when the colonel stepped down. Morrígan tried to catch Berrian's eye as he followed his superior, but he turned away and marched back to the inn with the rest.

"What point is there in keeping us so informed like this?" whispered Taigdh. "Why even bother telling us about the Simian weapons?"

"What do you mean?" she asked, careful to keep her voice low, although they were now alone in the Square. "Do you think Fearghal is right, about the war not being real and all?"

Taigdh shook his head. "Not like that but.... But they're manipulating us, Morrígan. They're controlling our lives, and there's nothing we can do about it."

Rather than stay standing in the centre of the empty Square, both Morrígan and Taigdh began walking up towards the High Road.

"Have you ever just felt...powerless?" asked Taigdh. "I mean, when it comes to matters like these?"

"What do you mean?"

"It's hard to explain...." he said, pausing as his gaze drifted off into the distance. "Remember when the harvest season started, and you told me that your father wanted to have you work earlier than usual on the farm, 'cause of the taxes that were coming in?"

She nodded.

"So, all of a sudden," said Taigdh, "you had to start working earlier than usual, to help pay for taxes you don't understand, all because a few Simians from across the mountains were causing trouble with the king. Now, because of them, I might have to leave Roseán for good once the new inn in Point Grey opens up, and there's nothing I can do about it."

It was a strange thought, that the dissident Simians of Penance could start a chain of events that led to her mother's death.

Then who is to blame? The troll who killed my mother, my father who forced us to work that morning, or the Simians who attacked the king?

"It's not the first time I've thought about it," continued Taigdh. "When I was younger, we had a really hot summer here. The grass outside the inn was all stiff and dry, and you could use your foot to pull the sides of the lawn up, like a big grassy blanket. Underneath would be all these insects; ants and lice that probably hadn't even seen the sky before.

"Anyway, my cousin was over from Point Grey, and I showed him the ants. Of course, we were fascinated with them. We used bottles to catch some, and then we started having races.

"Now, if you put an ant on the ground, it just starts running all over the place. So, we made tracks, using bits of twigs and branches and stones lying about. When we put the ants in, all they could do is follow the paths we made. A few tried to climb out, but we'd just push them back in again. We'd have these races, Fiachra and me, and then in the end we'd squish the loser and put the winner to another race. I don't even know why we did it. It just seemed like something boys do. Just because they can.

"Anyway, what I'm trying to say is that the ants only have small minds. There's no way they could have imagined that two little boys were making these trails for them, setting them adventures under glass bottles and over streams of water.

"Sometimes I wonder if it's the same with us. What if the king, or even the Gods, are like that? Just putting us through our lives, knowing exactly how we'd react. You saw how the colonel treated us when the battalion first arrived. It was like he knew that Father would give his family business away for a little gold."

He sighed deeply and turned to face her. He gestured back towards the town square. "So, all of this is happening around us, but there's not a single thing we can do about it. Even if we knew about it before, could we have really made a difference? They say the Lady Meadhbh has weaved our fate, but sometimes, it feels like she's ensnared us with it. It's like we're just tiny little ants to the Gods, and destiny is just the name of the stick they prod us with."

Morrígan considered Taigdh's words in silence as they made their way up to Yarlaith's clinic.

I'm not like the others, she wanted to tell him. *I'm taking control of my destiny, and someday nobody else will have to die like Mother did.*

"I don't know," said Taigdh. "It's just been bothering me more and more lately. Maybe it's just because Mrs. Mhurichú's sick now, and there's so little I can do to help."

With that, he took a step to leave. "Speaking of which, I've got to help Sorcha close up the shop. We might go over to visit her mother later on, if that's alright with your uncle. Will you be there?"

She placed a hand on the dead bird in her breast pocket. "No, not tonight. There's something I need to do."

***

In the darkness, Morrígan worked alone, long after the candles had died out. She used her hands and her magic to direct her efforts, not daring to break her concentration by leaving her workspace to fetch another light. There was blood all over her new needle, but she kept on sewing, her eyes strained and focused.

When she was done, she stood, took a step back, and admired her creation.

Now...now we are truly on par with the Gods.

She was about to call her uncle, but light footsteps on the stone floor told her he was already near.

"Morrigan? Are you still awake?"

"Yes! Yarlaith! Come look! We've made another breakthrough!"

"Wonderful!"

Light washed over the table as the old man approached, candle in hand, revealing the finer details of Morrigan's art. She expected him to cheer, or congratulate her, but instead he gasped with terror.

"Morrigan! What have you done?"

The rat screeched in agony as it rolled over on its broken spine. Two twisted, black wings hung from its back, sewn jaggedly into its shoulders.

Morrigan raised her voice. "I've done exactly what you did with Fionn, but better!"

The old man's face was pale, the whites of his eyes standing out in the darkness. "No...no Morrigan, this is wrong. This is unnatural...."

"Exactly!" She picked up the bloody needle and carefully pushed it into the rat's belly. The poor creature began flapping its wings furiously, trying to get away.

"See," began Morrigan. "Naturally, a rat's brains don't know how to make wings move like this, but that didn't matter. His spine is broken, and he can't move his legs, but look! I've given him wings, and he already knows how to use them!"

Yarlaith sank to his knees beside his niece. "No, Morrigan, what you are doing is unnatural. It's *wrong*."

Morrigan stood, feeling taller than the little old man.

"Wrong? What does that have to do with anything? Is it wrong that you saved Fionn's life? Is it wrong that you want to bring Mother back? What makes this more unnatural than keeping Mrs. Mhurichú alive with all those potions and spells? What makes this more profane than curing a sick child with medicine? All of those things are unnatural, Yarlaith, but who is to say what is right and what is wrong?"

The healer took a handkerchief from his pocket and rubbed sweat from his forehead. She noticed he was shaking.

"I don't know who is to say what's right and what's wrong, Morrígan." He picked up his candle and placed a hand on her shoulder. "But maybe that's just for the Gods to decide."

Defeated, the old man bowed his head and left Morrígan alone with her chimera.

For the Gods to decide? Morrígan flicked two flint-rings on her fingers together. They formed a spark, which she turned into a ball of fire with a gentle push from her soul. With half a thought, the flame leapt from her fingers and engulfed the crippled rat, its screeches drowned out by the crackle of burning flesh.

What makes the Gods so special?

CHAPTER 10: CHESTER THE LUCKY

"Murder! Murder! Aggravated assault and murder!"

The city crier woke Farris with a jolt. The booming voice penetrated the walls of his tiny waterfront hovel.

They must have found the body. He climbed from his bed. The memory of Chester's corpse floating down the canal the night before was still strong. *I was too rash. He didn't need to die.*

Farris stood and carefully pulled open his bedside dresser. The alcohol hadn't left him with much of a headache or a tremulous stomach, but his movements were slower and clumsier than usual.

He dressed himself in black trousers and a plain white vest: typical attire for a Simian of low social standing. An iron pot of water at his bedside quenched his dried lips, though it tasted metallic and tepid. Under his bed he kept a small pack of bare essentials, which he slung over one shoulder as he reached for the door.

When he emerged into the blinding morning light, he found himself facing a crowd that had gathered around the city crier. The crier stood elevated on a stone wall across the street and held a big brass bell in one hand. There were men and women, Humans and Simians, dressed in a variety of clothes that marked them of high and low stations.

There's so many of them. What if the crew aboard the ship had also caught wind that one of their navigators was dead?

When the crier spoke for the second time, Farris's first fear left him, replaced with a heavier, burrowing terror.

"The Chief Engineer of Penance, known as Santos, was murdered by Simian dissidents two nights ago. King Diarmuid, Third and Nineteenth, was mortally wounded in the attack, known now to be led by Argyll the Silverback, terrorist and criminal mastermind of the separatist movement."

Panic and dread rumbled through the crowd as the crier spoke, and Farris's knees grew weak.

So that's that. He turned away as the crier repeated his message. *The king really does mean to go to war, and he wants everyone in Alabach to know about it.*

Farris considered the only other possible explanation for the assassination attempt, but it still didn't make any sense. Even though Santos dreamed of bringing Humans and Simians together with his railroad, the Silverback would never *murder* him for that, especially not in plain sight of the king.

King Diarmuid must be lying. He must be....

As he turned towards the docks, Farris attempted to calm himself for the coming mission.

The gas, that's the key. He shuffled past a group of young Simian boys drawing on the cobblestones with sticks of chalk. *The other spies won't know that it's not flammable.* It certainly wasn't much to go on, but as a means of identifying the other agents aboard *The Glory of Penance*, it was all he had.

Pier Street connected the north and south coast of Cruachan together, acting like a spine through the docklands. The street itself was wide enough for a horse and carriage to be pulled through, but cargo from the docks usually came through the other winding roads of the waterfront, as Pier Street had fallen to overpopulation and neglect over the past few years. Tenement blocks and crooked wood hovels lined the path, their windows open and presenting damp clothes to the world, giving the buildings a dishevelled, patchwork appearance. As he eyed a Simian tramp sleeping uncomfortably close to an open gutter, Farris realised how relieved he was to be returning to Penance.

We've got sewers there, and even in the Dustworks, shit doesn't flow through the streets.

Farris gasped as he emerged from the archway, now with Davis Quay in full view. It was immediately obvious which airship was *The Glory of Penance*. It dwarfed every other boat, ship, and building of the docklands. The huge, lumbering wonder was as large as the Grey Keep itself, but slender, and pointed at both ends. The body was strong and ridged, unlike the malleable, flexible envelopes of the smaller aircraft.

She was built for power. Farris spotted four external engine-carts extending from either side of the ship, like the outstretched legs of an insect skimming water. Each was attached to the ship's gondola, which hung just below the massive hull. At the back were two more engines, larger than the others, with their propellers pointed downwards at an angle to avoid grazing off the gas-filled container.

The quay was alive with the typical excitement of an airship about to leave port. It happened in Cruachan every other day, but still the children were always eager to see a ship disappear into the clouds. Farris understood the appeal. In the Dustworks of Penance, seeing the ships leave the city was one of the few things he and the other slumfolk had to look forwards to.

A wooden walkway led up to *The Glory of Penance*, and two men stood guard at its base, amidst a bottleneck of people looking to board. Fortunately, one of them recognised Farris as Chester the Lucky.

"Ha! There he is! Aodhán told me you won his wages last night!"

Here it goes.

Farris turned his head slowly and squinted towards the Human.

"Who's that? I was up all night drinking his money, and my brain isn't working so well."

The stranger laughed. He was young, barely a man, and dressed like a simple deckhand. He stood with his arms folded, in a stance more intimidating than his appearance.

"Ha! Chester you ol' sot! You must be in a bad way if you don't remember your buddy Eoghan! I heard that you're gettin' the good cabin today. Probably best you go lie down as soon as possible!"

More people had gathered behind Farris. He stepped aside to let them by, not wanting to confront anybody else. King Diarmuid had mentioned the resemblance, but Farris was somewhat surprised that he was recognised as being Chester, even though Humans often made jokes about how all Simians look alike.

There must be some truth there.

A red-haired man in the white plate-armour of a knight pushed past and swore at Farris, shoving a rolled parchment into Eoghan's hands.

"Three," he grunted, and made his way up into the ship. Although he appeared to be dressed for battle, a heavy white cape hung over the knight's shoulders, gathering dust and sand as it dragged along the wooden planks. The three interlocking circles of the Trinity shimmered like sunlight from his back. He walked with an arched back, broad shoulders swaying with each step.

This one is no stranger to attention.

Two more Humans, a man and a woman, followed the knight up the ramp. The woman was dressed in fine silks, clear and white as the few cotton clouds that remained in the sky. Farris could tell that she was beautiful, as far as Human aesthetics were concerned, and even caught himself staring at the way her silks swayed with the movement of her hips. He didn't get a good look at the other man, apart from his hooded cloak, deep and crimson.

"I don't like the look of that."

A Simian stood at Farris's side, pointing at the red mage.

"Bad enough the Church has us take them on board," he whispered, "but a *Pyromancer?* He puts one finger in the wrong place, and the gas will burn us straight out of the sky." He cursed loudly as he strolled up the gangway after them.

Farris smiled as he painted a mental picture of the Simian: short and stocky with broad shoulders and thick arms covered in coarse black hair, darker than the other Simian crewmen. He didn't wear a shirt, just loose grey trousers and opened-toed sandals.

One.

Once Farris committed the spy to memory, he stood up straight and walked into the ship, mimicking the knight's confident gait. He took one last glance back at Cruachan; the city was stirring awake for the coming day. The people would soon learn about the attack on the king, and perhaps they'd demand the Crown strike back. Someone would find the body of Chester, too, but Farris would be far away by the time the City Guard could pretend to care.

He stood in the landing deck, with two hallways stretching out in both directions. On the opposite wall, a huge iron door opened and two Simians in blue overalls climbed in, their forearms stained black from coal. Farris gave a quick glance at the door before it closed. It led to one of the engine-carts on the airship's exterior. The two Simians closed the door over, chatting idly as they bolted it shut. They walked past Farris towards a pair of double doors leading down to the stern of the ship. Farris managed to steal a peek through these doors as they opened, confirming his initial instinct that they lead to the main engine room.

A spiral staircase lay before him, twisting upwards onto the second deck. Overhead, the red mage and his female companion reached the final steps, and Farris managed to get a better look at his face.

He's young. Surely too young to have graduated from the Academy.

Mages couldn't join the Academy until they were fifteen years of age and would usually study there for a minimum of four years. In his investigations of the Church, he learned that this was almost always the case.

Except for the most extreme of circumstances.

"Ah, it's always tragic when one as lovely as that takes the cloak!"

Eoghan patted Farris on the back, his eyes fixed on the woman in white. "So, Chester, you know where you're kipping then?"

He had no idea, but Farris nodded in the direction of the white mage, who giggled softly as the Pyromancer helped her up the stair.

"I assume I'll be bunking in with them?"

Eoghan laughed. "Oh, if only! Mister *Sir* and the mages are taking the royal suite for themselves. Yours is the one closest to the bridge, on the left."

Farris would have asked for more information, but it was safer to go on alone to find his room. All it would take was a single misplaced question for him to be outed as an imposter.

Since he wasn't an engineer, or even accustomed to air travel, the rest of the ship did not meet Farris's expectations. The gondola's interior was grubby, like any sea-ship designed without catering to the impressions of passengers. Plain sheets of grey steel made up the ceiling; they almost grazed the top of Farris's head as he walked through. Long timber planks lined the floor, splintered and stained, creaking under his footsteps as if threatening to suddenly snap and send him falling into the water below. Farris shuddered at the thought of being hundreds of feet up in the air, with the same floor separating him from miles of empty sky.

Other men and Simians passed him without paying him much mind, though he had to stop more than once to let a passer-by shimmy past through the cramped corridor. Both walls on either side had heavy iron doors, raised a full foot above the ground. Farris glanced inside one left slightly ajar, which led into a tiny room full of half a dozen bunks bound to the wall.

The ship has a large crew. It would probably take an average airship just under a day to travel from Gorán in the south all the way up to the Elis Point. A journey of that length certainly wouldn't warrant a bed for every person on board....

But the Glory of Penance wasn't designed for flights this short, Farris remembered, looking back at the main door that was now shut closed to the city outside.

Eoghan called down the corridor to Farris.

"See you in the mess hall at noon! And I'll be bringing my own dice this time!" He disappeared off towards the engine room.

While nobody was looking, Farris paused to gather his bearings. *This corridor connects the bridge to the engine room, with the crew's cabins on either side.* He closed his eyes, trying to picture how big the gondola was from the outside. *If there was a cabin either side, of equal size, there wouldn't be room for much else on this deck.* The mess hall, then, was probably upstairs near the royal suite, but he had trouble imagining what either room would look like.

Cautiously, he hurried down the hallway. A crewman wouldn't stop to examine each cabin, but Farris needed to learn as much as he could without seeming suspicious. Another door to his right was open. Without stopping, Farris caught a brief glimpse of the cabin inside. This time, the beds and furniture had been removed, the room filled entirely with boxes of uniform shapes and sizes.

Further down, on the left, another open door confirmed his initial suspicion. Half of the cabins were being used to store cargo. The other half were crammed with extra beds to host the crew.

No wonder Chester was so happy to get his own room.

The end of the corridor yielded a brass door, larger than the others, with a likeness of Penance and the Tower of Sin etched into its surface. Farris smiled. It wouldn't be long until he got to see the city again.

Assuming that this led to the bridge, Farris pushed at a door adjacent to it. The cabin was smaller than the others but contained just a single bed and a bedside locker. A brass porthole with a hinged window looked out over the city, drawing in some of the sun's morning rays. Farris closed the door behind him and sat on the bed.

Now I wait. The floor began to rumble softly beneath him. The dull whir of the engines drowned out all other ambient noise, and outside, the docks began to crawl away. Some people from the shore waved and chased after the ship as it gradually gained speed. Farris thought it only appropriate to wave back.

The sound of the engines amplified significantly, and Farris's weight shifted as the ship rose upwards. The scene outside quickly began to fall away, but Farris felt as if his stomach wanted to stay grounded. Fighting the urge to gag, he grabbed the window ledge, looking outside at the buildings shrinking in size, with acres of farmland surrounding the city like hundreds of tiny patches on a quilt. A wisp of white mist grouped at the glass, followed by another, and then the sight was shrouded by a sea of pale clouds. The ship began to slowly level out, and Farris's insides adjusted to the momentum.

He lay down on the bunk and pulled a tiny brass watch from his pocket. He propped it upright on his pillow.

Four hours, he reminded himself, as his eyelids grew heavy. *Four hours before my final performance as Farris, the double-agent of Cruachan.*

***

Farris slept for a typically irregular few hours as the ship sailed over Tulcha and the Woodlands, following the Godspine north towards the Clifflands. He woke to check the time at intervals, plunging in and out of a deep sleep until the clock face read noon.

He dreamt he was there during the Fall of Sin. He and the surviving Simians from Móráin's Conquest had come together to build a great tower, a feat of Simian engineering and ingenuity to dwarf the so-called achievements of the Gods. According to the teachings of the Church, once the tower reached a height greater than Mount Selyth to the south, the Lord Seletoth caused the earth to shake, sending the tower crumbling to the ground. In his dream, Farris was the one who placed the final stone when Lord Seletoth Himself appeared before them. *This tower shall crumble*, he said, each word burning through Farris's sleeping mind like wildfire. *For it is nothing more than a manifestation of Sin.* The voice echoed as a jarring discordance in his ears. *When it falls, your kind will be forced to live forever in its rubble, as this shall be your Penance....*

With a jolt, Farris woke, his heart racing as sweat pumped out from every pore.

"Penance," he muttered, trying to recall the fleeting details of his dream. The Fall of Sin had occurred over three hundred years ago, but with the Silverback's recent actions, it was certainly on everyone's mind once again.

Despite the deepness of his slumber, Farris had woken just in time for lunch. *Perhaps the Light of the Lady is still on my side.*

When he stepped outside, the corridor was empty. He guessed that the crew were all up in the mess room. He walked quickly down the hallway past the ship's entrance. A large window on the door revealed a surreal sea of clouds, rolling out to the horizon where silver met sapphire in the distance. Just below, a flock of birds flew along the side of the ship, delta in formation. It was a strange sensation, to be flying so high, with such speed, and not feel the wind in his face. *It's not all that different from a steamboat, really.* For a moment, this amusing thought was enough to make him forget about all the hundreds of feet beneath his own two.

He climbed the steel staircase and emerged onto another deck, wider than the last. The centre of the ceiling curved downwards with the shape of the hull above. Several rope-ladders dangled from trapdoors and swayed gently as the ship rocked back and forth.

They must lead up to the ship's gasworks. He craned forwards to see inside.

"Excuse me...sir? Do you know where the food is being served?"

Startled, Farris turned to see the young Pyromancer from before. His sleeves were rolled up, revealing two skinny arms that Farris imagined he could snap in half with little effort. A mass of unkempt tangles and curls sat upon his head, like a black mop. In contrast, there was a bright freshness to his face, with skin smooth and clear like a marble sculpture.

This one knows comfort. The woman in white and the knight joined them, the latter in a fouler humour than before.

"The mess room is this way, begging your pardon," said Farris enthusiastically, beckoning the three in the direction he guessed the food was being served. They walked under the hanging ladders, and Farris caught sight of the ship's huge stomach above. Another engineer in blue swiftly climbed between two massive gas ballonets, shapeless and grey like the clouds outside.

To Farris's relief, the first pair of wooden doors he opened led into a dining area, with several circular tables in the centre, and a long food-bar along the walls. More workers dressed in blue stood in a queue with empty trays in hand.

"Just grab a tray and join the end of the line, I suppose!" he suggested, laughing meekly. The knight and the Pyromancer didn't look impressed, but the woman smiled and thanked Farris, giving him an opportunity to disappear into the crowd of hungry crewmen.

There were some Simians already seated, and they wore fine, white suits and dined with paper napkins tied under their chins. In comparison to the grubby mechanics and engineers, Farris reckoned these were the officers and navigators. *The real Chester would be eating with them.* He picked up a tray for himself.

The others took their seats as he noticed an obvious divide between both groups.

Chester would be with the whites, but they might recognise me and pry for details. He shuffled towards the servers as the line shifted forwards. *On the other hand, it might seem strange if I join the wrong group.* A tall Human chef in grey overalls grunted as he tossed two boiled potatoes and a quarter stick of butter onto Farris's tray.

After some consideration, he joined the mechanics and deckhands, deducing that if there were other agents on board, it was more likely that the king would have them impersonate those who didn't require years of experience to be there.

After all, the Crown didn't even know Chester was a crewman in the first place.

Farris took a seat opposite the dark Simian he had already identified as an agent. A Human beside him spoke enthusiastically of recent events in the capital.

"Tragic, that Santos went the way he did, but that's the nature of political terrorism. The Silverback claims that we were wrong to take his land by force, so he commits more murder to make a point."

"Hear, hear!" exclaimed another Human, raising his cup in agreement.

There were eight of them in total, and Farris was quick to note that even the Simians were nodding as the first man relayed the details of the attack on the king. The black Simian agent sat mainly in silence.

Another Simian sat to the left of him. He was thin like a rail, with a wiry wisp of a red beard under his chin. He sat relatively confidently compared to his neighbour, adding to the conversation whenever the speaker took a breath.

"He claims to be fighting for us all," the thin Simian said, his tone heavy with aggression, "but I still see him as a murderer and a fool. A fool who's fighting a war nobody wants him to win."

The door to the mess room opened, and more crewmembers spilled in, queuing for food as others grabbed a table just behind Farris.

How many of them are there? There still must be some working to keep the ship in the air.

From the corner of his eye, Farris saw the knight and the mages sitting on their own. If one of the mages were on the same mission as Farris, it would mean that the Church was involved too.

Good thing neither of them are Wraiths, at least.

It was a comforting thought, as Farris figured that the Church surely would have sent Wraiths on board instead of the mages if the king had commanded it. That still left the knight, however. He was wealthy, that much was clear, but he spoke and walked like one who was insecure or overcompensating. Farris grinned.

Or acting.

The table behind him was full now, and the white-shirts across the room looked as if they were getting ready to leave.

A sudden pang of terror struck his chest, as a hammer would a gong. His heartbeat accelerated, each beat sending quivering waves of fear through his bones.

This could be his only chance to have so many crewmembers in one room. Once those senior members went back into the bridge and closed the doors, they probably wouldn't be seen again until landing. Once the other mechanics climbed back up into the hull, well, Farris could follow, but that would raise far too much suspicion.

I could wait. Another wave of panic crept up his spine and grasped at his throat. *I could wait until we land in Penance and kill the spies there and....*

He closed his eyes, figuring out the possible outcomes.

If I get caught, I can explain from a jail cell. If I fail, I could run and warn the Silverback but....

But in truth, he didn't know what the king was planning from there. The strike on Penance could take place a day or a week from now.

Farris's teeth began to chatter as another bolt of anxiety shook his skull. Stars and sparks danced in his vision. The others still talked to one another, exchanging friendly banter, completely unaware of Farris's condition.

I've gone too far. I've dug too deep and now I've gone too far.

He tried to take a deep breath, but another shudder took him, as if every bone in his body was screaming, begging him to curl up and die.

Then he saw it. A tiny tray in the centre of the table, made to collect ashes and embers from pipes and cigars. The sight brought so much joy, it may as well have been filled with gold. The panic passed, disappearing as quickly as it had come, and he leaned back in his chair and reached for his own pipe.

A joke was said, and Farris pretended to laugh along as he began unrolling a measure of bacum, tapping the residue into his pipe. As he did, he felt a small prod at his elbow from behind.

"Hey, friend, I don't think that's such a good idea."

Farris turned to face a fat, bearded Human seated right behind him. He was leaning back to whisper into Farris's ear, but kept his eyes focused forwards, still locked in conversation with his own group.

"You better put that away, before one of the officers sees."

Two. Farris smiled as he reached for a light in his other pocket. *This is too easy.* He held the pipe in his mouth and struck the match in cupped hands.

"Oi! What the *fuck* do you think you're at?"

Another crewman, a Human, now stood across the table, pointing a quivering finger at Farris's pipe. "You trying to get us all killed?"

Farris paused. *Three.*

A thick hush fell onto the room. Even the officers about to leave stopped in their tracks. One of them, with blue and gold stripes over his shoulders, approached the man.

"What is your name and station, sailor?"

The third spy hesitated. "Fenian. Fenian Malroy, sir. Mechanic."

The officer took a step closer. "And how long have you been a mechanic of this ship?"

"Just...just under a year, sir."

"How *much* under a year?" The officer's voice grew louder. "Eleven months? Six months? Three? Two?"

"Ten. Ten months, sir."

"Ah," said the officer, turning away to face the rest of the crew, still sitting in shocked silence. "And in those ten months, Malroy, how many times have you seen the inside of the engine room?"

There was a scatter of nervous laughter, as if some crewmen didn't realise the gravity of the situation. Farris did, but he laughed along anyway.

The officer stepped right up to the spy, staring him down and leaving barely an inch between their faces.

"Are you not who you say you are?" he rasped. "Are you not Fenian M—"

Farris often considered himself an agent of chaos. When there were too many factors to consider, too much thinking to be done, he'd ruffle up some feathers, cause some disorder, and rely on his own instinct and improvisation from there. It had worked before with the Guild, and many times back in the Dustworks. However, nothing could have prepared him for the chaos that erupted there and then, thousands of feet in the sky aboard *The Glory of Penance*.

Seemingly out of nowhere, a man dressed in blue overalls leapt up and grabbed the officer from behind. Before anyone had a chance to react, the attacker took a knife and opened the officer's throat from ear to ear.

The female mage was the first to scream, as the officer fell with his white shirt stained with a spray of speckled blood.

Some men jumped from their seats, others dived towards the murderer. Amidst more roaring and shouting, two Simians climbed across the table and wrestled Malroy to the ground. The black Simian Farris had identified as an agent joined the fray. A glass whizzed by Farris's ear, smashing against another Simian's face.

He turned and saw the white knight unsheathe his sword, charging towards the murderer who stood fighting another pair of Human crewmen.

Suddenly, Farris found himself knocked to the floor. Looking up, he saw the fat, bearded agent crouching over him, and felt cold steel against his throat.

"I don't know what you were planning, rat, but I'm gonna make sure you regret it."

In a flash of light and a burst of flames, Farris was free. The bearded agent rolled across the floor on fire, screaming as his life burned away. Farris got to his feet, and another ball of fire flew past, narrowly missing a now standing Fenían Malroy before it erupted against the wall.

What does he think he's doing? A pair of brawlers stood and charged towards the Pyromancer. The boy yelled, and streams of fire poured from his hands, engulfing the two men and lighting up the floor beneath them.

"Chester!"

Farris looked down to see Eoghan, crawling across the floor, his face covered in blood.

"Chester...run, warn the captain. We need to land...engines...right below us."

Farris sprinted across the room without hesitation, the wooden floor already starting to burn. He pushed open the door and made for lower deck.

"Fire!" he yelled through thick smoke, hoping those up in the hull would hear. "Fire in the mess room!"

He tore down the stairs in a single swing, but the ship violently heaved as he did so, sending him stumbling to the floor. A Simian engineer standing at the hull's entrance yelled down to him.

"What the hell is going on up there?"

"There's a fire," Farris rasped. "The mage, I —"

"Tell the captain that we need to descend." The engineer's voice was incredibly calm. "We can use gas from above to repel the fire, but we'll lose altitude. Hurry!"

Farris turned and ran as the engineer bellowed commands at others in the engine room, but the crackling flames raging overhead quickly drowned out his voice.

The ship rocked again as Farris approached the bridge. He pounded on the door with both fists, and it opened almost immediately. A hand grabbed him by the shoulder.

"Get in! Quick!"

Next thing Farris knew, he was in a room unlike the rest of the ship. Brilliantly white floors and walls surrounded him, and a huge window looked out over beautiful green hills and mountains below. An assortment of switches and machines filled the room, with several men and Simians tending to them frantically.

"Chester! What's happening up there?"

The door to the bridge closed again, as the officer who pulled Farris in locked it with three cross-bolts. It was the captain who spoke, at least Farris assumed so, considering she was dressed in the same immaculate manner as the other officers and navigators, but with more stripes and badges across her chest.

She thinks I'm Chester too?

Farris didn't know where to start.

"There...there was a fight, and then the knight, and the mage...the red mage joined in and...."

He had seen death at the hands of men and Simians. He had seen people die slowly to hunger and to cold. He had seen many terrible things in the criminal underworld of Penance, but he had never felt so afraid. He was trapped, up in the sky, with nowhere to go but down. He spoke up again.

"The engineers, they said we need to land."

One of the navigators snorted. "We can't land here; we're flying over the Godsforsaken—"

A crash and a surge of screams came from outside. The whole room shook again, knocking Farris off his feet. Even as he hit the floor, he still felt as if he was falling, spiralling through the air. It took his brain a moment to orientate himself, but when he did, he noticed that he now lay on the windshield, the rest of the room upside-down.

His final thoughts were of the man who murdered the officer. He closed his eyes as he painted another mental portrait of the spy. *Blue overalls, dark hair, stubbled jawline.* He smiled.

Four. The glass began to crack beneath him. *That makes four out of four.*

CHAPTER 11:
THE INVISIBLE WAR

Morrígan waited in the darkness for her uncle to give the signal, the other half of his resonance crystal clutched tightly in her hand. She was in an unfamiliar chamber; one her uncle had found before she joined his research. Although a flick of her wrist would reveal the cold, damp walls of her surroundings, she found herself growing more comfortable with the absence of light. She stood in silence as the funeral continued above the ground, just over her head.

It had taken little effort to kill Mrs. Mhurichú. All she had to do was omit the vital fungal ingredient in her medicine, and the old woman died in a matter of days.

I did her an honour. If bringing the end to a life half lived is what it takes to end death for all, then so be it.

Mrs. Mhurichú had died painfully, but slowly enough to not rouse suspicion. The hardest part was convincing Yarlaith to steal the corpse once the funeral ended.

Does he want all this to be a waste? Does he want these bodies to rot beneath the soil—food for worms and maggots—instead of being used for something great?

She heard the faint rumble of voices from above ground.

Poor little Sorcha. You'll never get to be the mid-summer's maiden now.

There was supposed to be a festival later to celebrate Mid-Summer's Eve, but Sorcha's mother had been well loved in the community, so it was cancelled as a mark of respect.

It's as if her death had come as a shock. How fortunate she was not killed by a bloodthirsty troll!

The rumble of voices grew louder, and Morrigan wondered if it was a sign that the funeral was almost over. Sure enough, the resonance crystal in her hand began pulsating slowly, bringing illumination to her immediate surroundings: Yarlaith's signal that it was time for her to act.

Morrigan clicked her flint-rings together. A tiny spark formed where they collided, and with a subtle tug of Pyromancy, the spark erupted into a ball of fire in her hand. She motioned towards a pair of torches on the opposite side of the wall, filling each with a bolt of flames. In the light, she examined the markings her uncle had left on the ceiling, indicating where the coffin was being lowered. Rolling up her sleeves, she reached up and pushed the power of her soul up into the rocks overhead.

Morrigan and Yarlaith had rehearsed the sequence of events many times before, and there was little time to act. Topside, she knew her uncle was lowering the coffin into the grave himself with Geomancy, while the rest of the mourners looked on.

In a matter of seconds, Morrigan had a firm grasp on the cavern ceiling, focusing on the chalk markings upon the stone. It reminded her of Necromancy; the need to concentrate on the specific parts of flesh was more important than the amount of power that went in. She kept an eye on the crystal as it resonated softly through the darkness. Like sand running through fingers, her power merged with the rocks and soil overhead.

The crystal, now discarded on the ground, omitted a constant glow, confirming that Yarlaith was ready for her to take full control of the coffin.

With a gentle sweep of her free arm, the rocks slowly cracked along the white lines on the ceiling. As the last fissure formed, the weight upon Morrígan's shoulders increased tenfold. Her knees buckled with effort. Tensing her shoulders and gritting her teeth, she took a step backwards as soil and stones trickled down onto her head.

How on earth did Yarlaith manage this by himself?

The rocks were loose now, and Morrígan held all of their weight with her power. Slowly, she brought both hands down as the rocks broke free from the ceiling. The coffin emerged from the trickling soil, suspended on a bed of stone.

With a soft thud, the coffin landed on the cavern floor. Using Geomancy to grasp at the wood, she pulled it from the stone bed and set it aside. Now accustomed to the weight and the feel of the rocks overhead, Morrígan plugged the hole she made with little effort.

I'll be ready for the Academy in just a few more weeks, but I'm already on my way to becoming a master.

Once she had finished fixing the ceiling, Morrígan turned her magic to the coffin and cracked open the lid in a flurry of splinters. She was used to the reek of decaying flesh, but the scents of perfumed ointments and salves took her by surprise. The woman inside had both hands crossed on her chest, with a tiny gold chain wrapped between her fingers. On the end of the chain hung the three interweaving circles of the Trinity, flat on the silk fabric of her burial gown. Morrígan wondered if Mrs. Mhurichú had made the dress herself, recalling that her own mother was dressed almost identically for her funeral.

The plains of Tierna Meall must be a confusing place, with everyone dressed in the same white gowns and black suits.

Morrígan sat beside the coffin, waiting for her uncle to return. She placed a hand on Mrs. Mhurichú's forehead. The undertakers had done a great job making her seem alive and warm, but one cold touch was all it took to remind Morrígan that the woman was dead. A thick layer of makeup did well to cover her wrinkles, adding colour to otherwise pale cheeks. The skin around her lips tightened into a crooked smile, but Morrígan paid it no mind. In her research, she learned that people in larger cities usually weren't buried until a day or two after they died. Although no Necromancy was involved, it was customary to "wake" the dead by bringing them back to their old homes, where family and friends would stay up all night with them, drinking and singing to celebrate their life. Taigdh had once attended a wake for his grandfather in Point Grey, and he insisted that over the course of the night, the dead man's smile slowly grew wider and wider as festivities continued around him.

Although Taigdh was adamant that this was a sign his grandfather was enjoying their company, Morrigan knew from her work that this was simply the result of the tightening of muscles and skin after death.

"Morrigan, how did it go?"

Yarlaith the White appeared out of the darkness, a Pyromancer's torch in his hands. He seemed wearier and paler than usual.

"It was easy," she said. "Do you need help with the corpse?"

Yarlaith smiled. "No, you've done enough. I'll look after her from here. But I have a quick errand for you to run instead."

Leaving the burial chamber, they followed the eastern tunnel towards the underground lake, guided by Yarlaith's torch. Morrigan shied her eyes away from the light as they walked.

They came to what looked like a dead end to the unfamiliar eye, but Yarlaith raised a hand and pulled at the false wall, removing the rocks and stones that blocked the path. Most of the entrances to the lake had been carefully hidden this way, but any good Geomancer would be able to spot a fake wall in a second.

This is all that lies between us and a burning stake.

There was no need for Yarlaith to light another torch as they walked towards the lake. Several rays of sunshine glared through the ceiling, dancing on the surface of the dark, still water.

Another false wall blocked the entrance to the workshop, and it too fell with a sweep of Yarlaith's hand. As the rocks crumbled, the familiar scent of rotting flesh and festering blood drifted through Morrigan's nostrils. The nearest wooden table had been scrubbed clean in preparation for the arrival of Mrs. Mhurichú.

"The colonel asked me to lend a few supplies and potions to the battalion," said Yarlaith as he shuffled across the chamber, his white cloak trailing along the blood-splattered ground behind him. "He may have some of the best 'mancers in the kingdom, but only half of them have any basic experience with alchemy. This isn't the first time he's asked me, you know."

Still fuming, he opened a small chest on a wooden shelf above the alchemy lab. Morrigan glanced inside to see other scattered ingredients and vials of fresh blood potions. Beside these was a little cloth satchel, tied shut with brown string. Yarlaith took this and handed it to Morrigan. It was heavier than it looked.

"Where will I find him?" she asked, placing the satchel inside her beadhbh cloak. "At *The Bear*?"

"Yes, maybe. If not, you can just leave it with whoever's in. Now, I better get our next set of experiments ready." The old man turned to leave, but Morrigan had one more question.

"Yarlaith, what am I supposed to say if someone asks why I wasn't at the funeral?"

Her uncle turned and shrugged. "Well, everyone in the village was there today. But to be honest, I doubt anyone noticed you were gone."

***

The villagers were still gathered around outside the chapel as Morrigan approached. At the gates, Taigdh and Daithi the Blessed tried to comfort an inconsolable Sorcha. She certainly didn't look as pretty as usual. Mottled streaks of makeup ran down her face as she cried, her cheeks blotched red from rubbing away tears. A black silk dress tailored to hug her hips and bosom hung loosely over her legs.

I wonder if her mother made that dress knowing it would be worn to her own funeral.

Nobody noticed Morrigan as she passed, the sound of her shuffling beadhbh feathers drowned out by Sorcha's barrage of sobs.

I didn't cry that much when Mother died, and I even saw it happen with my own eyes!

Morrigan was tempted to catch Taigdh's attention but decided against it. She'd be wasting her time repeating platitudes to poor Sorcha, who had probably already heard them all already.

Oh, she's in a better place now. You're mother's happy up there, in the clouds, in Tierna Meall with all the other dead folk.

Morrigan kicked at a loose stone in the curve of the road as it turned into the Square. With a subtle pull of Geomancy, the stone changed direction mid-air and hurdled over the blooming bushes that surrounded the chapel.

Oh, you'll be reunited someday, so don't cry now.

Morrígan looked back at the chapel.

Sure, what's the point in living, when there's an eternity of paradise ahead of us?

A mixed group of battlemages marched by the inn. The six men nodded curtly at Morrígan, and she responded by shrugging her hips in a half-bothered curtsy. She watched as the soldiers left, their cloaks flowing lazily in the evening breeze: two reds, two blues, a green, and a grey. She paused to imagine which colour she'd be wearing once she graduated from the Academy.

She pictured herself returning to Roseán, clad in the colours of a fully trained mage, as the door to *The Bear and the Beadhbh* swung open.

It wasn't the absence of the mural behind the bar that struck her first, nor was it that the rows of arms and armour that had replaced Padraig's wooden kegs. It was the absolute emptiness of the building that caused her to gasp. Even on slow days, there had always been at least a few people in the inn, but now there was no one. All of the tables and chairs had been removed, along with the wooden-framed paintings that once hung on the wall. The whole place seemed much more spacious than before, and Morrígan walked slowly across the plain wooden floors, taking in every detail of the strange, new environment.

"Hello?" she called, her voice bouncing back as an echo upon the walls. "Is anybody there?"

A panicked voice responded from behind the bar.

"HELP! HELP! THEY WON'T LET ME GO!"

Fear rushed through her veins. In a heartbeat, she vaulted over the bar and darted into the back room. With a kick, the door swung open, revealing two men; a bald, thickset battlemage dressed in blue, and a Simian, with both hands chained to the wall.

"Help! Please! He's torturing me!"

"I told you to shut up!" The Hydromancer punched the Simian in the ribs; he turned towards Morrigan. "Don't listen to a word he says, ma'am. He's a spy for the dissidents."

The Simian rattled his irons. "I told you, I'm not! There's been a mistake. I'm just a cartographer working for the Triad!"

The mage sneered. "Working for the Silverback, more like."

"The Silverback *is* the Triad now, you dumb boar! I've been mapping these areas my whole life, and this is the first time I've ever had any hassle from your lot!"

"This is the first time you've been a prisoner of war."

With rolling eyes, the Simian moaned. "How many times do I have tell you? THERE. IS. NO. WAR!"

An abrupt guffaw escaped the mage's lips. "So why has the Silverback sent the Triad's elk cavalry out to scout the Clifflands? Why has he locked the gates of Penance to all arms-trade with the Strongholds?"

"I have no idea what you're talking about. And neither do you!"

This only elicited a blank stare from the mage. From where the cuffs had bruised and grazed the Simian's wrists, Morrígan could tell that he had been there for quite a while. His fur was brown, but dark enough to appear black in the dim light of the inn. The whites of his eyes stood out in the darkness, and both were fixated on Morrígan.

He recognises me, she realised with a shock. *He's the one from the caves!*

Morrígan turned to the mage. "What did he do?"

The mage stood up straight and proud. "We caught him spying on our drills. He was taking notes on 'em, collecting intelligence on the size of our battalion and such. We found another assortment of maps, too, when we captured him."

He pointed a finger at the prisoner. "You were mapping out them tunnels, weren't ye! Looking for a way to sneak in with the other rats from Penance while we're all asleep!"

Morrígan gasped. *The catacombs!* Her heart pounded. *If they find out that Roseán sits upon the Lost Catacombs of Móráin's Conquest, every scholar and historian in the kingdom will be flooding those tunnels before summer's end.*

She eyed the mage as he scratched his head and stared off into space, unaware of the storm that raged through Morrígan's mind.

If he questions the Simian any further, and if they send even one solider down there to investigate, then....

She turned her attention to the Simian. He hung from his chains, sobbing and wiping his face into his shoulder.

If he really is a spy, then the Simians would know about those caves already.

She took a step to leave. "I'm sorry I disturbed you. I was just looking for the colonel. Is he about?"

The Hydromancer shook his head. Wasting no more time, Morrigan bolted for the door.

The Square outside was empty, and Morrigan frantically examined her surroundings, praying for sudden inspiration. The sun descended over the hills to the west, throwing a fiery glow over the wattle-and-daub buildings across the way, further down the Low Road. She turned towards the chapel and saw vague outlines of mourners in the distance. The trees and bushes along the High Road basked in the sunset too. On seeing this, a smile crept across Morrigan's lips.

She checked that nobody was looking, and flicked her wrist, causing the flint-rings on her middle and fourth finger to form a spark. Then, she pulled the power of her soul into the spark, turning it into a flame that burned in her fist. With a well-guided throw, the foliage by the chapel caught fire. It took a moment for the villagers to notice, but when they did, their cries of fright joined the sounds of crackling and burning as smoke filled the sky. Morrigan ran back inside the inn..

"FIRE!" she cried. "FIRRRRRE!"

The Hydromancer stumbled out from the back room, stopping to straighten the blue cloak on his back. Before he had a chance to ask, Morrigan pointed in the direction of the raging inferno and he staggered out past her, eyes widened in fright. The fire now threatened every building on the eastern side of the Square.

He's a Hydromancer. She watched the mage hobble as fast as he could towards the flames. *Putting out fires is just about all he's useful for.*

More blue mages appeared on the scene as Morrigan reached the back of the bar. The trees outside had been much dryer than she'd expected, but she still had no idea how much time she had left.

The Simian stared up at her as she opened the door.

"Is there a fire?" he said. "Am I in danger?"

"What did you see in the caves?" said Morrigan. "How much have you explored?"

"Excuse me?"

Morrigan slammed the door closed behind her. "Tell me now or I'll burn this building to the ground."

"Ah yes, the caves!" The Simian smiled nervously. "Oh, queer formations, those are. The paths change shape and size, you know. Strange magic going on too. There are dead bodies down there. Corpses and skeletons and...."

He leaned towards Morrigan, as close as his restraints would allow. "I've seen 'em walking around too," he whispered.

"What!"

"Well, I haven't seen them walking, but I know they do. They've changed places. You see a big stone sarcophagus there one day, and the next, the lid's open, and it's empty!"

Morrigan sighed. "Does anybody else know of this?"

"Of course not! Those dumb brutes caught me just as I finished revising my maps. I've had nobody to tell 'til you asked!"

Morrigan stole a glance out through the far window; the fire still raged on. She considered the Simian again.

It would be easiest to just kill him.

She could use her magic to pull the chains from the wall, and maybe carry his corpse back to the caves, but it would be hard to do so without getting caught. She eyed the Simian; he looked strong, but it would be easy enough to overwhelm him if he remained restrained.

"What do you think they'll do to you?" she asked. "The soldiers, I mean."

The Simian laughed nervously. "Haven't you heard? I'm a prisoner of war! There's not much I can hope for until the war's over. I'll be waiting a while, then, considering there isn't one."

"What if I let you go?"

"Well, if you let me go, sure, I'll run, but you'll be hung as a traitor once the 'mancers get back." His brow furrowed. "But why on earth would you do something like that?"

Morrigan flicked her wrist; another ball of fire appeared in her palm. The Simian recoiled, his widened eyes reflecting the glow of the flame.

"Don't hurt me! Please, please! I've nothing to do with anything!"

Morrígan slowly brought the flame closer to his face. "Listen carefully. I'm going to let you go if you give me your word that nobody, I mean nobody, finds out what you saw in those caves." The fire was close enough to singe his hair, but Morrígan had full control over the flame and kept it at a barely safe distance. "On the other hand, it would be easier to just silence you myself...."

"No!" the Simian wailed. "Wait! Please! I've got a better idea! A better idea! Just get that thing away from me!"

The flame vanished, and the two stared at one another in silence.

The Simian's eyes were still tightly closed. "In my pack. The soldiers left it under the bar. Bring it here. It'll benefit both of us, trust me."

He nodded towards the bar, and Morrígan did as she was told. She carefully considered every word he said, suspicious that it might be a trap of some sort. She was well aware that in the old stories, Simians were often depicted as thieves and rogues. With another glance through the window, she saw that the fire was almost quelled outside: four Hydromancers worked together, pulling water out from the well and spraying it over the burning trees.

"Hurry!" called the Simian. "Bring it in here!"

Morrígan brought the pack to him, placing it on the ground. Fashioned to be strapped over two shoulders, the bag was designed to carry a heavy load. Despite its weight, however, there was little inside.

"No, no. Don't open it that way!" The Simian pointed a heavy traveling boot towards the pack. "There's a false opening on the bottom, see?"

Morrígan pulled all the contents out: several rolls of parchment and a dozen or so inkpens of different colours. Once empty, she turned it upside down, but saw no way to open it. She looked up at the Simian.

"Like this?"

"No, there's...see those things that look like steel teeth along the bottom? On the other side, there's a tag you can pull across to open it."

Morrígan's fingers found a piece of metal, hidden under a flap of fabric. With a gentle tug, it ran smoothly along the bottom of the bag, opening it up like a gaping mouth.

"Now, there you'll find some lock-picks. Just take one and bring it here. Quickly!"

There was another strange object in the compartment that Morrígan hadn't seen before, but she ignored it and grabbed what she assumed was a lock-pick. It looked like the needle Sorcha had given her before, but shorter and heavier.

"Here, give it to me. In my mouth."

She tentatively walked over to the prisoner and placed the pick inside his large, protruding mouth. She had never seen a Simian up close before, and she noticed for the first time that he did indeed have lips, slightly darker than his skin. The Simian opened his mouth wide, wider than Morrígan imagined her own could. With a flick of his tongue, the pick vanished, and the Simian smiled.

"Now," he said, his speech still surprisingly articulate, despite his mouth being full. "There is an instrument in the bag: gold, with a wooden handle. I need you to take it and hide it. If these fellas find out I've got it, they'll behead me on the spot."

Morrigan reached inside and placed her hand on the instrument. Picking it up, she found the object to be much heavier than it looked. About as half as long as her forearm, it curved at the end, as if designed to fit neatly in one's hand. A silver inlay adorned a golden sprout, wrapped around the handle like a string of thorns.

"What is it?" asked Morrigan, holding it up to her eyes.

"It's dangerous. That's all you need to know. Take it and leave. I'll escape myself when the time is right."

Morrigan thanked the Simian and carefully put the bag back where she'd found it. Leaving the inn, Morrigan found the fires outside almost fully extinguished. Those who had stood to watch had already returned to their homes.

As she crossed the Square, she held the device tight in her hand. Remembering what the colonel had said before about the intercepted Simian cache, Morrigan reckoned it must be something like that: a weapon.

Yarlaith needs to see this. She wondered if the power of the Simian engineers was indeed stronger than their magic.

She suddenly realised how strange it was that she had thanked the prisoner, even after threatening him with fire moments earlier.

Perhaps he was a spy? Maybe he manipulated me into freeing him?

Unable to find an answer to these questions herself, Morrigan carried on home. She jogged back to the caverns with the Simian weapon held tightly against her chest, and her uncle's satchel forgotten in her pocket.

CHAPTER 12:
THE FLOWERS OF THE GLENN

Farris licked dirt from his lips when he woke. He tasted blood. His face was pressed against the ground, and it took him a full second to notice the dull ache that plagued every inch of his body.

I drank too much again. He opened his eyes to nothing but darkness.

Voices came from all around him, screaming, crying, calling for help. He tried to move, but barely managed to shuffle his body inside the tiny, confined space. Finding some room, he attempted to move his arms, but they were stuck, wedged awkwardly under his own weight. He attempted to shift his legs but felt little sensation below his hips.

With a sudden pang of terror, Farris realised that he was trapped under the wreck of *The Glory of Penance.*

His heart began to pound as he wriggled his head, curling his lips to the side to catch a breath, but he could only manage a muffled cry of "Help!" A great weight pressed down against his chest; his lungs clogged as if filled with mud. Again, he called for help, but he quickly realised that he wasn't the only one in trouble.

The ship...the crew...they're all trapped too.

Farris's body convulsed as he began gasping erratically.

I'm trapped. I'm trapped, and I'll suffocate and starve. I'm trapped and there's nothing I can do until I suffocate or starve.

The thoughts repeated in his head as the anxiety tore through his body. *There's nobody left to find me. I'll die in this coffin because there's nobody left to find me.*

He screamed again, even though he had no idea how many others had survived the crash. Still...he heard the voices. He tried to twist his neck again, barely moving it an inch, and in the corner of his eye he saw a speck of daylight through a gap of twisted lengths of wood and steel.

"Help me!" he called. To his relief, the light flickered.

There's someone there!

He took a deep breath, ignoring the grains of soil that rolled into his mouth, and roared again.

"In here! I'm in here!"

Another voice spoke, louder than before, but still Farris couldn't make out the words. A soft sound quivered overhead, and a tiny stream of debris trickled down onto the nape of his neck.

It's caving in. It's collapsing now, and it'll cave me in.

Then followed a slow, dull movement in the wreckage, and the weight on Farris's back lessened, ever so slightly.

"You, down there. Can you move?"

It was a woman's voice, gentle as a hymn and warm with hope.

Farris's heart raced. "I...I can't move, but...please...get me out of here!"

There were tears in his eyes for the first time in years.

What if she walks away? What if she leaves me?

He coughed as more dust danced in his lungs.

My life...my life and everything I have ever done, everything I have ever known, lies in the hands of this stranger.

He knew what it was like to hold that kind of power over someone, but he usually held it against the edge of a blade.

Another rumble came, and more light spilled through the gap. Less trapped now, he shifted himself onto his back. There, he saw the sky once again. Trees of green stood high overhead, with branches like interlocking fingers blocking out the sunlight and throwing a mesh-like shadow over his body. His legs were still confined, but a fresh breeze met his face.

Two figures stood over him, cloaked in red and white. One of them, a man, spoke.

"Can you move your legs?" The man crouched, peering down through the steel remains of the ship. Farris looked down at his waist for the first time, and his heart jerked when he saw blood seeping through his white vest.

"Barely..." he muttered, clenching his teeth as he tried to bend his knees. The red mage seemed calm, but Farris saw pure terror in his wild, blue eyes. The white mage remained silent, her hair mottled with mud and dirt. She whispered something into the Pyromancer's ear.

That's it. They'll leave me. I can't walk, and I'll only slow them down. They'll surely leave me.

It was a surprise, then, when the mages began to drag him from the debris. As they pulled his limp legs across the ground, Farris saw the extent of the wreckage. The main bulk of the ship hung in the canopy overhead, entangled in the branches as several fires still blazed within. It looked as if the ship's bow had broken off during the crash; the front part of the gondola lay in a thousand pieces along the forest floor. Other survivors picked through the rubble, climbing over piles of steel and charred wood to gather what they could. Some were visibly injured, and others lay on their backs, motionless, with their faces covered.

The mages dragged Farris under a large tree and propped him up against its trunk. The woman in white put a skin of water to Farris's lips, and strength returned to him with a single gulp. She placed a gentle hand on his waist.

"Do you feel anything here?" she said. Farris nodded. She carefully rolled up his blood-soaked vest, revealing a scratched and grazed stomach, brown and red under thick hair. The abrasions stung with a low, grating consistency, but when the woman touched them, the pain vanished instantly. Farris stared with wide eyes as the wounds began to heal, as if an invisible hand were painting the skin with a fresh coat where it had been torn.

"Wounds of the flesh," she said, eyes focused on her work. "They're deep, but you haven't lost much blood. I wouldn't worry too much about those." With another hand, she pressed her fingers hard against Farris's left knee. He grimaced in pain. "This, I'm more concerned about."

After some more poking and prodding, she turned to the red mage. "I think I can help him. Go back and help Sir Bearach with the others."

The young man turned and darted back to the wreckage.

The woman offered Farris more water, but he declined. He reached into his own pocket and produced a tiny brass vial of thainol. With a quick swig, the liquid rolled down his throat, warm and soothing. It did much more to take the pain away than the water did. The healer laughed.

"Never been a better time, I suppose." Her voice was weary, and her eyes heavy with exhaustion.

How long have we been out here?

"What's your name?" she asked, placing a hand on his forehead.

"Chester," he answered without hesitation. It would take a lot more than an airship falling from the sky for Farris Silvertongue to forget that the future of the Simian race rested on his shoulders. "I'm one of the ship's navigators, but today I travelled as a passenger."

She smiled. "I'm sure you were hoping for a better day off than this."

"Aye, but I could do with the overtime."

She laughed and placed a hand on his knee again.

"Now Chester, there's some damage done to your bones, and the underflesh that binds them together has been torn. I can fix the bones easily, but the underflesh will require a fully trained healer, and a lot more supplies than we have out here. I'll give you a temporary patching up now, though, so at least you'll be able to walk."

She cupped both hands around his injured knee, and he felt soft, pulsating warmth against his flesh.

And before Farris had a chance to remember how much he detested the Church and its servants, his pain disappeared.

"It worked!" he said, barely able to contain his surprise. "How...I mean...I thought you said you weren't a proper healer?"

"Not yet," she replied, rubbing her hands together. "I used to be a Geomancer, but I changed schools shortly after I earned my Earthcloak. I've got one year of study left in the Academy chapter of Penance, and then you'll be able to call me Slaine the White."

"Sounds far more majestic than Slaine the Green."

Farris tried to bend his knee. It was difficult, as if someone kept pushing in the other direction. But with some effort, he rotated his lower leg slowly in circles. He looked up at the trees, noticing that many were still full and green despite it being well into the autumn months.

"Where are we?" he said.

Slaine smiled. "That reminds me, you better not eat anything you see lying around. We're in the—"

A sudden, sharp scream rang out from the wreckage. They turned to see the red mage sprinting back towards them.

"Run!" he said, panting and waving his arms. Just behind him, four strange black shapes scuttled through the clearing.

Each moved with deadly speed and precision, darting over the ship's debris and falling upon those who were too injured to run.

The red mage paused to regain his breath, and then yelled once more.

"Beadhbhs!"

Farris frantically tried to pull himself to his feet as panic erupted all around him.

Although shaking with terror, he couldn't take his eyes away from the creatures; he was strangely fascinated by the way they moved. Some men tried to fight them off, but they died for their efforts. Others tried to flee, but they were killed for their cowardice. The beasts attacked always in pairs, closing in on their prey with startling synchronisation, as if sharing the same thoughts. More beadhbhs flooded in from all around, pouring out from the dense forestry and vastly outnumbering those unfortunate enough to survive the crash.

The Glenn. My luck had to run out as some point.

Nearby, the knight named Sir Bearach swung his claymore in large arcs, cutting down any bird that crossed its path. He moved through the carnage, roaring curses and raging with bloodlust. When he had a moment to spare, he called towards Farris and the mages.

"We need to leave. Now."

"Chester," Slaíne said, grabbing Farris's hand, "can you walk?"

Farris smiled. "I'd rather run."

As he spoke, two more beadhbhs fell upon another wounded survivor across the clearing, his cries drowned out by the sound of flesh torn by talons. Some of the other men had climbed up on top of the ship's remains, but the beadhbhs surrounded it, shrieking and squawking as they leapt upwards. One beadhbh broke away from the flock and charged directly at Farris, its path curving away from him, ready to attack from the side. Farris noticed that there was another, following an opposite but otherwise identical trajectory.

He was about to call out and alert those still capable of fighting, but there was no need. The red mage took a step forwards and fire burned in his hands. He made no move until the beadhbhs were upon them, but as they leapt through the air, the mage threw his arms towards the sky, engulfing the birds in flames. The beadhbhs shrieked as they fell burning to the ground.

The battle raged on by the wreckage, but several more survivors had joined the mages, obviously aware that magic was their only chance of escaping in one piece. Without saying another word, they turned and ran from the clearing, deep into the poisonous valley of the Glenn.

He had no more pain, but Farris felt the bones in his knee bend and grind with every step. The path wriggled through ditches and streams as they went, but their pursuers never gave up the chase. Every so often, Farris heard a scream, or a cry for help from behind, and he knew that another beadhbh had satiated its hunger.

But still they ran.

It was clear that no Man or Simian had taken this route in a long time. The plants and flowers that sped past seemed beautiful. Farris didn't give them a second glance. Twigs and leaves scratched against his face while upturned roots threatened to trip him, but he didn't slow. There was little material between his feet and the forest floor, and he felt every stone and blade of grass roll beneath him.

Still, he blindly followed the figures of Sir Bearach and Slaíne before him.

If we reach a dead end, we'll be trapped between that and the beasts.

As the trail evened out for a small stretch, Farris quickly glanced behind. Perhaps a half-dozen more men still followed, but four beadhbhs came closing in, leaping through the foliage with ease. Farris turned his attention back to those running ahead of him.

As long as there are more of us than them.

The cold air caught in his throat, and every breath jabbed icy daggers into his lungs. A thousand voices in his head begged him to stop, to rest, to catch a breath, but he ignored them.

The trees above his right shoulder fell away, revealing the full splendour of the Glenn below. On the other side of the river, the hills rose up green and grew darker towards the top until they became jagged peaks, like stone teeth splitting the sky.

Another Simian blocked the beautiful view, overtaking Farris. Just as the crewman was about to pass, one of the beadhbhs caught up and sprang onto his back; they both went tumbling to the ground. Farris didn't look back to see what happened next.

The Pyromancer ran the furthest ahead, his cape flapping wildly behind him. As the path veered back into the dense forest, he glanced back.

"We can't outrun them forever!" he cried, vaulting over a fallen tree covered in thick green leaves. By the time Farris reached it, the others cowered behind the red mage and Sir Bearach. Both men stood facing Farris.

"Get behind me, and don't move!"

Farris ducked under the knight's outstretched claymore and turned just in time to see the last beadhbh spring over the tree, its talons stretched out and pointing forwards like curved knives. Everything seemed to slow as the beadhbh glided gracefully through the air. Sir Bearach spun on the spot, bellowing obscenities as the beast connected with the blade.

An instant later, the knight crouched over the severed body of the black beadhbh.

A man in white uniform stood by his side. Farris recognised him from the ship's bridge.

Another navigator, perhaps?

"Sir," he said. "Are...are you sure it's safe for us to stop?"

The knight grunted. "Just as safe as it is to keep running. We'll need to catch our breath if we're to outlast the rest of them."

The two mages approached the corpse, along with two more of the crew. One was the thin, red-haired Simian Farris had been sitting across from in the mess room, the other a bearded man in blue overalls, like the mechanics and engineers from the ship. He appeared to be crying.

"Where are we?" he said, blubbering under the thick black beard that consumed half his face. "What happened up there?"

Sir Bearach pulled a dagger from his boot and dug the blade deep in the bird's corpse. "Beadhbhs: predators of the Glenn. They're rarely seen outside of the valley, but—"

"No! What happened up *there*?"

Farris knew the answer to that. He pointed at the red mage. "It was this one. He's far too fond of his fiery magic."

"That's not fair!" The mage turned and marched towards him. He was tall, but still stood up on his toes to look Farris straight in the eye. "I saved your life when you had a knife to your throat! And it was you who started the fight, when—"

"Fool!" The red Simian waved a dismissive hand. "The fight didn't start until Officer Brádaigh had his throat opened. When one man murders another, we can deal with it. When one man decides to burn the ship from the sky, that's a fuckup that can't be fixed."

The other men argued, but Farris remained silent. Sir Bearach had started skinning the dead beadhbh. The knight's white cape was laid out on the ground with strips of feather-covered flesh piled on top of it. Slaíne the White noticed and strode over to the knight.

"What do you think you're doing?"

Bearach ignored the woman, continuing his work. His armour was thick and heavy, but his crouched stance seemed agile. He looked as if he could spring up and cut the healer's tongue out before she had a chance to use it again.

Slaíne didn't seem to have the same opinion. She raised her voice. "As a servant of the Trinity, I command you to stop, now!"

Bearach didn't stop as he spoke. "The road ahead will be long and treacherous, my lady. The feathers of a beadhbh make a powerful blood potion, and right now we would be wise to carry some." The knight paused, his knife weeping with blood by his side. "Just in case."

Slaíne stood with her arms folded, as if protecting herself from the knight's reasoning. "I'll have you know that I am a powerful and capable healer. There will be no resorting to forbidden magic in my presence."

The knight pointed the blade towards her, smiling. "But what if something happens to you? Who would be left to heal the healer?"

Apparently, her silence was an adequate answer, and he returned to his work.

"I'll keep the meat too. The vegetation in this region isn't famous for its flavours, and anything else that walks through these woods can kill any one of us in our sleep. Instead of hunting some more hunters, we'll make do with what is already dead."

He picked up a handful of bloody flesh and placed it on the outspread cloak, next to the feathers.

"And if we do survive, we'll sell what feathers we have left over in Penance, and I'll share the profit with everyone else who's listening!" His raised his voice for the last word, but the others were still arguing over what happened up on the ship.

"It wasn't a mutiny, fool!" said the navigator. "The ship was infiltrated! You heard Brádaigh before he died. The man who claimed to be Malroy was a fraud!"

"I knew it, I knew it!" said the mechanic. "He barely spoke to me when he boarded today."

The navigator hesitated. "There were others, too, right? Otherwise a proper fight wouldn't have broke out like that." He turned his attention to the red Simian. "What if one of them was you, huh? How do we know you're not in with them?"

"Who's *them* now? Can you answer me that? Why did all this happen in the first place?"

"Quiet! All of you!" Slaíne stepped into the centre of the group. "Regardless of how it happened, it still happened. It doesn't matter who was involved, but who has survived." She looked up to the sky, the sun glaring across from the west. "Now, does anybody know where we go from here?"

The others looked down at their feet, but something stirred in Farris's head. Maps he had seen long ago, embedded somewhere in his memory. He closed his eyes to fetch the image, and he remembered Garth.

"Yes!" Farris said, catching the attention of the others. "I...my brother was a scout for the Triad."

The others paused and leaned closer, as if afraid they'd miss a word. Farris realised it was the first time all day he had told the truth.

Oh, fact really is more riveting than fiction.

"So, you know where to go?" asked the red Simian.

"Not exactly, there's no roads that traverse the Glenn, and it's usually sparse of travellers for obvious reasons. There are roads that bypass the Glenn either side, but we'll have to ascend and descend a mountain before we can access those...."

The Pyromancer stepped forwards. "I sure hope the next word you say is 'but.'"

Farris smiled. "But there may be another way." He crouched down and began drawing a rough outline of the area in the soil.

"Garth used to tell me all about his adventures through the Glenn, hunting down beadhbhs and fleeing from wolves." This much was a lie, but it was better that the others have confidence in his story, even the little details. He pointed towards the western side of the crude map, etched into the dirt. "Here, he said that there were caves which he used to get in and out of Penance. The Triad commissioned him to find out about routes that lead from Penance, through the Glenn, and out into the Clifflands. We could use those, but I have no idea how far we are."

The navigator crouched down beside Farris and jammed his finger into the soil. "I saw a map of this area once, and there's a clearing right here. They call it the Scalp of the Glenn, 'cause it rises up over all the other hills and trees. We could gather our bearings better if we reach there."

"Not a bad idea," said Sir Bearach, who now stood over the two, covered with red specks of beadhbh blood. His cape was slung over his back and tied into a sack that hung heavy and dripping. "But what if we've already passed it?"

"Then we still should travel west," answered Farris. "If we've already passed the Scalp, we'll stumble upon my brother's caves instead, and then we'll be in an even better position."

"Well, that settles it," said Sir Bearach. "Let's move. Don't fall behind if you want to live long enough to taste my famous roast beadhbh and blood potions."

**

The seven strangers continued westwards towards the setting sun. Only slivers of light made it through the dense canopies, casting staggered streaks of shadow and light along the ground. It was only at this point that Farris could really admire the landscape. Like a twisted parody of Nature, the Glenn seemed to mock the travellers as they went, with some plants as out of place as they. The flowers were similar to those Farris recognised from other regions, aside from a few subtle differences. Some looked like typical foxgloves and tulips, but their colours were more vibrant, as if fluorescing with their own light as dusk settled in overhead.

That would be the poison.

He passed what looked like a tangential path made entirely of dark blue roses, weaving away from the track. The trees seemed to grow away from the tiny blue flowers, as if afraid to touch them. For a moment, Farris wanted nothing more than to break away from the company and follow the bizarre path, wherever it led.

A child wouldn't last an hour in here. Wolves, bears, and beadhbhs notwithstanding.

An hour passed with little said between the companions. They paused a few times, but Farris only spoke to Slaíne during those brief intervals while she checked his wounds and eased his pain.

He never asked for the names of the others. The Pyromancer walked first, his hands always alight with fire. The red Simian followed, and every so often he'd throw another question at the young mage, who responded with the same calm, collected certainty each time. The mechanic and the navigator walked in front of Farris, separating him from the inquisitive Simian.

In a way, it was a relief to be thrown into such a dangerous situation. There were no more lies to keep track of, no politicking to stay updated on, and Farris felt himself adapt to the situation rather quickly. Here, the Crown didn't matter, nor did the Silverback and his war. There was no

Church. No Wraiths. No Captain Padraig Tuathil with his empty accusations, however accurate they happened to be.

It wouldn't even have been all that detrimental if Farris had let it slip that he wasn't Chester the Lucky, because none of that mattered anymore. The number one priority now was survival, and Farris welcomed all the chaos that the valley threw at them.

I'd rather fight a hundred beadhbhs than have to lie to another king.

As the sun sank, the company was about to give up and camp in the middle of the dense forest when the ground sloped upwards. The others ahead of Farris ran, and he followed reluctantly as his leg began to ache again. When they reached the top of the Scalp, however, he welcomed the day's last view of the valley before them.

The hills beyond the river were still as high and steep as they had been before, but this time a river slithered down from the mountains beyond. Farris found peace in the silent dusk, and for a moment it seemed as if the trees weren't filled with poison and the valley wasn't crawling with predators.

The Scalp itself was barren, the ground uneven. The others walked in circles around the dirt, looking for a place to sleep. It quickly occurred to him that they'd be sleeping out in the open, with only their own cloaks for warmth. It didn't bother him; he had slept under far worse conditions back in the Dustworks of Penance. To be safe, he figured that Chester wouldn't be too happy with those arrangements.

"I sure hope you don't expect me to sleep out here," he said to Sir Bearach, who opened his sack of beadhbh feathers to examine their contents.

"Well," Bearach said, shooing away some flies that had gathered around the meat. "You can stay up and keep watch. If you'd prefer that."

Farris certainly would have preferred that, but he answered as Chester. "I'll take the first one, then, and I'll sleep out the rest of the night."

"Works for me," the knight said. "You can take the first watch with Fionn."

***

The meat wasn't all that wonderful as far as normal food was concerned, but Farris gladly devoured his portion. Some of the other men grumbled, but there was no point. Unless they were to hunt down another beadhbh, it was likely this would be their last meal for the foreseeable future.

As they ate, the red Simian told bawdy tales of his drinking nights back in Cruachan. Farris laughed along with the others, though it was easy for him to pick out the lies in the story. Too much detail here, a strange description there...each anecdote served to make the Simian out to be the victor, and everyone's words sounded too good to be real dialogue.

This one has a lot to learn, he thought, though he laughed along with the others and commended the storyteller on his conquests and campaigns amongst the female Simians of Cruachan.

There was little banter after that, and each made their way to their own camp-spots. Farris found himself left with the young Pyromancer named Fionn. They stared into the fire in silence.

"Did you make this?" Farris asked eventually, nodding towards the flames. "Did the fire come from your fingers, like before?"

The young mage sighed. "Nothing can ever be truly created or destroyed. That's what all the masters said anyway. It's basic Nature." He pointed at the huge oak trees that stood like sentinels at the edge of the clearing. "Trees like those, they grow out from the ground. They take in light from the sun, nutrients from the soil, and water from the clouds. Then they just keep on growing. Up and up and up, until they drop another seed and it all starts over again. Nothing was created, I mean really created, but the very first trees and the very first seeds."

"And who made those?"

"Lord Seletoth," he said. "But I don't know who made Him. I've asked before, but none of the druids I've spoken to ever gave me a good answer."

"What about the fire?" asked Farris, watching as the smoke twisted up into the sky. "Where does that come from?"

There was silence, as the mage considered the question.

"The sun," he said, eventually. "It takes light—sunlight—to make the trees grow. If you chop down a tree and apply the right amount of heat, then the power of the sun is released again. That's what fire is. Pyromancers like me can manipulate fire. We can make it bigger, smaller, hotter, colder, but we can't make it out of nowhere. If we could, we'd be able to make another sun, and it'd never be night again."

The mage reached out to the fire and commanded it to sway back and forth as if it were connected to his fingers with invisible strings.

"As long as I carry a spark with me," he said, causing the fire to shrink down into a tiny flame against the wood, "there'll always be light."

Each word Fionn said faded into the night, quivering with fear.

He's only a lad. I was the same at his age. Afraid of most things dark. Farris reached into his pocket, found his vial of thainol, and tossed it to the boy.

"Drink this," Farris said. "It'll make you less scared, and it'll warm up your insides. I bet you magic folk haven't found a way to do that, eh?"

Fionn laughed meekly. He took a gulp and shook as he swallowed. "Gods be good, what's in there?"

Farris laughed. "Why, it's only liquid fire, forged by Simian hands. Here, watch this."

When Fionn handed back the vial, Farris splashed some of the thainol into the fire. With a whoosh, the flames turned bright blue, crackling and raging more violently than before. The young Pyromancer almost jumped from his skin.

"That's...that's incredible! Where did you learn that? I mean, they never showed us anything like that in the Academy!"

"Aye, but they teach it to kids on the streets of Penance. On a cold night, a single spark and stolen bottle of thainol might be the only thing that keeps you from freezing. They call those beggar's flames."

Fionn smiled as he watched the blue flames dancing. He pointed a finger out to the fire, and the smile vanished from his face.

"I can't grasp it. Are you sure this...this is truly fire?"

Farris laughed. "Well, I don't think it came from the sun, if that's what you're asking. Who knows, maybe someday us Simians will make our own sun!"

Some time passed while they watched the blue flames slowly return to normal as the last of the thainol burned out. Fionn told Farris about the other schools of magic. There were Geomancers, capable of manipulating the earth itself, and somehow that even included wood, iron, and steel. There were Hydromancers, who worked with water, ice, and steam, and then there were Aeromancers. Fionn struggled to find a practical application of Aeromancy, though. He said that they used to be popular on ships, but that was before the Simians learned how to make engines that ran on steam.

As Fionn began talking about alchemy, Farris felt a gentle hand on his shoulder.

"Bearach and I are to relieve you two," Slaíne said, taking a seat beside him. "Chester, I want to examine your wounds again before you go."

Fionn nodded to Farris as he passed, and Slaíne placed her hand on Farris's knee. Once more, he felt a soothing power resonate in his flesh, like thainol running through his veins.

Not quite sure where to look, Farris found himself staring at Slaíne's necklace as she worked. It depicted the three interlocking rings of the Trinity, and he felt a burning question slip from his lips.

"Why are you helping me?"

"You say that as if I need a reason," the healer said with a smile.

Farris shook his head. "Seriously, though, why go through all this trouble to help a stranger? You risked your life to save mine. Why?"

"Well...I am helping you because you need help. I am tending to your wounds because I need practice in the mending of wounds. I protect the weak and heal the sick, because I took an oath to do those things, whenever it is in my power to do so."

She leaned closer to Farris, her voice dropping to a whisper. "But why you? Why here? Why now? Because the Gods have willed it, Chester. I live my life in the Light of the Lady, and She shines Her light upon you too. I am only doing what I have been destined for. You may not realise it, but you, too, are bound by fate. We are trapped here because the ship crashed, and the ship crashed because there were imposters on board. Why that was, I don't know."

Because the king is delusional. Because he wants war.

The healer's eyes met his, and Farris knew she sensed his apprehension.

"But," he began, "if the Gods are watching over us, then why would they let something as horrible as this happen?"

He asked because he wanted to keep the conversation away from the motives of those who infiltrated the ship. Deep down, however, he was eager to hear how she'd respond.

"It's fate, Chester," Slaíne said, casting her eyes up to the sky. "Everything that happens to us has already been fated to be. I can't say what role we have in the Lady's plan, but I have faith that She will lead us to happiness."

Farris had nothing to say to that, but Slaíne seemed to know what he was thinking. "But you don't believe in fate, Chester, do you?"

He nodded, staring into the waning flames. "My choices are my own, nobody else's. I've made lots of decisions in my life. Some I stand by, some I don't, but nobody chose them but me."

The healer smiled. "I used to be like you, Chester. Not a nonbeliever in the Trinity, but an advocate of free will. Of course, these choices seem like your own, but...."

She paused and closed her eyes, running her fingers through her dry, straw-like hair. "But then I met Catríona Ní Marra. She was the daughter of the Earl of Dromán, back when I started studying white magic. The Mage's Academy looked out over the manor's courtyard, and it was a common sight to see the little lords and ladies playing amongst the flowers. The Earl took ill during my first autumn there, and he passed away some weeks later.

"Shortly after he died, when winter had really set in, young Catriona fell from her horse and hit her head. It was quite serious. Her elder brother brought the unconscious girl to us, and we did everything in our power to save her. The master healer saw that she was still breathing and put us on shifts to monitor her condition through the night. Although there were three of us taking turns to watch over her, Catriona's brother never left her side. Not even once.

"The Academy is an institute of research just as much as it is an institute for education. We were ordered to take records of everything we observed. There was no need, though, for I'll never forget what I saw.

"I was on duty when she finally came to. Her brother was there, so happy to see his little sister alive and awake again. She looked confused at first, which was to be expected. Head injuries often affect the memory, and patients usually wake asking what happened, or where they are.

"Catriona Ní Marra didn't ask anything like this. Instead she gazed out the window, out into the dark, frozen courtyard, and asked, 'Where have all the flowers gone?'

"Her brother smiled and told her that she had just bumped her head and would be better very soon. We had told him to expect some memory loss, so he knew that the last thing she remembered was probably seeing the courtyard outside alive with the colours of spring.

"Then she asked, 'So I missed my birthday?'

"He laughed, and said that she did, but she'd remember again in time. He told her about the feast they had to celebrate and described the jesters, bards, and fools that performed for all the guests. She was laughing at this point, until she asked, 'And how is Father? Is he still unwell?'

"Desperately, he looked to me for help, but I was just a student then, and I didn't know what to do. The poor lad was left with no choice but to tell the girl about her father's death, and little Catríona mourned for him all over again. She cried for several minutes as her brother sat there in silence. Soon afterwards, she stopped. Her eyes, barely dry, were drawn again to the window.

"Then she asked, 'Where have all the flowers gone?'

"He told her about the accident again, the memory loss, but still she asked, 'So I missed my birthday?'

"I sat and listened to the same details—the jesters, the bards, the feast—as the little girl laughed and smiled in delight. I knew what was coming next, but I prayed to the Gods that she wouldn't ask again.

"'And how is Father? Is he still unwell?'

"For a whole hour, they had the same conversation. Over and over again. For a whole hour, Catríona mourned for the death of her father. Each time she cried in exactly the same way: soft sobs followed by a slow building wail, then silence. The way she paused and looked out the window was the same every time, as was the way she wiped her tears away with the back of her sleeve.

"Again, and again. Every. Single. Time.

"Eventually the gaps between her periods of memory-loss decreased, but still she always asked the same first question: 'Where have all the flowers gone?'

"Those words have been burned into my soul since that day. Whenever her crying stopped, I wanted nothing more than for her to remain silent, but always she asked, 'Where have all the flowers gone?'

"From that day on, Chester, I knew that our will has never been free."

Farris paused when she finished her story. It was a strange tale. "But...but what does that have to do with fate?"

"Everything. Consider this: If our memory of this conversation were to be erased, your response, 'But what does that have to do with fate?' would be the same if we were to have it again. If we were all to relive this day from the start, we'd still end up here, stranded in the middle of the Glenn. If you were to be born again, with no knowledge of the life you have already lived, everything would turn out exactly the same.

"Like an alchemical reaction, the output will never change if the ingredients are consistent. I don't know what you are going to say next, but the Gods do. The Gods do because your next answer has been determined before I started speaking. It was determined before your father met your mother. It was decided before the Fall of Sin, before Móráin's Conquest. From the moment the Lord created the Firstborn, He knew how each of their lives would unfold, along with the lives of their children, and their children's children. It is said that the

Lady guides us through our lives, but there are some who argue that She only knows what will happen. Because She sees life like alchemy. Formulaic. Predictable. Predetermined. Catrina Ní Marra's injury gave us an insight into what it would be like to lose your memory and relive a few moments over and over, and her story leaves very little room for free will."

Farris pressed his hand onto his forehead as he considered the healer's words. He was put on board the ship because he had earned the king's trust. He had earned the king's trust because of his work with the Guild of Thieves. He was sent to Cruachan because of the Silverback's wish to rid the land of Humans, and the Humans never would have landed on the shores of Alabach if it wasn't for King Móráin the First, and the Grey Plague. Everything was suddenly traceable back to a single point.

The moment of Creation.

This was an unsettling thought.

Slaíne stood up, unaware of the turmoil inside Farris's head. "Now, get some sleep while you can. Only the Gods know what tomorrow holds, but you better make sure you are strong enough to handle whatever's in store."

Dear Yarlaith,

I'm sorry I couldn't tell you this in person, but I'm tied up with work on the new inn, and I needed to get this message to you as soon as possible.

Cormac is alive. He's here in Point Grey. I have him staying in the inn for the time being, but he's in a bad way. Seems like he's been homeless for the best part of a year.

I know you two have never really seen eye to eye, but Gods above and below, he's your only brother. I have a healer looking after him now, and he'll hopefully be ready to go back to Roseán by the time the moon turns.

I know how bad he was as much as you do, and I'm all too aware of what the others have been saying about him fleeing when Aoife died, but he needs help more now than ever. He can barely string a coherent sentence together, and I've no idea what he's been doing on the streets of Point Grey to survive all this time.

I can understand if you don't want anything to do with him, but he can't stay here forever. Please come as soon as you can. If not for me, for Morrígan. She's had a tough year and needs to know her father is still alive.

Yours in the Light of the Lady,
Peadair O'Briain.

CHAPTER 13:
MORRÍGAN THE BLACK

The sun set crimson over the Eternal Sea, bathing all the houses on the High Road in fiery light.

Morrígan gazed out from the clinic. *The days are growing shorter.* Summer had somehow slipped by between all her glass beakers and broken bodies. It was almost a full year since her mother died.

She sighed and turned her attention back to her patient. Darragh went on chatting casually as if he hadn't almost sliced his own finger off with a meat cleaver an hour earlier.

"...and his da's new inn is gonna open soon, too, over in Point Grey. We should all go visit them soon. What do you think? I've never been outside Roseán before."

"Is that so?" said Morrígan, concentrating again on Darragh's wound. It was clean and deep, with bone exposed right across his knuckle. She had applied some pappavar oil to alleviate the pain, but she thought her job would be much easier if the fool would just pass out in agony.

"Yeah," he continued, his eyes hazy from the medicine. "Never even put a toe outside the village, so I haven't. Sure, there's no need to! What do the other cities have that we don't?"

He waved his free hand across the room. Yarlaith's clinic was empty, cleared entirely of its contents, the healer himself down in the caves. Morrígan desperately wanted to finish fixing Darragh's stupid wound so she could assist in Yarlaith's final experiment.

"Hold still," she said, her fingers pressed firmly on either side of the gash. Reaching out and grasping living flesh was quite similar to Necromancy, she found.

To think, every white mage in Dromán has been dabbling in arts so close to sin. There isn't much difference between healing and heresy.

The Human body was capable of a sort of white magic, too, Morrígan supposed, as she watched the blood clot and coagulate under her control, slowly forming a dark scab across the boy's knuckle. With a little more time, it would have healed itself just as easily.

As she dabbed the wound with cleaning solvents and solutions, Darragh filled Morrígan in on the funeral of Mrs. Mhurichú. He didn't ask where Morrígan had been, and for that she was especially grateful; she hadn't come up with a reasonable excuse to miss such a big day.

Maybe I'll tell them where I've been after we bring Mother back. Maybe they'll understand, once they see what we can do.

The battlemages had formed an honour guard, but some villagers saw it as more an insult, considering Mrs. Mhurichú strong position on the Crown's "occupation" of Roseán, as Darragh put it.

Sounds more like his father's words. Morrígan turned to tidy away the vials and solutions she had used for the procedure.

"It hasn't been the same, you know?" said Darragh, standing from the bed and flexing his healed finger. "Ever since Mrs. Mhurichú died, that is. Sorcha hasn't left her house in weeks, and I've only seen Taigdh once or twice. He told me that he wants to be there for Sorcha, but it seems like she just wants to be alone."

"I know the feeling," she said, hoping he'd take the hint.

Darragh bowed his head in response. "I'm...I'm sorry, Morrígan. I know it must be awful to lose someone like you have. Even though the whole town is upset over Sorcha's ma' right now, it doesn't mean we've forgotten about you."

Morrígan placed the bottles and vials inside a glass cabinet beside the bed, locking the tiny doors. "Oh, don't worry about me," she said. "Anyway, I better get back to my studies, Darragh. There might be some scarring there, so try not to touch it for the next few days."

Darragh looked down at his hand, eyes opened wide in amazement. "Wow, that was fast! Thanks, Morrígan!"

He took a step towards her, stuffing his newly healed hand into his trouser pocket. He shuffled for a bit, as if in hesitation, and then finally pulled out a long silver chain. Staring at his feet, he held the chain out to her.

His face turned red as he stammered. "I...I know it's not much, and I know you and Yarlaith don't normally ask for anything...but I wanted you to have this."

Oh, what now? Morrígan took the chain in her own hand. The links were heavy, but delicate and intricately designed with silver inlays of swirls and spirals. At the end hung a small pendant of three interlocking circles, each dotted with tiny stones of blue, red, and gold.

"It's the symbol of the Trinity," said Darragh, stating the obvious as usual. "It used to be my mother's, before she left."

Although she was eager to return to her uncle, Morrígan found herself transfixed on the necklace.

It used to be his mother's? She had never really given much thought as to why Darragh lived with his father.

"Darragh, what happened to your mother?"

The boy looked away, the colour fading from his chubby red cheeks. "I don't know. I never knew." He paused, eyes glancing past hers. "One day, when I was little, I came home from my reading lesson with your uncle, but when I went to look for my ma' in the house, she was just gone. I found my da', alone in their bedroom, crying and drunk, and nothing he said made much sense. He just kept saying that it'd just be the two of us. Then it was just up to us to look after the shop, and I've never heard anything else about her since."

Morrígan's first reaction was to sneer, to say, *Oh, at least your mother isn't dead,* but she stopped herself. Ever since her own mother died, she had thought her own lot was far worse than anyone else's. Sorcha's mother had died peacefully, and

Taigdh's parents were just off with his grandmother in Point Grey. Their grief and sadness couldn't possibly compare to hers, who still had to live with the image of the mountain troll etched into her mind.

But Darragh's situation was different. Worse, even. His mother didn't get sick. His mother wasn't murdered. She had made the sober, calculated decision to abandon her husband and son. And somehow that seemed a far crueller fate than being smashed against the ground by a blood-crazed beast of the Glenn. Morrígan's mother was just up in the plains of Tierna Meall, waiting for her, as the others would say, but what about Darragh's? Sure, she could be dead somewhere too. But what if she had just moved on? What if she was somewhere else with a new lover, living a happy life without sparing a thought for the little boy she had left without saying goodbye?

Morrígan tried to picture herself in Darragh's shoes, but she couldn't. Instead, something stirred in the back of her mind. It no longer seemed so bad to be left without parents, as long as she remembered that her mother always loved her. Her memory drifted back to the words of the Simian after her mother's funeral: *As long as you remember your mother, a piece of her will live forever.* Looking back, it seemed like an eternity ago. Before Mrs. Mhurichú got sick. Before the mages came. Before she found out about her uncle's caves—

Her gaze flashed towards the trap door in her uncle's study. For just a moment, she had forgotten that down there, her mother was finally ready to be brought back from the dead.

"Sorry, Darragh, but I really have to go. Thanks for the gift."

And she was gone, leaving the butcher's son behind the firmly shut door to the study. The key was already in place, and she carefully twisted it, locking the door without making a sound. As soon as she heard Darragh leave, she descended down into the damp, bloody caves.

Once her feet touched the ground, it all came back to her. The hard work she and Yarlaith had gone through, the hours she had put in, down in the darkness, researching, studying, experimenting.... All it took was a stupid necklace to distract her from the fact that they were on the verge of changing the world. With a spring in her step, she made her way to her uncle's chamber.

As she turned the final corner and saw her mother laid out in the same spot she had been in all year, the words of the butcher's son were entirely forgotten.

This was what it meant to conquer death, to take control of the Lord's gift, to wield more power than the Gods themselves.

Yarlaith was busy shuffling through pages of notes on his desk. Beside them, the tiny Simian weapon lay dismantled. It was a simple device, and elegant in its design. Yarlaith had been fascinated with its mechanisms when Morrigan first presented it to him. With the pull of a switch, it caused a tiny flint hammer on its surface to strike a tiny flint anvil, creating a spark in the same manner as a Pyromancer's rings. However, instead of using magic to manipulate and expand the flame, the spark ignited a strange powder inside the device, causing a small explosion that expelled whatever else was inside the chamber. When Morrigan had found it, there was just one little metal bead there, and just enough powder for one shot. Yarlaith had been thrilled with his findings, but Morrigan was unimpressed.

One weapon, one shot. Even our crossbows are more efficient.

The Crown had nothing to worry about, Morrigan reckoned, for Simian technology was far from ever competing with their magic.

"You're late," said Yarlaith. He held an envelope over a candle, letting its flame devour the paper.

"What's that?" asked Morrigan. The envelope was addressed to Yarlaith, written in a crooked scrawl.

Her uncle closed his eyes tightly in response. "A letter...from the Academy. They wanted an update on my work, but its best that I pretend it never arrived."

Morrigan watched as he turned the letter to ash.

If he wants to pretend it never arrived, then why bother burning it?

Part of her wanted to pry further, but she had more important things on her mind. "I'm ready, Yarlaith. I'm ready to bring back Mother."

The healer glanced up at Morrigan. For half a second, she could have sworn she saw tears in his eyes.

"We only have one chance at this, Morrigan." Yarlaith extinguished the candle and stood. "We can't turn back now."

We, he kept saying, as if they were a team. Morrigan knew all the spells, all about the Nature of Necromancy, but Yarlaith was the one who called the shots, no matter how many times he used the word "we."

Morrigan slowly stepped back as Yarlaith paced around her mother. White robes, mottled and damp, swung in heavy strides as he walked. When he reached the head of the slab, he paused and turned, eyeing Morrigan from over his foggy glasses. His hands shook; his brow furrowed. Slowly, the old man placed his hands on the stone. He took a deep breath, turned his head upwards, and closed his eyes.

Then there was silence. Not even the rats stirred. The trickling of running water all around them seemed to have stopped, as if the whole world had paused to witness the end of death.

Morrigan knew what her uncle's mind was going through behind those closed eyes. She knew that he was focusing on every part of the dead woman's body, from where her muscles were bound to bones, to the blood that ran through her veins. Yarlaith seemed much older now than he had before, back when Morrigan had last seen him in the light of day.

His lips pursed, moving slightly in whisper. His brow narrowed further, and his eyes began to twitch, as if in a dream. Then, his body jerked.

A long, low moan escaped his mouth. It rang through the caves with a chesty rumble.

He's done it! He's grasped her!

Morrigan glanced down at her mother. She still lay motionless under the veil of her funeral garb.

Is it not working?

She looked back at her uncle. A frown crossed his creased, wrinkled face. He began to shake his head, bringing his hands up to cover his ears.

Then her mother rose, slowly sitting upright on the stone slab.

It was a moment Morrigan had longed for every day and dreamed about every night. Her mother was there, eyes open, alive, and looking at her daughter for the first time in almost a year. Her eyes, though cold and dead, were as deep and as green as Morrigan remembered. Her skin, once porcelain and pale with tiny freckles, now sagged loose and grey under her cheekbones. She had been preserved through alchemy, but the months in the cave had taken their toll on her appearance. Some dust had collected on her white funeral gown, but to Morrigan, she still looked as beautiful as a mid-summer's bride.

"Mother...are you there?" Morrigan took a step closer. The dead women slowly twisted her lower body around, bringing her limp legs to hang off the side of the slab. She balanced herself with hands gloved in white silk and gave a gentle push until she stood on two feet.

Morrigan glanced back at her uncle, still in a trance with eyes closed and ears covered. In front of him, Morrigan's mother stood hunched. She turned and looked right at Morrigan, then raised a hand towards her daughter and opened her mouth to speak.

But only a low groan escaped her twisted lips.

"Uhhhhh...."

"Mother." Morrigan took a step closer, bringing a hand up to touch her mother's cheek. "It's me. Do you remember?"

"Morrrrr...."

"Yes! Morry. Your little Morry."

As Morrigan touched her mother's face, the dead woman's head drooped crookedly to the side, hanging from where her neck was broken. From there, a thick bone emerged, pressing against her skin. Her eyes, still fixed forwards, now stared down at the floor.

"I can't believe it. You're back, Mother. You're back!"

Then the dead woman opened her mouth wide and screamed.

It pierced the air and sliced through Morrigan's soul; it gripped her heart and pulled the air from her lungs. But she did not balk.

"Don't worry, Mother. It's over. The troll is gone. You're back now."

Morrigan reached up to her mother's chin and raised her head until their eyes were level.

"See, I've grown. I'm almost as tall as you, now, and I can use magic and...." Tears began to fill Morrígan's eyes. "Oh, Mother, there's so much to tell you. So much has happened!"

Morrígan embraced her mother, but the corpse did not respond.

"Don't you remember me?" she asked, looking up at the woman's blank expression, her dead eyes shimmering against the candlelight.

"Morrrrrrrrr...," responded the living corpse. "Morrrr...."

"Yes, yes, Mother. You can do it. Morrígan. I'm Morrígan."

There was another scream, lower, and laced with more agony than the first, but it didn't come from her mother. Yarlaith, his eyes wide with fright, howled with a burrowing terror unlike any Morrígan had witnessed. The woman suddenly collapsed to the floor in a heap, as dead as she was on the morning of her daughter's birthday.

Yarlaith stopped yelling and held his face in his hands.

"No," he sobbed. "I...I was wrong. I was wrong...."

Morrígan looked down at the trembling little man. "What are you talking about? It worked!"

"No...no, no, no. Not like this. It wasn't meant to be like this." He rocked back and forth. "I was wrong about Necromancy, Morrígan. I was wrong about everything."

"What does it matter? You brought her back!"

Yarlaith looked up at her, the whites of his eyes like tiny crystals in the darkness. "Don't you see, Morrígan? The Church was right. They were right to outlaw and banish magic as black as this." He brought himself to his feet, struggling and shaking. "I was wrong to do this, Morrigan. We were both wrong."

He stepped over the corpse and began walking towards the trapdoor into his house.

He spoke over his shoulder. "Come sunrise, I'm burning the bodies and tearing this place down."

"What?"

"If the Church found out we were practicing Necromancy—"

"But that didn't stop us before!" Morrigan stepped forwards, her heart raging in her chest. "We've done it! It's over! Why stop now?"

"Because Necromancy is not the simple manipulation of flesh, Morrigan," he whimpered. "I believed it was before but...it's the manipulation of the *soul*."

I don't care, Morrigan wanted to say. *She's back. She's no longer dead.*

"What difference does that make?" she said. "Yarlaith, we're about to change the world!"

Yarlaith gasped. "Don't you understand? What we've been doing hasn't been breathing life back into the dead. We haven't been undoing something natural but doing something unnatural, something far worse. We've been tearing souls down from Tierna Meall and binding them to our own, but I did not know until now. The voices, Morrigan, the voices you hear when you grasp at a limb belongs to the soul that once dwelled inside."

Morrigan glanced down at the corpse. "No," she said, heat boiling in her heart. "I don't care about the technicalities, Yarlaith. You must bring her back!"

The old man shook his head. "You might have seen your mother stand and walk, but I could see into her heart. She screamed, Morrigan. She begged me not to keep her trapped inside her lifeless body. I didn't stop at first, because I felt myself grow powerful. Far stronger than I ever felt in my youth. This is why the Church has been purging Necromancers, for magic is the power of the soul, and if even a single mage learns how to harness the power another soul then—"

Morrigan balled her hand into a fist. "Then they'd be a braver man than you've ever been!"

Yarlaith sighed. "I was wrong, Morrigan. I need to rest. It's over." He went to leave, but she stepped in front of him.

"We're not done, Yarlaith. It's not over. I thought you were braver than this, but you're just a coward. Afraid of the mages, afraid of the Church. Afraid of the very power we've worked so hard to uncover. I've worked far too hard to just give up now, and I have no intention to."

"Morrigan, you don't understand—"

"I do understand! Those other Necromancers, Earl Roth, Callaghan the Black, they were bad men. The problem with you, uncle, is that you're scared! You have the intellect and the power to change the world, but you don't have the courage to fight for what others might not think is right. If we could just convince the other villagers that all this—"

"We are not having this conversation."

Morrigan paused. She stepped to the side while the defeated white mage hobbled past her, slowly ascending the rope ladder.

It's not fair! We've sacrificed so much. We've come so far.

Before following her uncle, Morrigan considered her mother again. She was no longer laid out on the slab like a princess, but now on the cavern floor, useless, like the rest of the corpses that hung disembowelled from the ceiling and walls.

I'll show him. Morrigan walked through the workshop. On one of the wooden tables sat a pile of bones mottled with dried blood, some with hands and slender fingers still attached. The torso of Mrs. Mhurichú lay decapitated on the adjacent workbench; her arms and legs removed and hung up on the wall beside her severed head. A pair of cold eyes seemed to watch Morrigan as she passed.

With Geomancy, Morrigan opened up the secret entrance to the cave.

We took so much care in making sure we were never discovered. But was it all for nothing?

Coming towards the lake, Morrigan heard the familiar trickle of running water overhead. She recalled the first time she had seen the workshop.

I was so afraid at first, but now it all seems so normal.

She clicked her two flint-rings together, and a flame burned in her hand.

I've changed so much. I couldn't even light a Pyromancer's torch back then. The village had changed, too, but she hadn't spent enough time above ground to appreciate it. The realisation that she would have to go back to a normal life slowly dawned on her. Without the hope that her mother might be alive again someday, even going off to the Academy was no longer an exciting prospect. An empty, numb feeling ached in her heart, as if her mother had just died all over again.

"It's not fair," she whispered, walking through the winding tunnels. Most of the coffins that used to fill the cairns along the walls had been removed for their research.

There must be a way to convince him....

Although she considered going ahead alone, she knew there was no way Yarlaith would sit by as she took on the work herself. Working in secret wasn't an option, either, as no other place would be as perfect as these caves for such endeavours.

She toyed with the flame between her fingers, wondering what the others would think if she told them.

The soldiers would murder us, but the others....

She knew Darragh would be scared, of course. Sorcha might understand, but she probably wouldn't be too happy with the role her mother played in their work. Then there was Taigdh....

If anyone would understand, it would be him.

She stood back up and continued through the caves, along the same path she had followed the Simian all those months ago. Her pace quickened into a run towards the cave's exit.

Outside, the night was cold and cloudless; a full moon shone down over the fields leading to Roseán, augmented by a thousand tiny stars. She began sprinting towards the lights of the village.

Taigdh was worried; he was the most worried about where I've been. He'd have to understand.

Taigdh was surely intelligent enough to appreciate their efforts, and wise enough to see what their work would mean for the rest of the world.

The petrified troll loomed up ahead as Morrígan considered what to say to Taigdh.

Imagine a world without death, Taigdh, she mouthed silently as she ran. *Imagine if nobody, like my mother, like your grandfather, like Mrs. Mhurichú, would ever have to die again.*

The ground beneath her feet shifted from the freshly turned soil of the fields to the rough stony path of the Sandy Road. The Hazelwood stood tall and golden to the south, even in the darkness.

The road curved into Roseán, and her old home was one of the first buildings to appear ahead. The sight lightened her heart, even though she was breathless.

This is it. She reached the old familiar door. She raised a fist and rattled upon the wood.

"Taigdh! Taigdh!" she called, taking a step back to get a view of the second-story windows. It was a red-brick house, like the others along the Sandy Road, with cracked and stained wooden panels surrounding the windows. One window opened, and a head of short brown hair peered out.

"Morrígan?"

All of the words she rehearsed caught in her throat.

Where could I possibly begin?

"Just...come with me! I need to show you something!"

"What is it?" He yawned.

"It's hard to explain. It's...something Yarlaith and I have been doing. I need to show you!"

The window above closed with a bang. A moment later, Taigdh opened the front door, dressed in a dark green tunic and brown leather boots. He wore a heavy black cloak tied at the front with a thin, brass brooch. He eyed Morrígan with concern.

"Come on!" she said, turning back towards the fields. "It's this way!"

They ran in silence, back down the Sandy Road and over the fields.

He knows it's important. They were passing the petrified troll again. *He knows not to ask about it until we get there.*

They stopped outside the caves. Taigdh stared at Morrígan as she casually stepped inside.

"Morry, you know that leads into the Glenn, don't you?"

"Yes, but I've been in here a thousand times now, and it doesn't go straight into the Glenn. It leads into the catacombs first."

The two stepped inside. Taigdh looked around in all directions. "The catacombs?" he asked, as Morrígan started down the tunnel. "The Lost Catacombs?"

"Yes, those ones. That's not all though, there's more."

Morrígan trotted down the tunnel while Taigdh followed. She pointed out where there once had been coffins and sarcophagi, with bodies that belonged to the warriors of Móráin's Conquest. Taigdh didn't ask many questions, but Morrígan gave him plenty of answers. As the tunnels twisted deeper underground, she told him all about the Simian she had followed through the caves but left out the part where she had given him a means to escape from the battlemages. She didn't know for sure if he really did escape in the end, but she presumed so; the colonel probably didn't want to tell everyone in the village about it.

They reached the lake, and Morrígan told him about how the caves reached into the Glenn, and also out into Penance, which was why the Silverback and the Simians used them to go back and forth across the valley. Taigdh seemed more concerned with the rats, however, as Morrígan saw him flinch as two paddled by in the lake, leaving a trail of tiny waves as they swam.

"Here," she said, as they approached the entrance to the workshop. "We've been doing most of our research inside."

"Research on what?" he asked, as they got closer. He suddenly wrinkled his nose.

She took a breath. "We've brought my mother back to life, Taigdh. It's incredible! Come, I'll show you."

As they walked inside across the bloody chamber, she gestured towards the limbs hanging on the walls.

"Imagine, Taigdh, if nobody ever had to die again. Imagine if we all could just...live forever!"

The boy gave no response. Morrigan turned to see terror etched upon his face as he stared up at Mrs. Mhurichú's severed head.

She held his hand. "Don't be frightened, Taigdh, please. I was startled, too, at first, but Yarlaith said that this was all a means to an end, and we mean to change the world. You need to understand that."

Taigdh spoke, but his voice was barely a whisper. "Did...did you do this?"

"Yes, that's my mother over there, at the top of the room. Yarlaith was able to bring her back to life earlier, and I think I can do the same. Here, I'll show you."

Taigdh pulled his hand away from Morrigan's.

"No," he said, shaking his head. "I won't come any closer."

"What? Why?"

The lad took a step back. "This can't be real," he muttered, as if to himself. "This can't be."

"Please," whispered Morrigan. "You have to understand. Don't you know what this means?"

"It means you're a murderer. Worse. The bodies, Morrigan...where did they come from?"

"We took them from the graves. Well, some of them. We found most in the catacombs and—"

"You weren't there," Taigdh said, with startled realization. "I looked for you at Mrs. Mhurichú's funeral, but you weren't there!"

"Yes. I was here instead. Here trying to fix the world. And I need your help."

She reached out a hand to him, but the lad flinched.

No. Why doesn't he understand?

"Please, Taigdh. Why can't you see what we've achieved? Beyond the bodies and the gore, there's greatness here."

"Get away from me!" he cried, taking a quick look behind him. "You've changed, Morrígan. You're no longer—"

"A frightened little girl?" She smiled. "Of course not, Taigdh. I've learned to wield magic. I've learned to heal the sick and wounded. This is just one step further. This is —"

Before she could finish, the lad spun his heels and sprinted out towards the tunnels.

"No, Taigdh! Come back!"

Morrígan gave chase, but the boy was too fast for her. She lost sight of him as they passed through the tunnels, but she kept on running. She called out after him, but only the empty echoes of the cavern walls answered.

When she reached the exit looking over Roseán, she saw him run off into the distance and disappear towards the tiny lights of the village.

Tears filled her eyes.

What if he's right? She started running again, her pace slowing as she reached the troll and her old family farm. *What if he's right to be afraid? What if it's right to hate me?*

She remembered a time when she once felt as if she loved him, but that feeling had somehow passed her by.

Even when he started courting Sorcha. I wasn't even jealous.

In truth, she hadn't really connected with anyone since she started hacking corpses apart with her uncle.

What if it changed me?

Silver moonlight illuminated the petrified troll's weathered, stone face. Its mouth hung open with rows of familiar stone teeth.

Morrigan gritted her teeth. Inside her chest, her heart pounded to the beat of grief once more.

"It's all your fault!" she screamed, looking up at the beast. "This never would have happened if you never came here! Mother wouldn't have died, I wouldn't have gone to live with Yarlaith, and...." She paused, looking down at the flint-rings on her fingers.

I never would have learned magic.

That much she was glad for. At the cost of her mother's life, at the cost of her humanity, she had grown into a powerful mage. Without other capable trainee mages to work with, she had no way of really gauging how good she was.

What if I'm one of the greatest? What if I'm as powerful as the mages in the battalion?

She closed her eyes, focusing on her power, and touched the stone flesh of the troll. No, it didn't feel like touching stone with Geomancy.

Its flesh turned stone! I feel it with Necromancy!

The green-cloaks had said that they weren't even able to grasp the troll, but Morrígan could. It was there, in her hands, the stone and flesh as one.

She tugged at it, but it didn't budge. She tried again, thinking of the other tiny weights that pulled down on her heart—sorrow, joy, fear—but still nothing happened.

There was one more weight, though, stronger than the rest: the great pendulum hanging from her heart that had smashed the glass beaker when she first learned Hydromancy.

She reached in for it, feeling its weight in invisible hands.

This is for my uncle, the coward.

Power surged through her body.

This is for those too afraid to offend the Gods. This is for the battlemages, who blindly follow their orders. This is for the Gods themselves, who chain us with their ancient creeds. This is for the backwards people of Roseán, who will never understand what it means to change the world!

Her hands balled into fists and her nails dug into skin.

Taigdh took one look at our work and ran, but he will never understand what it is like to wield power as strong as this. None of them will!

She opened her eyes and focused on the troll.

I hate them. I hate them all.

As the pendulum swung forwards, a huge force pushed back against her, knocking her to the ground.

In a daze, Morrígan raised her head; the troll was nowhere in sight. She jumped to her feet and ran towards the edge of the cliff, just in time to see the stone beast crash into the retreating tide below.

CHAPTER 14:
THE GODSLAYER

Morrígan didn't sleep much that night. She shuffled in her bed, painfully aware of the painting of King Móráin the First on the opposite side of the room, his golden wings glimmering silver and grey in the moonlight. The scene depicted the Apotheosis of the Trinity: the moment King Móráin transcended to godhood, sprouted glowing wings behind his back, and blinded the Simian natives with their holy light.

All it took was for him to claim this land for him to become a god.

The wind howled outside, beating against a wooden gate somewhere across the street. The trees along the High Road crackled and rustled in response.

Again and again, just as she was about to fall asleep, she woke startled, remembering what had happened.

We did it. We achieved what mankind has been struggling with for centuries. She balled her hand into a fist. *Healers and alchemists strive to prolong life; how are we different from them?*

She closed her eyes as her mind recalled the image of Taigdh, sprinting across the fields.

He was just startled. She rolled over again in the bed. *If only I just had another chance to explain.*

It seemed like an impossible task: using rationality to fight the irrational. She knew the people of Roseán, knew that they were blinded by their faith, and that left little room for reason.

They live their lives in the shadow of the Gods, ignorant of the light of which they are deprived.

Morrígan opened her eyes. Her beadhbh cloak hung on from hook on the wall like a black figure, watching her in the darkness.

"Creation," she whispered, remembering one of Yarlaith's lessons from long ago.

Nothing can be truly created or destroyed, he had said, *for Creation is an artform reserved for the Gods.* Morrígan's hand reached up to her chest, and her fingers found the silver necklace Darragh had given her.

We both witnessed Creation tonight, but Yarlaith was the only one afraid of usurping the Gods.

Morrígan ran her finger around each of the three rings.

Some of the bravest warriors and the wisest scholars live by the teaching of the Trinity. Would they all be in agreement, if they too had seen Man overcome death? Surely, they've lost the ones they've loved too....

Her mind dozed off to a shallow sleep as the hours drifted by, despite the arrhythmic beat of the gate outside.

* * *

Her dreams were formless and intangible, as if her sleeping mind was too exhausted to conjure up anything solid. When she woke to the sounds of voices outside, all Morrigan could remember from her dreams was a bathing blue light, pulsating and penetrating through her soul.

She pushed those visions aside as she focused on her surroundings. It was much later now, and the light of the moon had vanished, replaced by a darkness thicker than before.

Her bedroom door swung open; Yarlaith the White stood in its frame.

"They've found us," he said, his voice low and calm. "Grab what you can and run."

There was terror in his eyes, like none Morrigan had ever seen. A loud crash came from downstairs, and the sounds of men shouting and roaring filled the room.

She leapt from her bed and threw her beadhbh cloak over her head. Then she shoved her feet into a pair of leather boots on the floor.

Outside her room, at the end of the landing, three men dressed in red cloaks appeared, balls of fire clenched in their fists. They were joined by two Geomancers, standing at the top of the stairs. With a bang, the door shut, leaving Morrigan alone in the room.

"Run!" screamed Yarlaith from the other side.

Morrigan scrambled across the bed and pulled herself onto the window ledge, stealing one last look.

Does this make me a coward? She pushed the window open and looked down. A cobblestone path meandered out from the front door, curving to the High Road below and leaving a soft patch of grass several yards from the window. Across the green, a crowd gathered at the gate: men and women from the village along with battlemages, all huddled under the light of raised torches.

Morrigan dove from the window, rolling as she hit the grass. More villagers appeared down the road, striding from the direction of the chapel and blocking Morrigan's only means of escape. Luckily, they had yet to see her, and she knew a short cut to the Low Road.

A cheer erupted from the crowd as the two Geomancers kicked open the door to present Yarlaith the White, his hands bound behind his back.

Morrigan spotted a Hydromancer searching around the back of the house. She pulled the hood of her beadhbh cloak up and ran to the end of the High Road. A fence of rotted wood blocked the way, where a twenty-foot drop led down to the Low Road and the Reardon Forge.

A voice called out through the night as she jumped, but Morrigan didn't look back. She swung herself around the highest branch of a tree and landed below without making a sound. Over her head, a group of men with torches peered down from the ledge. Fortunately, Morrigan found her feet quickly and set off down the Low Road.

The houses along the way were vacant, many with their doors left wide open. Morrigan ran through the silence, thinking about what she should do next.

Do I run? Will I confess? Will I just hide up in the Glenn and live amongst the bears and the beadhbhs 'til the end of my days? From the look of things, it didn't seem like she had any other options.

As she turned the final corner, past the butcher's shop into the Square, she skidded to a halt, scratching her heels along the ground. A huge crowd of people had gathered in the centre of the village, and they all looked on as Colonel Eodadh addressed them from atop the stone well. A line of Pyromancers stood behind him; mages dressed in green pulled two large wooden stakes upright with Geomancy.

Morrigan almost let out a cry of shock.

Two stakes. They mean to burn me too.

"Darkness has fallen over this community!" boomed the colonel, venom and fury in his voice. "But it is not from a foreign enemy. The Simians, who spit at our Gods and our faith, are not the ones who have brought us to arms tonight, but a man! What say you, who have lived amongst a heathen: should he be punished in the sight of Gods and men?"

The crowd roared. Some men clutching farm implements in their hands, raising them as they cried.

"He's a sinner! Let the Gods punish the sins of Man!"

"Burn the heretic!"

Why won't anyone defend him? Morrigan spotted Fearghal and Mr. Cathain chanting with the rest. The Reardon brothers stood at the back of the crowd, their fists held high in the air. Morrígan tried to find other familiar faces amongst the villagers, but many of their features were warped and twisted with anger, distorted beyond recognition. There were some children amongst the rabble, too, clutching their parents' hands as they added their voices to the chorus.

From the opposite side of the Square, Morrígan saw the mob march down from the High Road past the chapel, with the tiny figure of Yarlaith the White shuffling in front of them.

Two stakes. The thought of attempting to free her uncle flared in her mind again. She could do some damage, perhaps, but Morrígan knew that the rest of the battalion, and indeed the villagers, could overwhelm her in seconds.

He wanted me to run. He wanted me to leave him.

As soon as she turned her back on the crowd and slipped down the Sandy Road, she accepted that she was a coward.

It won't end here. I'll recover the notes; I'll hide deeper in the cave, away from the prying eyes of the Gods.

She climbed over the wall and sprinted across the fields, tears beginning to fill her eyes. The mountains of the Glenn loomed overhead as she ran, her chest burning with every breath. She paused and looked back. From here, she saw the Square, the gathered crowd, and the now burning stake.

But clearer than anything else, she heard the triumphant cheers of the villagers.

"No!" Morrígan shrieked. She dropped to her knees, unable to hold her own weight. With a barrage of sobs, she buried her face in her hands, and her world went dark.

"He dedicated his life to saving yours!" Her voice was hoarse, and only a thin column of rising smoke responded. "He mended your bones...cured your ailments...he healed your wounds!" She thought of all the people he had treated: Mr. Cathain's leprosy, Ciarán's buboes, Mr. Mhurichú's smallpox and his wife's consumption....

He never asked for anything in return, not once. He gave them a life of health and happiness, and this is how they repay him.

Her fists tightened. Rage and despair ripped through her soul, and the pendulum hanging from her heart grew heavier than ever. Morrígan paused, recalling a memory from earlier that night, when she had succeeded at something a group of fully trained Geomancers could not even attempt.

There might still be time.

She squinted, reaching for her power, and felt the cold, coarse touch of Geomancy upon her fingertips.

Her eyes concentrated on the flaming stake. *So far away.* She reached out her arms and flexed her wrists, forcing her emotions into her hands.

It won't be as heavy as the troll. Further, yes, but not as heavy.

She stood in silence, reaching, touching, feeling through the air and across the field. Her power groped along what felt like the cold stone of the Square, punctuated with tiny shrubs and plants that had forced their way up through the cracks...and *there.*

She found it, hot and heavy, the wood from the flaming stake burning between her fingers. She pictured herself grabbing it with giant, iron fists, and pulled.

The force of the stake's weight refused to give way. Gritting her teeth and planting her heels firmly into the ground, she started to feel the base of the stake shift. She heard shrieks and gasps from the village as the burning wood began to tilt.

Morrígan held her breath and forced all of her might into one last heave, and like a burning harpoon, the stake shot towards the hills with an explosion of fire and splinters.

Morrígan opened her eyes. The stake was jammed into the ground next to her, the old man still tied to it.

"Yarlaith!"

His waist and legs were black and burned, bubbling with bloody blisters and charred bone.

He groaned. "Strong...please...take...take me down to her."

Morrígan crouched to lift the old man over one shoulder. Still attached to the stake, Yarlaith moaned in pain as Morrígan rose to her feet. She gritted her teeth as she stood, then turned her gaze back towards the village.

They'll regroup soon and come for us. There's nowhere else to hide.

Without knowing where else to go, Morrígan ducked into the cave and carried her uncle into the Lost Catacombs of Móráin's Conquest.

She waded through the darkness, ignoring the tears that burned in the corner of her eyes.

"We're almost there, Yarlaith," she whispered. "Stay awake. We're almost there. Please."

There were potions and salves in the workshop, but she had no idea how to apply them to a man half burned alive.

Is this what life we have left? With no hope, and not even the Gods to turn to?

Eventually, she reached her uncle's workshop. It had been raided; books and notes lay scattered across the floor. The corpses, however, had not been touched.

They have less respect for the living than the dead.

Morrigan placed her uncle on the stone slab where her mother used to lie. Yarlaith's eyes were closed, but he still breathed in quick, wheezing breaths. He reached out a hand and pointed down at Morrigan's mother on the ground.

"She's...here...thank you."

"Yarlaith, I'll help you! I'll grab some medicine and try—"

"No. Please...a moment." He closed his eyes and smiled. "Give a moment for the three of us to be...together."

He held a single hand in the air. "Seal this place...nobody can learn...and we can be together forever." His words came harder with every breath. "Thank you, Morry...I wanted...us...even just once...."

"No!" She held his hand and shook him, but the old healer did not stir.

Yarlaith the White died smiling.

Morrígan submitted to her tears, sobbing as they ran down her face.

He only wanted to help. He only wanted to save Mother.

Exhausted, she sat and quietly contemplated her uncle's last words. To seal the chamber off would mean all of their hard work and progress would be lost, but he and her mother could rest together for eternity. She looked down at the healer. He had lived his last days as though a shadow had been cast over his life. Now, it seemed that he was happy for the first time in months.

Why...why did you have to be such a fool! Yarlaith the White was a gentle man, certainly not cut out for the dark arts. *Why did you even try?*

Morrígan closed her eyes, trying to recall the first day she had seen him as Yarlaith the Black, the Necromancer. Her sobs echoed through the chamber, and her chest quivered in the cold.

It was Fionn. His arm...Yarlaith had tried to save his arm, and then he discovered Necromancy. They hadn't heard from Fionn the Red since, and Morrígan still wasn't sure why he and his companions had picked that fateful day to cross the Glenn, bringing the mountain troll to Roseán.

She shook the memory from her head, eyes fixed on the two dead bodies: her mother dressed in white, and Yarlaith burnt black. *Why did you risk it all? Why did you do all this for me?*

She paused.

"For me?" she whispered out loud. That's what she had assumed: that he was doing all this for her, because the loss of her mother had hit her so hard. Yarlaith had seen how distraught she was on the day her mother died.

"But why would he go to so much trouble?"

Then she saw it. Morrigan wasn't sure if it was the half smile that ran crooked across the old man's face, or the way his twisted finger seemed to be pointing down to the beautiful woman on the ground, but something stirred at the back of her mind, and everything made sense.

Yarlaith was my father's brother, but the two never got along.... That was his only connection to me. But still he cared. Still he loved me.

More things fell into place as she recalled what Yarlaith had said about the talent for magic. Passed down from parent to child.

The rest of her world came crumbling down.

"No!"

She didn't want to believe it. Her father was a drunkard, a coward, a fool. He was abusive and negligent. He even fled when they were attacked.

Another thought surfaced.

No, your father loved your mother. He helped raise you; he taught you how to use magic. He died attempting to bring his love back from the dead.

Morrigan screamed. All of her life she had wanted a happy family, a mother and father who loved her. Now in the damp cave, hundreds of feet below her hometown, with thousands of dismembered and dead soldiers, her family was finally reunited.

No...not like this. This isn't right. This isn't fair!

Hatred and regret clouded her thoughts.

They took it from us.

Why couldn't they have just understood? Burning tears filed her eyes.

Small-minded fools, too afraid of what they don't understand. If only they could see what we're capable of.

She raised a hand over the two corpses. She squinted and concentrated on the spell, on the flesh made dead.

Twist it. Make it whole again.

Nothing happened. She dug deep into her soul, and in the back of her mind, she heard an almost silent scream. As she focused more, the shriek slowly grew louder.

The screaming. That means it's working!

A man's voice joined the noise, but it was almost imperceptible.

Morrígan tried to forget about the noise and focused instead on her pendulum, the heaviest weight upon her heart. Both of the voices in her head suddenly amplified tenfold, raging through her skull like a storm. The screamer sounded like a woman, the voice that of an old man, and he was begging her to stop.

Morrígan opened her eyes and saw the two corpses rousing, as if waking up from a long slumber.

No, I will not stop. The man's voice in her head pleaded, but she ignored it. She looked within for more power and found two new sources within her heart.

The voices are of Mother and Yarlaith. What if I can draw on their souls too?

As she pulled on the fear and anguish of her two marks, the spell began to take hold. The two corpses slowly sat upright, and two pairs of lifeless eyes stared back at her. Their thoughts resounded through her mind, and the power of three people flowed through her body.

Within the cacophony, she heard other voices, those of many other men, soft like whispers. When she closed her eyes and focused on them, they too grew louder, speaking in a strange language. More joined in with other valiant war cries. Morrigan couldn't understand the words, but she felt anguish and despair within them. As each voice joined the dissonance, she grew stronger. Slowly, she opened her eyes.

Two dozen corpses stood to her attention. Rotted bones stained brown, bound to flesh by black sinew. Some were armed, others held old rusted shields. Many were nothing but shambling frames of old bones, swaying before her. Others from the winding tunnels of the catacombs joined, their voices adding to the rest.

Her audience grew as did her power, with some newcomers fully fleshed with bright armour. High-ranking generals and brave heroes whose bodies had been preserved for the afterlife stood ready to fight again.

The undead responded very sensitively to her own thoughts; she could move them all like a newly acquired limb. With half a gesture, the crowd parted, and she walked towards the cave's exit. The reanimated corpses of Yarlaith and her mother followed her.

"She has grown so much," said the voice of her mother.

Only Yarlaith seemed to be aware of what was going on.

"Morry...no.... This is madness. I beg you to stop. Please."

Morrigan rolled her eyes. *What does he know?* She was about to accomplish more than he had in a lifetime of hard work, and as sure as Sin, she wasn't about to give up so easily.

"Don't try to stop me," Morrigan said. "You of all people should know that they've brought this upon themselves."

"No, Morrigan. You don't understand."

But with the power of so many souls within her, Morrigan understood now more than ever. Mere moments ago, she would have been content with reuniting her family again, but a different desire consumed her now.

"Fine, then stay," she said, then dismissed the old man with a flick of her wrist. His corpse fell to the ground, lifeless again. Morrigan turned and made her way to the exit, with the souls of a thousand people raging in her heart.

When she reached the mouth of the cave, a cold sea breeze greeted her. She raised a hand to the sky, changing the direction of the wind with Aeromancy. With her own pendulum augmented by the power of the dead, manipulating the mood of the air was as simple as swirling a pool of water. She pulled clouds from across the sky, feeling the moisture between her fingers. She twisted her grip, and energy exploded from above, lighting up the sky as rain poured down from the heavens.

Morrigan smiled. *They will cower when they see what they created.*

She turned her attention to the swarm of voices in her head, each a part of her now. With barely a thought, an army of dead soldiers strode out from the cave.

She paused. *There is nowhere for me to go. They will chase me and hunt me through the Glenn when they find out what I am capable of. They have forced my hand.*

Thunder rolled overhead as she called to her army. In unison, the voices in her mind responded with cries in a dead tongue. The ground shook as they charged towards the village, more thralls emerging from the cave to follow their comrades.

There are so many. Ancient bones creaked under rusted iron and steel as they passed. Some were missing limbs, some were missing heads, but each marched forwards. In their wake, Morrigan followed the dead army, eager to see what she was capable of.

She commanded the horde as she reached the peak of a grassy hill. From there, she saw the battalion of mages emerge from the village. Colonel Eodadh stood on the front line, with Berrian the Green by his side.

Eodadh roared a strange command, and a salvo of rocks and stones washed over the undead soldiers. The stones collided with the horde, but the dead remained unmoved.

Again and again, the colonel gave the order and his men fired, but none of the corpses fell.

It is impossible to kill what is already dead. The Hydromancers stepped forwards and launched arrows and spears of ice at the wights.

Before the Pyromancers took their turn, Morrigan raised a hand and the dead legion charged. The mages yelled in terror and screamed in pain as they fell, but the undead soldiers carried out their massacre without a word. Morrigan's power touched upon the soul of the first mage from the battalion who fell, and with a slight push, she brought him back from the dead and turned him upon his brothers. As the soldier's soul merged with her own, Morrigan heard his voice echo through her head.

"Lord help us! This power, it...it's not like anything I've ever seen. They stood before us, in such silence...but then.... Is this it? Have I died? Is this what it's like to be dead? I...I was promised paradise. They told me I'd see my family again...."

Another soldier fell to one of her skeletal minions. His thoughts resounded in her skull too.

"I told them! I told them we should have burned the house while they slept! Eodadh, he wanted a trial first, a mock trial, and this is what he has brought upon us!"

Every dead man added to the discord. The power they brought her was far more significant than the old skeletons and corpses from the catacombs.

Of course. These are mages already skilled in the ways of magic. Where once there was a single, heavy pendulum swinging from her heart, now there were dozens: one for each of the battlemages who now rose to serve her.

Some of the remaining living mages broke from the fray and regrouped behind a stone wall that encircled the field, out of sight from the undead.

Morrigan focused on the new power she possessed. With the magic of half a mage battalion surging through her veins, her soul wrapped around every pebble and grain of sand along the road before her. She raised her hand, and a cloud of dust and stones erupted from the ground, surrounding the cowering mages like a whirlwind. Bringing her hand to a fist, the stones engulfed them, tearing through their flesh like damp parchment. Their screams surged through the night. Then there was silence.

She reached out for the remaining men's souls. The power inside her amplified further as more servants rose. The colonel was one of them, but now he stood hunched over with his broken spine, his face torn to shreds.

"He warned us. His Highness warned us of power gathering in the north." Colonel Eodadh's voice did not resonate with fear as the others had but was deep with repentance and lament. "Power strong enough to bring the Gods to his knees, he had said. Could this be it? Were we wrong to be wary of the Silverback? The Godslayer, he called him. Could he have really meant this...girl?"

Morrigan toyed with her new power as she walked towards the Sandy Road, passing over the blood-stained fields. She pulled at a wooden barn in the distance, crumbling it into a pile of splintered timber with little effort. After a sweeping gesture, the trees of the Hazelwood to the south collapsed in unison. A black cloud of birds rose from the distant wreckage, their cries echoing through the night.

She commanded the soldiers to follow her into the village, all marching together. Mages walked with skeletons, and old war leaders in bright armour followed in the rear.

There was still some commotion in the Square. Morrigan saw that one of the remaining stakes stood alone and proud amongst the charred wood where Yarlaith had been burned.

The villagers screamed and scrambled into their houses as the dead marched in. Morrigan walked towards the old stone well and climbed to the top of it, granting herself a full view of the Square. Some villagers peered out from their windows, while others huddled in fear amongst the market stalls.

You have no battalion now. There is nobody here to protect you from the Simians of Penance, from the beadhbhs of the Glenn.

She flicked her wrist and brought the buildings behind her crumbling to the ground.

"Justice!" she screamed. "Tonight, you gave Yarlaith the White justice in the name of the Lord, but it was you who set fire to the stake. This is justice, but at the hands of something greater than the Gods."

The undead charged on the villagers; Morrigan watched in silence as the slaughter unfolded.

One skeleton hacked at a man pinned to the ground, while a bloody corpse threw a spear at a young boy running to his mother. The old woman shrieked as she saw her son fall, but her screams of anguish turned to screams of terror when his corpse stood up and pulled the spear from his stomach. Two headless skeletons with shields and swords chased Sorcha towards the High Road, but she took a crossbow bolt from an undead villager before she made it. Ciarán from the mill tried to fight off an unarmed solider with a pitchfork, but the wight did not fall, even when stabbed through the neck. The miller was quickly overwhelmed when others took notice of his attempted defiance.

The Reardon brothers tried to fight off their undead father with their own weapons. The elder brother was wearing a chainmail vest. Remembering one of her first lessons on Geomancy, Morrígan reached out to him, focusing on the chains, and twisted her fingers. The armoured brother fell to the ground, gasping for air as the mail tightened, slowly crushing him. The younger brother dropped his weapon and ran, and his undead father gave chase.

She saw Fearghal and Mr. Cathain cornered by a group of undead mages. With a click of her flint-rings and a gesture at the butcher and undertaker, a bolt of flames went hurling over their heads. The building behind the two caught fire, and broken, charred wood collapsed on top of them.

Morrígan grasped at the fire from atop the well and spun her body, covering the entire Square with a twisting inferno as the carnage continued.

In the corner of her eye, she noticed someone skulking towards her. As she turned, the figure of a boy emerged, a dagger clutched tight in a trembling hand.

"Make it stop, Morrígan. Make them stop or I'll bury this blade in your throat."

Morrígan laughed. "Oh, Taigdh, you don't understand. You were the one who brought this upon Roseán. If only you had trusted me. If only you had helped me, when all I wanted to do was make the others understand."

"Understand?" The boy's body shook. "I saw Mrs. Mhurichú down there, Morrígan. You left me no choice." He paused, lowering the dagger. "You...you killed her, didn't you? You were supposed to look after her, and you killed her. Why? Why did you do it?"

Morrígan pulled on her power and grasped the iron blade, still in the lad's hand. She tugged at it, raising it slowly up towards his bewildered face.

"You once told me about the ants you and your cousin used to kill. Remember?" Morrígan turned the dagger around, pointing it towards Taigdh's throat. She could feel a tiny resistance as he tried to pull it away, but he was just one boy, and she had the power of a full mage battalion behind the dagger's hilt.

"You used to race them, and drown them, and squish them, but you never told me why. When I asked, you shrugged, and said it was just one of those things little boys do."

A thin line of red trickled from Taigdh's neck as the steel touched his skin. His eyes rolled back in pain, but she pressed further.

"Like ants to children, you are to me."

Taigdh's knees buckled, and he collapsed to the ground, twitching. Morrigan pushed on the blade until the tip emerged from the back of his neck.

"I do these things," she whispered, "because I can."

She pulled the dagger free and set it flying at a woman trying to escape across the road. She never had a good throwing arm, but guided by the Geomancy of twelve dead mages, it quickly found its way deep between the woman's shoulder blades.

All those who died had risen again to serve her, growing to far greater numbers than before. Looking around, she saw the body of a lad lying close to the burning butcher's shop. She strode over and reached for his shoulder, rolling him over to face her.

Darragh's bloodied face stared back, the whites of his eyes all that she could see under his mop of bloodied red hair. Staring up at Morrigan, he raised his hand slowly.

"Maybe I should have told you instead," she said. The boy reached for something dangling from her neck. "You wouldn't have told anyone. You would have been too *scared*."

Darragh coughed, sputtering blood across her cloak. In his eyes, she saw a final flash of defiance as he pulled her necklace, snapping his mother's pendant from the silver chain. He held it tightly to his own chest and went still.

Morrigan stood to admire the butchery. The wights under her command now stood in attention again.

What next? The fire crackled and swayed lazily in the wind. She touched upon the power flowing through her body.

This is from just one battalion, but there are more, stationed in every settlement across the Clifflands.... She smiled as she tried to imagine becoming even stronger.

Why stop there? She crouched down beside Darragh's corpse. *There are garrisons all over Alabach, in each of the Seachtú. Then there's the Academy in Dromán, where there'll be a thousand mages in training....*

She knelt and pulled the pendant from Darragh's fingers. Morrígan rubbed her thumb across the three rings.

And in the capital city of Cruachan, King Diarmuid Móráin, a living God, sits upon the Throne of Man.

She gazed to the south. She knew Cruachan was down near the Sea of Storms, but she had no idea how far away that was.

In a flash, the sun broke over the Glenn, casting morning light over the burning village. She looked up at the sun and smiled.

"It's my birthday," she whispered. "This was supposed to be the day I become a mage."

She turned back towards her army of corpses. In the sunlight, she saw every detail of the twisted, broken skeletons and bodies that stood to her attention. The dead villagers still clutched their improvised tool and weapons. Women and children, soldiers and mages, all waiting for her next command.

We'll build our numbers. We'll take the Seven Seachtú. We'll claim the power of the Academy. Then we'll march on the capital, and I'll take the king's power for myself.

Morrigan smiled. *They called my father Yarlaith the Black, but soon I shall be known as Morrigan the Godslayer.*

CHAPTER 15: MORNING

Sleep didn't come easily to Farris that night. Every bone in his body was weary, every muscle fatigued beyond measure, but he would not let them rest. Not now. Not here. Not out on the Scalp of the Glenn, where anything that walked was a predator, and anything still awake was hungry.

But aside from the pain, Farris's thoughts lingered on Slaíne's words. Whether he liked it or not, fate was guiding him. To freedom? To death? Only the Lady Meadhbh knew. Whatever was in store for Farris, he was heading for it, whether he liked it or not.

No, thought Farris, turning where he lay. *I will not let destiny enslave me. I won't go down without a fight.*

Slaíne and Sir Bearach returned to the camp, marking the end of their shift. Farris watched with a half-opened eye as Slaíne crouched down next to the other sleeping Simian and gently informed him that it was his turn to take watch. From the way he woke, Farris supposed the Simian was having trouble sleeping too.

How much longer must we wait? He rolled over to face the eastern horizon, with dark mountains glowing in the full moon's light.

His eyelids grew heavy, but he fought back against their weight. He sat up and shook himself of his exhaustion. Across the camp, the trees shuffled softly as they swayed in the wind, surrounding the Scalp like a great wall of wood. In the shadows of their trunks, dark shapes shifted through the clearing.

There was no noise. No screeches or cries for mercy like before. All Farris saw were the two black figures converging where the red Simian stood guard.

"Run!" Farris yelled, squinting through the darkness. It was fortunate that the moon was out; otherwise they would have truly been lost. The silver outline of two beadhbhs feasted on their kill, their plumed tails pointing upwards, swaying like black wraiths in the night. More came charging through the trees, shrieking with that familiar, vicious cacophony.

Sir Bearach rose quickly, already fully armoured.

"This way!" he bellowed as the others scrambled awake. The knight held his great claymore tight in two gauntleted fists and dashed past Farris into the trees. Without thought, Farris followed, away from the reach of the moon and into the dark of the undergrowth.

The forest was denser than before, but Farris welcomed the branches and thorns that swept past his face. *Can the beasts navigate through here?* Without a thought for who else had made it from the Scalp, he kept running, ignoring the lingering pain building in his knee. No words were spoken; only the rustling of trees and the cracking of twigs whispered as they pushed further into the forest.

The forest around them grew thinner. The mountains of the Glenn stood above, like stone giants watching over the night. The path curved towards the river; the ground slowly rose upwards below Farris's feet. As the last trees fell away, he skidded to a halt. Before him, a huge wall of rock and stone stood in the way, towering twenty feet overhead.

"We need to climb!" roared Sir Bearach. The others appeared from the woods, too, but Farris didn't stop to count how many had made it. Each threw themselves against the wall, searching for a foothold. Farris took a spot right under where Bearach had started climbing. He couldn't help but admire how the knight scaled the rocks so swiftly, despite the weight and restrictions of his armour. Sir Bearach still carried the beadhbh feathers in his cloak, fastened around his neck to keep his arms free.

The things we do for gold. Farris pulled himself off the ground, fingers pressed against the cold rock. He heard quick, soft footsteps below as he reached upwards for another grappling point.

"Chester!" cried Slaíne from above. "Hurry!"

He didn't need to be told, for a quick glance was enough to inform him that the beadhbhs were right below, clawing and biting at the corpse of one of the crewmen. Two beadhbhs stood with their beaks covered in blood while three more hopped in circles, flapping their useless wings in a feeble attempt to gain height.

When Farris reached the top, only four others had made it: Slaíne, Fionn, Sir Bearach, and the bearded mechanic dressed in blue.

What a strange company we make. The bards should surely write a song about this adventure! He rolled onto his back to catch his breath.

After a moment's peace, the beadhbhs still shrieking below, Sir Bearach stood to speak.

"We can't linger here any longer. They can't reach us, but as long as they keep up that racket, more will join them." He pointed into the darkness, northwards towards the other side of the valley. "We'll keep the river over our right shoulder and make our way west. I don't care if we have to fall, roll, or plummet down the other side of the mountain, we'll be safer than we are now."

There was certainly no arguing with that, and the others pulled themselves to their feet. Slaíne the White gasped when she saw Sir Bearach fixing his improvised sack onto his shoulder.

"You're still carrying that?"

She marched over and pulled the cloak from his back, spilling the beadhbh feathers onto the ground.

"You fool!" she said, jabbing a finger into the knight's armoured chest. "You've brought them upon us! The beasts have come all this way, hunting us, stalking us, all because they were following the scent of the cursed feathers you stole from them!"

At this, the others chimed in with their own words of contempt, but Sir Bearach barely flinched. Farris smiled.

Just tell them. Tell them that black market gold is more valuable than the lives of a few strangers.

"Please, Slaíne," Sir Bearach said. "Feel free to make as many accusations as you want once you take the time to read a book or two." He turned to the others and raised his hands in submission.

"Beadhbhs are birds," he began. "They do not fly. They hunt Humans and other large mammals, true, but they are still birds. Like other birds, they lack the sense of smell mammalian hunters are famous for, relying on other senses to track their prey. As sure as the poison that fills this valley, I am not the one who brought these beasts upon us." He turned his attention to Slaíne. "It's simply a matter of magnitude, my lady. With so many packs of beadhbhs pouring through these lands, it's a wonder we haven't been spotted sooner."

The healer rolled her eyes but didn't press the matter further. Sir Bearach retrieved his loot and strutted past her, whistling softly into the night. Slaíne sighed and beckoned the others to follow the merry knight deeper into the hills.

***

The route through the rocks proved difficult to navigate, especially in the darkness. For the most part they walked, but often they had to stop and climb over piles of rockfall and steep slopes. As they left the valley behind, Farris glanced back every now and then, checking if the beadhbhs were following.

"They'll find their way up eventually," said Sir Bearach, sensing Farris's anxiety. He pointed towards the forest below. The cliff was less steep there, with a slope low and gentle enough to walk through. The knight shook his head. "If one of them picks their way through here, the rest will surely come. They'll follow us out of the Glenn into the Clifflands if they have to."

"So, what do you propose we do?" asked Farris.

"We keep going, of course. No need to worry the others."

Farris nodded, then noticed something about the man's armour. The steel appeared to be white, but where the paint had been chipped and scratched, a faded blue tint shone out.

"Your breastplate, it's Simian-made, no?"

The knight smiled. "Aye, the Church prefers we stay away from the Simian smiths, but I have yet to find castle-forged steel of better quality." He tapped his shoulder with a heavy fist. "And besides, only the Simians of Penance have truly mastered the art of break mechanics."

"Break mechanics?" It was a long time since Farris had been inside a Simian smithy.

Sir Bearach raised his arm, revealing a thin, wiry cord dangling under his shoulder. "Geomancers defeated the Simian soldiers by crushing them in their own armour. If I'm assaulted by a mage now, all I need to do is pull here and my whole suit will collapse to the ground."

"Clever," said Farris. "It's a shame we didn't think of that before Móráin's Conquest."

The knight shrugged. "Well, the Simians never had a need for it until we came."

Each of the rock faces looked the same, and Farris found himself wondering over and over if they were even heading in the right direction. Twice they met with dead ends and were forced to trace back on their steps. They tried to keep the river on one side as Sir Bearach had suggested, but with the winding path bringing them deeper into the mountains, the valley was often completely obscured from view. Not to mention the darkness that seemed to fall heavier as the hours drifted by.

When they reached the third dead end, Fionn groaned with frustration.

"I'm so tired," he said. "We'll never find a way out."

Farris was hoping that Sir Bearach would have something smart to say, but the knight held his own tongue. Nobody spoke, as though they all secretly agreed with the Pyromancer.

The night was filled with a calm stillness, despite how deep into the wilderness they had travelled. The nocturnal clamour of a typical countryside was replaced with a deadly, harrowing silence. Only those that feasted on meat lived in the Glenn, and they made little noise in nightfall.

But there was one sound. A single, smooth trickle of water, echoing all around despite there being no river in sight.

"Do you hear that?" said Farris, raising a hand to alert the others.

"Caves," whispered Sir Bearach. "The stone in this region is weak, and rivers have burrowed deep beneath the mountains, forging their own routes under the ground. These river-caves run all over the Clifflands"—he threw a smile towards Slaíne— "and we seem to be standing over one."

The two Humans seemed to share a moment of mutual understanding, but Farris was still as lost as they had been all night.

Then Slaíne the White spoke. "Everyone stand back. I'm going to try and open up a way down."

She walked in a circle along the path, her arms held out to either side. *She's a Geomancer too.* Slaíne continued to walk slowly about the clearing, as if following a track long lost. Eventually she stopped, waving her arms to catch the attention of the group.

"The ground is weak here!" she called. She crouched and pressed her hands against the stone.

The rocks rumbled softly below Farris's feet. Slaíne stood and raised both arms over her head, and the tremor suddenly amplified in magnitude, as if the mountain itself was shaking. She stepped back, and the floor fell away, revealing a huge, gaping hole. The crashing of the rocks resounded all around. A tiny, rising anxiety fluttered in Farris's stomach.

The healer stood at the other side of the pit, smiling and beckoning the others to follow, but he saw something shift amongst the rocks behind her.

Sir Bearach laughed with delight as he stepped forwards, but the joy drained from his face as his eyes were drawn to the slow, lumbering movement. He let out a roar before Farris saw that those rocks were not rocks, but the limbs of a massive, grey mountain troll.

"Down!" the knight yelled and threw himself into the pit. The others followed, as did Slaine, without turning to see the brute. The troll glared down at Farris with huge, bulging, bloodshot eyes, peering out behind a shapeless, bulbous nose. It stood thirty feet tall, on two thick legs like stone columns.

Panic washed over his body as the troll beat its chest with fists like boulders, knuckles scratched and scarred.

As soon as his wits returned, Farris darted towards the edge of the pit and jumped down after his companions.

He landed with a splash in a shallow stream. Moonlight from above poured down onto the water, glimmering like liquid steel below his feet. The others were already running deeper into the caves, led by a flame in Fionn's hands.

Farris followed, praying that the beast would not follow them into the pit. However, a sudden loud thud from behind reaffirmed Farris's old convictions that Gods did not exist. He scampered off into the tunnel, following Fionn's glimmering magelight in the distance.

This is your territory now, Garth. If only he had paid more attention to his little brother's sketches. If only he had listened to his lectures about the caverns of the Glenn.

If only I listened when he told me to stay away from the thrice-damned Silverback and his rebellion.

The cave floor shook as the troll followed behind them, its steps slow and lumbering. The others ahead stopped, and when Farris caught up, he knew that they were doomed, caught between death and a dead end.

"We're trapped!" cried the mechanic. He rubbed the damp walls with his hands, as if feeling for a way out.

Sir Bearach drew his sword. "Then we'll fight. If I am to die, I'll be armed and fighting."

"Wait!" commanded Slaine. She pressed her hand against the wall. "I can forge a way through. Stand back!"

The stone was already crumbling before they stepped away. Farris heard a deep snort, and he glanced back to see the mountain troll plodding towards them, its hungry eyes leering through the dark.

A fresh sea breeze washed over Farris's back as the wall fell away.

When he turned and saw the rolling green hills of the Clifflands spreading out into the distance, the weight of the last few day's trials seemed to lift free from his shoulders. He wasn't going to die in the depths of the Glenn. He wasn't going to fail in his mission to warn the Simian people of the king's plans. Farris Silvertongue—known to many as Farris the Turncloak, to others as Farris the Swift, and to some as Chester the Lucky—was going to live.

"Run!" cried Slaine, beckoning the others out into the freedom of the fields.

"Don't stop!" roared Sir Bearach as he went, the earth shaking with each thundering step of the troll. "It'll be morning soon! We just need to keep going until the sunrise!"

Of course. The morning mist was forming along the ground. The earth was different now. The rocky terrain of the Glenn had been replaced with the sandy, tilled soil of the Clifflands. Stout, stone walls surrounded the fields. From the even troughs running beneath his feet, Farris realised they were on a farm.

Terror began to rise in his chest. In the distance, he saw the blurred silhouette of wattle-and-daub buildings. *A town. We've brought a damned mountain troll to a village.*

It seemed as if Sir Bearach had noticed too.

"This way!" he yelled, drawing his claymore and pointing it out with his right hand. "We'll steer it away until the sunlight!"

As they began to veer away from the village, Farris glanced back to see that the troll was quickly gaining ground. Fortunately, the direction Sir Bearach had chosen was westward, away from the buildings and towards the slow-rising sun.

"It's getting closer!" roared Fionn, as they approached one of the stone walls. "We're running out of time!"

Farris vaulted over the wall. *We're lucky it's still early, otherwise these fields would be full of—*

It was at this single thought—not the death of the crewmen aboard the ship, not the ferocity of the beadhbhs of the Glenn, not the monstrosity of the mountain troll—but this idle musing that brought more terror to Farris's bones than anything he had witnessed since leaving Cruachan.

He saw the cart first, bound to an old draft horse that barely looked fit enough to walk. Before the cart stood three peasants—a man, a woman, and a young girl—quietly tending to their crops.

"Troll!" he yelled, hoping it would at least alert them to the hulking death that was following. "Run fo—"

His ribs cracked, snapping like twigs in a child's fist. Before he realised that the troll had struck him, Farris lay on the ground, face down with a mouthful of dirt. Using the last of his remaining strength, he forced himself to look up.

The troll stood in the middle of the field, both arms raised in the air with the bearded mechanic held in one beefy fist. Sir Bearach and Fionn stood to fight, the latter with fire burning in both hands. Slaine helped the woman and girl climb into the cart; the man frantically tried to mount the horse.

The troll roared and threw the limp, lifeless body of the mechanic towards the head of the cart. It landed in an explosion of splinters. The horse reeled on its hind legs, whinnying violently in response. The farmhand, knocked from its back, fell to the ground with his foot caught in a stirrup. As soon as all four hoofs hit the ground again, the horse bolted off into the morning mist, dragging the screaming man behind him.

Sir Bearach charged at the troll, roaring valiantly as Fionn shot bolts of fire at its face. The beast barely flinched when the flames burst against its skin; with an effortless swoop, it picked up the knight. Farris watched in horror as the knuckles of the troll's fist whitened, crushing the knight inside his armour.

Slaíne the White stepped forwards, away from the wreckage of the cart. She stretched her arms outwards as a cloud of stones and soil rose before her. With another elaborate gesture, the salvo of debris shot towards the lumbering beast. The troll roared in agony, but still stood strong. As the dust settled, the beast trudged towards the mage, huffing and grunting as it moved. Slaíne tried to flee, but the troll reached her in a few long steps. It lurched, and sent the woman tumbling through the air with a kick. With a sickening crack, she landed at the far end of the field.

The troll turned and trudged towards the red mage. The young man stood his ground and threw another burst of fire at the hulking mass, but the beast did not slow. With incredible ease, the troll reached out and snatched the mage's arm as he passed, dangling him high above the ground. With another hand, the troll grabbed Fionn's swinging legs and began to pull. After a few painful seconds, a scream of agony and a spray of blood tore through the air; the mage's body parted from his arm.

The troll paused to admire the carnage, eyeing the shattered corpses and blots of blood littering the field. Its gaze eventually landed on the two peasants, still hiding under the broken cart.

"No!" groaned Farris, forcing his knees under his body. "Run! Just run!"

He closed his eyes and gritted his teeth, pulling himself to his feet. He grimaced as a sharp, shearing pain grated at his knee.

I can't run, but by the Shadow of Sin, I'll fight it.

Farris groped the ground until his fingers found a rock. He heard a scream, for the troll had grabbed the woman in one hand, beating her against the ground like a child with a broken toy. In shocked silence, the young girl looked on, her face pale as stone.

The troll sneered and tossed the woman's shattered body aside, turning its gaze on the girl.

"Over here!" yelled Farris, forcing himself to stand straight despite the agony chewing at his ribs. When he found his balance, Farris shifted his weight onto his back leg and threw the rock, adding every ounce of his strength its arc.

For the second time in his life, Farris prayed. The stone soared through the air, and as sure as Sin, the Gods did listen. The stone hit the troll between the eyes, and the beast howled in pain.

"Come on!" yelled Farris. The troll turned and came lumbering towards him. He quickly scanned the mountains to the east, glowing gold with the rising sun. As it approached, the troll stooped down and picked Farris up off the ground.

He saw every detail of the monstrous face as he hung in the air. A long, wet tongue hung from its mouth, lips twisting into a hungry smile. The sides of its cheeks were wrinkled, but almost seemed like cracked rock in the light of the morning sun.

With a grunt and a heave, the troll hurled Farris across the field.

It doesn't matter. I've silenced the agents. I've prevented the ship from reaching Penance. The king's plans have already been foiled. Even as he hit the ground and went rolling off the edge of the cliff, Farris didn't care.

The sun has risen. I've caused the death of many today, but I've saved the life of one....

His body fell broken amongst the jagged rocks of the shore.

Farris stared up at the trees and bushes along the top of the cliff, their branches and leaves bare in comparison to the warped splendour of the Glenn. His neck was twisted, his throat dry, but still he managed a final, crooked smile.

Where have all the flowers gone? A gentle wave washed over his face, filling his lungs with saltwater.

EPILOGUE

"From here, the tracks continue all the way to Penance, Your Grace. A single, straight line, uninterrupted as the raven flies."

Chief Engineer Santos rode next to King Diarmuid Móráin, pointing out the details of the Simian railway tunnel. The journey from Cruachan had been long, but Santos still spoke with the brimming enthusiasm of a salesman lying through his teeth.

"There are five more outposts between here and our city. If it pleases you, we wish to show you just one more."

Aye, and then we'll have to travel all the way back. Diarmuid sighed. They had been riding for hours, deep under the surface of the earth, and all Santos wanted to do was show him how brilliant the Simians had been in their design of Alabach's first underground trade route.

If the next outpost doesn't have a brothel or a beerhall, I'll scrap the damn project myself.

The king travelled with Santos and an escort of five Simian guards, but being the only Human there only bothered him slightly. Although his predecessors had been small-minded bigots, his own reign was meant to usher in a new age of unity between the two races. This magnificent hole in the ground was supposed to do just that. It would have been easy, if it wasn't for the Silverback and his dissidents, raising their fists and beating their chests over in Penance.

The Silverback's rebels are a tiny minority. Diarmuid's eyes focused on the steel railway tracks shimmering under his horses' hooves. Argyll was nothing more than a common criminal, but he claimed to have plans for the future of his people. They were always *his* people. They never belonged to the Crown. They never belonged to the Triad, or to Borris Blackhand, the one they had elected to power. They never even belonged to themselves. Argyll the Silverback was the authority on who belonged to whom and claimed that he'd rather die than see his Simian people ruled by a Human king.

So why doesn't he do just that?

"Here we are!" announced Santos, reining his mount to a halt. The Chief Engineer of Penance was thin for a Simian. The hair that covered his body was chestnut brown, with tufts of greys and white speckled across his shoulders. He had been grinning since they left Cruachan, but his eyes always lied. He constantly assured the king that everything was going smoothly, according to plan, but Diarmuid knew about the deaths. Four Simian miners lost their lives during the construction of the railway, buried alive when one of the tunnel ceilings collapsed. Four deaths, and Santos was willing to brush it away with a smile and a refrain of "Your Grace."

To Diarmuid's utmost despair, the outpost was vacant of barmaids and whores. The tunnels had been narrow and alive with the light and buzzing of oil lamps, but the outpost was wide, empty, and eerily silent in comparison.

"Santos, is there anyone present right now?" he asked, climbing down from his horse. Diarmuid spoke in his usual kingly voice, which normally caused the common folk to scurry and flee before him.

"No, Your Grace," answered Santos. "Of the twelve outposts, only those adjacent to Cruachan and Penance are occupied as of now. However—"

The Simian paused, tearing his eyes away from the king.

"It was nothing, Your Grace," he said, shuffling in his saddle and running a hand across the back of his neck. "Just some of my men...they claimed they saw something as they excavated the site. They begged me to show you but...well, it's silly really."

King Diarmuid nodded. "Show me, and we'll head back. My horse is tired, and my arse is sore."

"Of course, Your Grace, this way. It was nothing but an oddity."

Santos led him to the edge of the clearing, and the royal Simian guards followed in silence. The outpost itself was a steel construction, built to accommodate off-duty engineers and provide a quick route up to the surface in case of emergency. They walked past the outpost, however, towards the edge of the cavern.

"Here it is, Your Grace," Santos said, pointing to a space on the stone wall.

The walls through the tunnel had been grey and damp, with only the occasional cluster of fungi to break the monotony. Here, though, there was something peculiar. The wall was uniform, for the most part, but there was a strange slab, pushed right into the centre, just below eye-level. Unlike the curving, circular stones that surrounded it, the slab was jagged and irregular in shape. Diarmuid counted seven uneven sides, each extending out at a different angle. This wasn't the most peculiar thing, however.

The stone slab was blue.

Brilliant, blinding, bright blue against a sea of browns and greys. The slab appeared to be manmade, like the steel door of a mining shaft. Diarmuid peered closer at the stone, and gasped.

"That's right," said Santos, standing behind the king. "This is why we wanted to show you personally."

Etched into the surface of the stone was the symbol of the Trinity: three interlocking, looping circles, identical to the one that shone brightly on the king's own cloak.

"What...what is this?" asked Diarmuid, running a finger over the carvings.

"Well, Your Grace, we were hoping that you may—"

As Diarmuid's finger touched the image, a single crack broke through the stone like crooked lightning. Pieces of rock crumbled away from the top, trickling down before the king's feet, and light spilled through from behind the wall. Eventually the slab was gone, and all that it left behind was a tiny passage, with stairs leading down into gleaming, blue radiance.

"This...this hasn't happened before," said Santos, who stood quivering beside the huge, unresponsive guards. "We just thought you'd want to see the stone and—"

Diarmuid nodded. "So, I presume you'd like to take a look then?" He stepped into the opening.

The walls inside were of similar stone to that of the slab, all jutting out at crooked shapes and angles. Each step of the stairway downwards was different in size. Some broad enough for two full feet, others barely big enough to fit half a toe. Columns stood all along the hall, some short and wide, others tall and thin, and each with similar strange scribblings etched into them. The irregularity of it all put the king on edge.

Where the Holy Hell are we?

At the bottom of the stair, they faced what looked like a massive stone altar, flanked by two huge, circular sconces.

Santos stood next to the king. "This place...is it some sort of temple?"

Before Diarmuid had a chance to respond, he heard a voice. A terrible, wicked voice, brimming with more hatred than Diarmuid knew existed. He threw his hands up to his ears to block its sound, but it did not help. The voice was like hot daggers, digging deep into his skull, twisting with every word.

"Heathens, be gone! This is a sacred place. You have rejected our ways for far too long, and do not deserve to look upon the face of a God."

Santos immediately grasped his throat, gasping as he dropped to his knees. All around Diarmuid, the other Simians started coughing and sputtering, clawing their necks and falling to the ground. A moment later, Diarmuid stood alone, and six dead Simians littered the floor.

"Show yourself!" he roared, not sure where to turn. "I am King Diarmuid of Alabach, Third of My Name, Nineteenth Incarnate. In the name of Gods and men, I demand you reveal yourself!"

At the foot of the altar, the blue pulsated, slowly forming a glowing figure. Then there was a flash, and King Diarmuid found himself face to face with a beautiful, naked woman, made entirely from light.

No! This cannot be!

Diarmuid fell to one knee before the stranger. He had seen Her face a thousand times before, on the stained glass of every church and chapel in the kingdom.

"Holy Mother of Kings and Men, Lover of Gods, Weaver of Destiny and Fate: This humble king bows before you."

Lady Meadhbh of the Trinity stood before the kneeling king, Her body glimmering in the darkness. Diarmuid dared not look upon Her modesty, lest he offend the God any further.

"Stand!" She commanded. There was something in the sound of Her voice that made Diarmuid's soul feel like it was screaming. He looked into Her eyes as he stood, and all he wanted to do was gouge out his own, lest he'd ever set them upon anything less beautiful.

"Why have you graced me with your presence?" he asked, tempted to fall onto his knees once more. His mother had been a good queen, wise in the ways of etiquette, but she had never told him how he should act before a God. He wanted nothing more than to look upon Meadhbh forever, but he prayed that she did not speak again.

"It will all end soon," She said, Her voice like a whip. "The kingdom your forefathers have built was destined to fall before they were born. And you will be the one to witness the end of the Age of Man."

The same magnificent blue light surged through Diarmuid's mind, and he saw it: the fall of his kingdom. He watched as the land burned, with ruins of castles, cities, and towns left in the wake of a massive, marching army. Some of its soldiers wore armour, others wore nothing, but some had no flesh at all, just walking masses of bones. Dead, undead, whatever they were, they climbed the walls of Cruachan and spilled into the city streets.

Diarmuid's words failed him. As he stuttered, Meadhbh spoke for him.

"How will this happen?" She smiled. "Are you sure you want to know? Are you sure you want to know how your kingdom will crumble under a power greater than the Gods? Are you sure you want to see how even the Gods themselves will be brought to their knees?"

All King Diarmuid managed to do was nod.

With that, a thousand images flashed before him, like hot coals pressed hard against his eyes. He saw himself meeting with a Simian agent named Farris back in the capital. Then an airship burned through the sky and crashed into a mountain. Men, mages, and Simians ran through dense forestry. He saw a troll, charging towards a young girl in a field right before it turned to stone. Then there was a battered Simian corpse lying face down at the base of a cliff. A squadron of battlemages fought off a flock of black beadhbhs in the middle of a village. There was a cave, with severed limbs and bloody bones hanging from the ceilings and walls. An armoured Simian spied on a group of green battlemages as they trained. Diarmuid saw the city of Penance, in all its glory, and a contingent of elk cavalry marching out from its gates. Then he saw a rat, stretched out across a stone table, black wings sewn onto its back.

A girl in black feathers. A knight in shining white armour. A young Pyromancer with one arm, screaming as blood sprayed from a severed stump. A woman in silks. Two Simians drinking together in a dark tavern. A child crying before a gravestone. Each image appeared and vanished before he could make sense of it. Then, he saw a great crowd of Simians in Penance cheering as Argyll the Silverback took a seat on the Triad.

Finally, he saw himself, King Diarmuid, Third of His Name, Nineteenth Incarnate of Seletoth, drinking alone in his chambers while his city burned. The North Wall was on fire, and a thousand dead men charged towards the Grey Keep.

"What is this?" he demanded, gazing up at the Lady. "I don't understand what I'm seeing. I don't know what you want me to do."

Meadhbh stooped down and placed a hand under the king's chin. Her cold hands seemed to grasp his very being, but Her fingers barely touched his skin.

"There is power brewing in the north. Power forged by mortals, over their heads in power they are forbidden to understand. Soon, the Godslayer shall march south, and the fall of your kingdom shall follow."

Suddenly, everything became clear.

The Silverback! Of course! Sin take them all!

"My kingdom will not fall so easily." the king said, stepping back. Courage began to rise in his voice. "We have faced Simian rebellions before, and we can quell another!"

There was a pause, and Meadhbh stared back in silence. Diarmuid prayed that it was over, that She'd let him return to the city to make preparations, but She spoke again.

"These events will unfold as you have seen, for even the Gods themselves cannot turn the tides of destiny. The Godslayer's army will march south, and it will not be stopped. You will return to your city, you will lie to your most trusted men, and you will prepare for war. You'll build up your defences, you will tax your people, but in the end, your city will be breeched. You will die as a coward, King Diarmuid, and you will die alone."

"No!" cried the king. "We will not be broken so easily! You have shown me this, yet you expect me to sit back and watch as the Realm of Man falls? You have shown me what I must do, and I must throw back this enemy, whatever the cost!"

He took another defiant step towards the shimmering God. "As long as I am alive and breathing, as long as I am willing to fight, as long as my choices are mine and mine alone, there will always be hope."

The Lady tilted her head, and Diarmuid saw a smile twisting across Her face. There was a terrible mischievousness to Her grin, and it terrified Diarmuid more than all the images and visions of death he had seen.

"You speak of hope, but you don't understand the nature of destiny. No matter what you do, the things I have shown you shall come to pass, exactly as you have seen them. Your efforts have already been destined to fail, King Diarmuid, for every man, woman, and child lives and dies a thrall of fate. No, there is no hope. There never was."

GUIDE TO ALABACH, HER PLACES, AND HER PEOPLE

AC: After Conquest. The Thralls of Fate begins in AC403.

Aoife Ní Branna: Morrígan's deceased mother. *(Ee-fa Nee-Branna)*

Ard Sidhe: One of the Seven Seachtú of Alabach. *(Ard Sid-heh)*

Argyll the Silverback: Leader of the Simian dissident movement in Penance, formally the head of the Guild of Thieves.

Barrow's Way: Commercial district of Cruachan.

Beadhbh: flightless bird of prey from the Glenn. *(Bayve)*

Berrían the Green: Geomancer stationed in Roseán. *(Berry-Ann the Green)*

Borris Blackhand: One of the Triad, the governing body of Penance, along with Cathal Carríga and King Diarmuid Móráin III, XIX.

Cathal Carríga: One of the Triad, the governing body of Penance, along with Borris Blackhand and King Diarmuid Móráin III, XIX. *(Ca-hal Carry-ga)*

Chester the Lucky: Crewman aboard the Glory of Penance.

Ciarán: Miller of Roseán. *(Key-ear-on)*

Colonel Eodadh: Commander of the Battalion of mages stationed at Roseán. *(Colonel O-dah)*

Cormac O'Branna: Father of Morrígan.

Daithí the Blessed: Local druid of Roseán. *(Daw-hi the Blessed)*

Darragh: Son of Fearghal, the butcher. *(Darra)*

Derelith: Pawnbroker, and fence for the Guild of Thieves.

Divine Penetrance: Also known as the Gift of Immortality, this is a power passed from father to son through the Móráin line, ensuring the royal bloodline stays intact.

Dromán: Capital of the Woodlands of Alabach, home to the Academy of Mages. *(Dro-mawn)*

Dustworks: A residential sector of the city of Penance, home to Simians of low social standing.

Earl Roth: Earl of Terrían in AC178.

Elis Point: Northernmost point of Alabach, where the Simian Elis Highwind tested the world's first airship.

Eternal Sea: Sea to the west of Alabach, with no known land beyond it

Farris Silvertongue: A double agent infiltrating the Crown, relaying information back to the dissident Simian movement of Penance.

Fearghal: Butcher of Roseán. *(Fear-gal)*

Fionn: A young Pyromancer. *(Fyun)*

Gallows Head: Headland north of Roseán.

Garth: Brother of Farris Silvertongue.

Geomancer: Mage capable of manipulating the earth and Her fruits

Grey Keep: Residence of King Diarmuid Móráin, Third of His name, Nineteenth Incarnate of Seletoth

Grey Plague: Mysterious force that the Firstborn fled 400 years ago. Some speculate it was a sickness, others claim it was a supernatural blight on the earth.

Iron Concordant: Peace Treaty written up following the Fall of Sin. Promising Simians would not interfere with the workings of the Church and Crown.

Jane: Barmaid of the Stained Glass in Cruachan

King Diarmuid Móráin: Third of His Name, and Nineteenth Incarnate of Seletoth. Son of King Flaithrí IV, Diarmuid spent his reign attempting to bridge the gap between Man and Simian. *(King Dear-myid More-ain)*

Lady Meadhbh: One of the Trinity of Alabach. Called the Mother, the Lady, and the Weaver of Fate. Said to have determined the destiny of every living soul in Alabach. *(Lady Mayve)*

Lord Seletoth: One of the Trinity of Alabach. Called the Father, the Lord, and the Creator. Believed by some to be the One True God, rather than one of three as the Church teaches.

Mahon Family: Wealthy landowners who have residence near Point Grey.

Moiré: Wife of Peadair, originally from Point Grey. Returned to her hometown after her mother fell ill. *(Moy-ra)*

Móráin Hall: Main hall of the Grey Keep, Cruachan.

Móráin I: The First King of Alabach, also known as the Old, or the Great. Instead of accepting true divinity from the Lord, he chose to be with his wife. As a compromise, Seletoth bestowed upon him Divine Penetrance, in order to ensure that the Móráin line would never be broken.

Morrígan Ní Branna: Daughter of Aoife Ní Branna, and niece to Yarlaith the White, Roseán. *(Morry-gan Nee Branna)*

Mount Selyth: A lone peak said to be the residence of Lord Seletoth, though no person has climbed the mountain and returned to confirm the myth.

Mr. Cathain: Undertaker of Roseán. *(Mr. Caw-hayn)*

Mr. Mahon: Landowner of Roseán.

Mrs. Mhurichú: Dressmaker of Roseán. *(Mrs. Vir-iku)*

Mrs. Natháin: Mason of Roseán. *(Mrs. Nay-hain)*

Old Donal: Beggar of Cruachan, informant for Farris.

Padraig Tuathil: Captain of the City Guard in Cruachan. *(Pad-rayg Twa-hill)*

Peadair O'Brian: innkeeper of *The Bear and the Beadhbh*. *(Pee-yadar O'Brian)*

Penance: The home city of the Simian people following the Final Conquest; named by Lord Seletoth following the Fall of Sin.

Plains of Tierna Meall: Human version of an afterlife, with rolling green hills and summers that last forever. *(Plains of Tear-na Myall)*

Point Grey: Capital of the Clifflands of Alabach.

Pyromancers: Mages who manipulate fire.

Reilighs: Family of Hunters outside of Roseán (*Rail-lees*)

Resonance Crystal: Crystals that, when paired with another, can be manipulated by a crystallographer to relay messages over long distances.

Rosca Umhir: Capital of the Midlands of Alabach (*Ros-ka iv-er*)

Roseán: Small town in the Clifflands of Alabach, adjacent to the Teeth of the Glenn. (*Row-shawn*)

Santos: Previous Chief Engineer of Penance – deceased.

Seven Seachtú: Provinces of Alabach. (*Seven Shock-two*)

Simian: Native people to Alabach, holding science and technology to a hire esteem than faith and magic.

Sin: The name given to the remnants of a once great tower in the centre of the city of Penance.

Sir Bearach: Knight of Keep Carríga. (*Sir Byar-ak*)

Sláine the White: Healer of Dromán. (*Slaw-nya the White*)

Sorcha Ní Mhurichú: Daughter of Mrs. Mhurichú, dressmaker of Roseán. (*Sorsh-sha Nee Vir-iku*)

Southern Waterfront: The only dock large enough to house airships in Cruachan.

St. Aisling: The Patron Saint of Healers. (*St. Ash-ling*)

St. Durnagh: The Patron Saint of Blacksmiths. (*St. Durn-ah*)

St. Lorcan: The Patron Saint of Architects.

St. Mhórthos: The Patron Saint of Bards. (*St. Vor-tose*)

St. Moira: The Patron Saint of Hunters.

St. Ruadh: Saint of Sailors (*St. Roo-ah*)

Taigdh: Son of Peadair, the innkeeper. (*Tie-g*)

Terrían: Capital of the Godlands of Alabach. (*Terry-Ann*)

The Academy of Dromán: Educational and academic institute based in the Stronghold of Dromán. Thrives on research into the Nature of magic and training young mages. (*The Academy of Dro-mawn*)

The Bear and the Beadhbh: Inn and alehouse in Roseán, owned by Peadair.

The Black Sail: A smuggling group operating in Cruachan.

The Clifflands: One of the Seven Seachtú of Alabach, its capital city is Point Grey

The Fall of Sin: An event in the history of Alabach where a tower build by the Simians was cast down by Lord Seletoth for exceeding the height of Mount Selyth.

The Firstborn: Early Humans who conquered Alabach 400 years ago.

The Glenn: A valley separating the greater Penance region from the Alabach's Seven Seachtú. Uninhabitable as all flora are poisonous, and all fauna, carnivorous.

The Glory of Penance: Airship built for long-distance travel. Decommissioned and used as a trade vessel.

The Gutted Fish: Tavern on the Waterfront of Cruachan

The Kinglands: One of the Seven Seachtú of Alabach, its capital city Cruachan houses the seat of King Diarmuid III, XIX.

The Reardon Brothers: Twin brothers who work the forge of Roseán.

The Seven Seachtú of Alabach: The kingdom's seven provinces. They are (capital cities in parentheses): The Clifflands (Point Grey), The Godlands (Terrían), The Midlands (Ard Sidhe), The Woodlands (Dromán), The Wetlands (Rosca Umhir), The Floodlands (Tulcha), and Cruachan (Cruachan).

The Stained Glass: Tavern in the commercial district of Cruachan.

The Teeth of the Glenn: Mountain range north of Roseán separating the Clifflands from the Glenn.

The Triad: The governing body of Penance, comprising of Borris Blackhand, Cathal Carríga, and King Diarmuid III XIX.

The Trinity: The three Gods worshipped by Humans in Alabach, comprising of Lord Seletoth (The Father), Lady Meadhbh (The Mother) and King Móráin the First (The Son). The current ruler of Alabach is said to be an incarnation of King Móráin.

The Twelve Saints of the Trinity: Twelve men and women who accompanied Móráin I to Alabach.

Tulcha: Capital of the Floodlands, one of the Seven Seachtú of Alabach. Named after the river that runs through it. *(Tul-ka)*

Wraiths: Mysterious cloaked figures, agents for the Church, but rumoured to be affiliated with Lord Seletoth directly.

Yarlaith the White: Local healer in Roseán, and uncle to Morrígan Ní Branna. *(Yar-layth)*

Acknowledgements

First off, I would like to apologise to all of those who had early drafts of this book forced upon them back in 2012. Even though it needed a lot more work at the time, you gave me the encouragement to improve as a writer. I would like to thank all the writers from *Scribophile's* Ubergroup, and the Candied Sea Urchins who helped me on that journey. Across those two groups, there are too many names to mention. It's through all your help and support that I was able to complete this project. Another big thanks to alpha and beta, readers who read the improved versions of this novel.

I'd like to thank my editor Lauren Humphries-Brooks for getting this book to its final form. Also, a big thank you to Cornelia Yoder for the wonderful map of Alabach, really helping to bring this world to life. The incredible art comes from the MiblArt team, a group I can't recommend highly enough.

Finally, I'd like to thank you, the reader, for picking up this book. Whether you've gotten here by skipping to the end or reading the story that precedes this, I am grateful for your time.

ABOUT THE AUTHOR

Alan was raised in the seaside village of Rush, County Dublin. He began writing fiction at the age of ten, starting with short stories about each of his classmates being eaten by dinosaurs. Fortunately, this behaviour was encouraged by both parents and teachers, allowing him to grow as an author.

The Thralls of Fate is Alan's first novel, written while studying for his PhD in Dublin City University. During that time, he also wrote a thesis on genetics and molecular biology.

Today, Alan works for the pharmaceutical industry, and spends most of his spare time playing Dungeons & Dragons and Magic the Gathering. He co-hosts two podcasts on the latter: *Skullcraic!* for the game's strategy, and *Uncharted Pages*, delving into its history and lore.

He has no pets.

@AlanHarrison

AlanHarrisonAuthor@gmail.com

Lightning Source UK Ltd.
Milton Keynes UK
UKHW022009161021
392325UK00012B/180